The *SPIN*

The SPIN

REBECCA LISLE

HOT
KEY
BOOKS

First published in Great Britain in 2013 by Hot Key Books
Northburgh House, 10 Northburgh Street, London EC1V 0AT

A CIP catalogue record for this book is available from the British Library.

ISBN: 978-1-4714-0023-0

1

Typeset by Palimpsest Book Production Limited, Falkirk, Stirlingshire
This book is set in 11pt Sabon LT Std

Printed and bound by Clays Ltd, St Ives Plc

FSC

Hot Key Books supports the Forest Stewardship Council (FSC), the leading
international forest certification organisation, and is committed to printing
only on Greenpeace-approved FSC-certified paper.

www.hotkeybooks.com

For fan-tastic Maud Mellish

PART ONE

1

Compost

Stormy felt as if he were being cooked – steamed like a pudding, baked like an apple pie. The kitchen was *so* hot he could barely breathe. He yawned. Scooped up the eggshells and onionskins into the bucket of scraps, yawned again.

Uh-oh. Otto the cook had spotted him.

'You! Stormy! Wakey-wakey!' A sieve sailed through the air towards his head. Stormy ducked. 'No yawning in here!' Otto yelled. 'Take that bucket to the compost heap! And be quick about it! No snoozing in my kitchen! Zero yawning! D'you hear me?'

'Yes, sir. No, sir.'

Stormy picked up the heavy bucket and got a whack on his ear. A *size five* whack.

Otto was tall, and as wide as the black stove, and when he hit you with a size five spoon it felt as if your head was splitting open, like a conker bursting out of its shell.

'Ouch! Yes, sir.'

He ran to the door as Otto reached for the number six spoons.

Stormy perked up in the fresh, cool air. He staggered across the yard, down the path and past the crooked bean-poles and rows of shrivelled sprouts, the bucket bumping against his thin legs.

If I were taller and stronger I'd give Otto what for! I'd show him. If I didn't have to do what he told me to do, I wouldn't do it!

The steaming compost heap at the very end of the path was hidden behind bushes. Beyond it, the garden sloped away in rocky terraces and giant boulders down the side of the mountain.

Stormy tossed the contents of the bucket onto the pile, set it down and stood a moment.

In the evening gloom, every edge and outline was beginning to fade.

The twilight sky was a beautiful purple, with tiny brilliant stars just beginning to appear like holes in the dark. Two spitfyres were wheeling around the Academy castle on the summit of Dragon Mountain. They were looping, tilting and swooping like birds, as if they were searching for something on the mountainside. It was unusual for winged horses to be out so late. He wondered what they were doing. Lucky things, those sky-riders. They weren't orphans like him; they had rich parents who paid for them to go to the Academy. He looked up at the spitfyres adoringly. If only he could get close to one, touch one – it was what he most wanted in the whole world.

A sudden chink of metal against metal made him spin round.

'Who's there?'

A man leapt out of the shadows, grabbed him and without a warning, locked his hands together round his neck and began to squeeze.

'Silence!' said his terrible voice. 'Don't move. Not a word!' His grip on Stormy's throat was like a metal claw, cutting off air, pushing him to the ground.

Stormy stopped breathing.

The man was strong, but no taller than Stormy. His long grey hair hung in rat-tails around his grizzled face. Inside his beard his few teeth were broken into yellow spikes. He was shivering and wet.

'I won't say a word!' Stormy managed to say, terrified. 'I'm not moving, only you're just about throttling me – sir!'

The awful hold on his throat lessened but did not go away. A dank, damp, marshy smell, a smell of wet undergrowth, cloggy soil and worms, crept into Stormy's nostrils.

'Name?' The man's voice was a croak, as if it hadn't been used for years or had been strained by shouting.

'Stormy. Sir.'

'God help us! What sort of name is Stormy?'

'The one the orphanage gave me, sir. Found on a stormy night, thunder and lightn—'

'You a norphan?' the man interrupted, looking around in a distracted manner as if he expected someone to appear.

'I am.'

'Listen then, norphan, and you'll not be hurt. I've a gang

back there in the bushes and if I give the sign they'll leap out and rip you limb from limb and chuck the pieces over the cliff for the vultures. They would, soon as butter a slice of bread.' Stormy nodded to show he understood. 'But I won't give the sign if you –' he looked about nervously and gave Stormy a shake, 'you bring me food. And a file for the chain. A coat if you can find one.'

'Food and a file and a coat if I can find one,' Stormy repeated. His heart was beating madly. The man held him so tight his toes barely touched the ground.

'A big file, mind, for this here big leg chain.' He rattled it softly. 'Strong. Come back at midnight. If you're not here by the time the clock strikes the last of the twelve, we'll be in that place there two ticks later.' He nodded towards the kitchen. 'I know where you sleep; know your very bunk. We'll come to you and slice your throat. Got it?'

Stormy gulped. 'Got it.'

The squat man pushed him away roughly, then he turned and limped away, holding his chain from the ankle cuffs so that it didn't clank.

Stormy stood frozen for a few minutes, waiting for other figures to rise up out of the dark. No one appeared. What a terrible man! Escaped from the Academy dungeons, no doubt – a convict, a *murderer*, probably, and he knew where Stormy slept . . . His very bunk!

Stormy crept ever so quickly back to the kitchen.

4

2

Otto

Otto's few strands of long grey hair were drawn over a scabby, turnip-shaped skull. His eyes were like two burnt potatoes and his nose was a knobbly ancient parsnip.

The only time Otto had left the kitchen was when his sister ran away to the circus. He went to bring her back, but before he could coax her home, she died in an accident. It was after he returned that he started throwing pans and counting the strawberries in a bowl, daring anyone to steal one.

Stormy was one of Otto's kitchen skivvies, the lowest of the low. They washed, cut, peeled, cored and mashed. They prepared plain food for the orphanage and fancy casseroles, puddings and tarts for the Academy.

The convicts in the dungeons got what was left.

Brittel ran the spitfyre kitchen, a much smaller place than Otto's kitchen, hidden away down a narrow corridor. Brittel was as thin as a stick and as mean as a snake. He prepared all the spitfyre food. He used strange ingredients

– rare herbs, minced bark, molluscs, special flowers and copious amounts of grass which he combined in mysterious, secret ways.

The food was sent up through the core of Dragon Mountain in lifts. The Winder, always the strongest boy in the orphanage, had the job of wheeling it up.

Stormy hoped to make it from skivvy to under-cook in Brittel's kitchen by the time he was thirteen or fourteen. He could never expect to get closer to a real spitfyre than that.

Stormy opened the kitchen door nervously, hoping no one would notice how long he'd been at the compost heap, or that he was shaking. His friend Tex gave him a wink.

'Where have you been, you little worm?' Otto yelled. He was a simmering pan with the lid off. 'It's taken you an hour to empty a bucket. Is our compost five miles away?'

'I –'

Otto picked up a size six wooden spoon and ran at Stormy, waving it. 'I'll show you, you cheeky little slice of sausage! How many ounces of flour in a three-egg cake? What ingredients in a chocolate sauce? Wasting my time, lingering and loitering! Time is food, Stormy! Lobster pancakes! How d'you make puff pastry? Crème caramel? Food comes first!'

The other skivvies sniggered. Stormy didn't mind – he'd laugh too if it were someone else being chased round the kitchen.

Sponge, Otto's old dog, staggered up on his stiff legs and pretended to nip at Stormy's ankles. He and Stormy were friends; Sponge would never really bite anyone.

Otto battered Stormy's back and shoulders with the wooden spoon, whooping every time he made a good, loud sound. 'Splat! Whack! Crack!' he cried. 'Batter! Smash!'

Otto was large and slow and Stormy was small and quick. After the first few blows, which didn't really hurt, Stormy escaped under the kitchen table. Sponge joined him, grinning.

'Sorry, Mr Otto . . . sorry, sir . . . sorry, Mr Otto, sir –'

'Moron!' Otto yelled at Tex, seeing him about to sweep bits of bread into the bucket. 'Keep those! Crumbs is food. No waste here! Don't forget the little birdies!'

'No, sir.'

Stormy was forgotten. He stayed under the table. His encounter at the compost heap had chilled him to the marrow, and despite the warmth he was shivering. Otto could be scary, but it was the wild man outside he was most scared of. There had been anger and misery in the bones and hard flesh of those hands around his throat.

The old dog sank down and snored, and Stormy crawled out, picked up a knife and began chopping.

Otto was standing by the window that looked over the mountain track, slurping a mug of mint tea. He watched that stretch of path a lot, as if he were expecting someone.

*   *   *

Stormy worked all evening, anxiously watching the time slip away. Ten thirty. Eleven o'clock. Eleven thirty . . . How was he ever going to get out to the convict with the food and the file by midnight?

At last the kitchen was tidied and cleaned, the food prepared, ready for breakfast. Team by team the staff left; the skivvies were the last. Stormy glanced at the clock. Oh, if only they would all hurry up! He let the other boys go out ahead of him, then went back to pick up an imaginary speck from the clean floor before following them, making sure he was the last to leave the kitchen. But he didn't climb the stairs up to his dormitory as they had done. He slipped quickly into the darkness at the bottom of the stone stairs, where Otto kept his coats and wellingtons. He pushed his way through the heavy mackintoshes and tweeds and slippery leather until he felt the cold stone wall. He was well hidden. He stayed very still, waiting. The smell of Otto was all around him.

The clock struck quarter to midnight. Sweat broke out all over his body. *Come on, Otto!* At last the cook shuffled out, Sponge padding beside him. He slept in a damp stone-flagged room beside the kitchen, dreaming of piecrusts, brandied cherries, apple crumble and cake.

He was yawning and scratching at his greasy head. His footsteps came closer and closer. Then stopped.

'What's the matter, Sponge?'

They were right there, right beside the coats!

Sponge was sniffing loudly. Stormy closed his eyes and prayed his shaking limbs wouldn't give him away. *Go away, Sponge! Go away!*

'Come on, you daft old dog. It's only a mouse. Bed!' And at last his bedroom door shut.

3
Stealing

Stormy waited a few minutes, then crept out from his hiding place, dragging with him a vast green tweed garment he had never seen Otto wear so would never miss. He put it on to save carrying it, and headed for the kitchen, the coat hem trailing on the floor.

He tiptoed in, feeling like a burglar; feeling like a thief.

Black beetles scattered, scurrying back into the cracks and crevasses behind the stove. The only sound was the crackling fire and the scratching of mice and lizards in the skirting board.

The great coat was suffocating in the hot kitchen but still he was shaking; even his lips were quivering. He almost couldn't do a single thing.

He went to the big stone larder. Otto knew every item of food on every shelf. If one thing was moved, he'd go crazy! Once he'd prepared a dish, he had it recorded in his brain forever. No skivvy had ever managed to steal so much as one mulberry from here without Otto knowing about it – nor lived to tell the tale.

But Stormy had no choice.

He shut his eyes. *If I can't see what I'm doing, I'm not responsible*, he told himself. He pushed back the enormous coat sleeves and let his fingers close around whatever food they happened to touch. Stormy's mouth watered when he opened his eyes and saw a muffin in his hand, baked golden with the red fruit oozing out of the top. There were four other muffins – it would be missed, but what could he do?

He lifted the cheese cover but the cheese beneath was cut into triangles and beautifully arranged in a swirl. The muffin, might, just might have fallen on the floor and got eaten, but not the cheese. He put three crumbs of muffin on the shelf and three on the stone slabs. There, it had fallen and Sponge had eaten it, or the mice. He put the muffin in the coat pocket. What else? There was a long loaf, and since the end was jagged he hoped Otto would not miss another inch or two. Then an apple, but as he reached for the apple, he set three others rolling off along the wide stone ledge. He froze. No one came. He left the fallen apples. A bat had got in or some rats, giant beetles or . . . There was the end of a fat sausage, just two inches of it; he added it to the rest in his pocket.

Now the file; where would he get a file? The man wanted something to cut through the chain that hobbled

11

his legs together; it would need to be a huge file. Otto kept tools for mending the stove and the turning spit beneath the stone sink. Stormy pulled the cupboard door open and rummaged around quietly. There was a heavy chisel and hammer, and he considered taking them before he spotted a massive pair of pincer things that Otto had used to cut the bars on the pantry window when his friend Purbeck had got his big head stuck through them. Otto had made Purbeck wait for two whole days before freeing him. It had been snowing at the time too.

The back door was locked, but the key was in the lock and Stormy turned it slowly. The clock in the tower began to chime the hour. Midnight!

He ran.

A dim yellow glow flickered in the dark by the compost heap. Stormy headed towards it, his heart booming, and his mouth dry. With his eyes set on the light, he saw nothing, only heard a hideous *wheeze* as the terrible man leapt out and flung him to the ground. The man was on top of him in an instant, settling on his chest like a heavy toad, and smelling like one too.

'Alone?' The convict's voice rasped close in his ear. 'Anyone see you?'

'No, sir.'

'Tell anyone?'

'I swear I didn't, sir.'

'Food?'

'Yes, here, if you'd just let me . . .'

The man rolled off him and, reaching for a shrouded lantern, opened it so a sliver of light shone out. Stormy managed to get his hands into the deep pockets of the big coat and squash the stolen food into the convict's hands. 'Sorry, it's a bit broken and –'

He didn't notice a folded square of paper escape from his coat pocket to the ground.

The little man grabbed the muffin with shaking hands and rammed it into his mouth. His teeth were chattering so badly that much of it flew out again and had to be scooped up several times before it was eaten and swallowed once and for all.

Stormy had a moment in which to nervously study the convict. His eyes were black and very round, like polished stones. And his ears, half hidden by the straggly hair, were pointed.

A *grubbin*! That accounted for the smell of old leaves and wet earth.

'What you starin' at?' the grubbin said, and food sprayed out of his mouth as he spoke. '*What?*'

'Nothing, sir, nothing.'

'Is it the ears? Is that it?' He chewed away furiously, swallowing in great hungry gulps; saliva dribbling down his chin. 'Ears? Been paying all my life for them ears. Locked up for years and years, little norphan, for a pair of ears. A pair of pointed ears! Locked up there.' He indicated the dungeons, the tiny black-barred windows set into the castle walls below the Academy.

13

'Get the file?' he added, gripping Stormy's arm tight. 'Did you?'

'There wasn't one,' Stormy said, quickly, pulling out the pincers. 'I got these. I hope they'll do. Otto's going to go crazy when he finds out!'

'Fierce is he, this Otto?'

Stormy nodded. 'Can be.'

'Well, I'm grateful to you, and sorry. There. Can't say fairer than that. I've done nothin' wrong and shouldn't be locked up, and that's a fact. I needs my freedom. What about you?' The grubbin stuffed the last of the sausage into his mouth and nodded at him. 'Know what it's like to need something? Need it bad?'

'I do. Yes. I *need* to be a sky-rider,' Stormy blurted.

'Ah ha. Good, good,' and the grubbin held out a dirty hand for the tools. 'Got a dream, lad, hold it. Now give me them.' He weighed the heavy pincers in his palm. 'Good. Done well.'

'Can I go now?' Stormy whispered.

'Yes. Thank you. You can go. Away to your bed before my men come back. 'Ere, give me the coat.'

Quickly Stormy stripped off the coat and the grubbin put it on. It was huge on him too, drooping off his shoulders and long on the ground, but he hugged it round himself gratefully.

'You done me proud, young man. Thank you. Thank you for your help and I hopes you get your dream. Brave lad. Here – don't forget this.' He scooped up the fallen

14

paper and thrust it into Stormy's hand. 'Might be important.'

He shut off the light and limped away into the darkness, hardly clinking at all, and was eaten up by the shadows.

4

Guards

Stormy could not sleep. His night was tormented by
fearful dreams where Otto roasted him slowly on the
spit above the fire or fed him live to Sponge, in bite-size
pieces.

He kept waking, thinking he heard the door to the
dormitory open, thinking Otto was coming to get him,
imagining he heard the low growl of Sponge as he padded
up to the bed, his wet nose sniffing loudly, scenting stolen
food.

He was amazed when he woke at six o'clock to find he
was still all in one piece, safe in his narrow bunk and not
dead. Images of the escaped prisoner came swiftly into his
mind along with the paper he'd handed him, which, after
briefly glancing at the night before, he'd pushed under his
pillow.

Now he pulled it out. It was a faded handbill, much
creased and fingered. He unfolded it quietly and read:

Cosmo's Circus
Wonderful Wild Winged Horses

THE GREATEST SPITFYRE SHOW ON EARTH!
COME AND SEE OUR DAREDEVIL
DEATH-DEFYING ACTS!
SEE THE MOST SPECTACULAR SPITFYRES
IN THE WORLD!

Cosmo's Circus presents the Great Renaldo!

The Great Renaldo was a young man, as round and sleek as a well-fed seal. He had a large black moustache with twirled-up ends and was wearing a sort of string vest through which his muscles bulged.

RENALDO
THE STAR OF THE SHOW!
TERRIFIC Tricks and Dazzling FEATS of Bravery!
Spitfyres tamed to submission!
Renaldo is fearless!
Don't miss the Great Renaldo!

Stormy stared at the confident spitfyre master with wonder and awe. To be in a spitfyre circus looked even better than being a sky-rider in the Academy.

Behind Renaldo were some of the tiny folk with very round faces and spindly legs known as *littles*. They wore tights and elaborate hats. They cartwheeled round the ring or rode on miniature ponies with star-studded harnesses.

Tex was stirring in the bunk below and quickly Stormy folded the handbill up again and slipped it inside a book.

'What happened to you last night?' Tex asked him, poking his head round from the lower bunk. 'Did Otto keep you?'

'Tummy trouble,' Stormy said. 'Stuck in the bathroom.'

Tex laughed. 'What did you eat?'

'I didn't eat anything! I wouldn't dare.' Stormy got up and started to dress. 'Otto has eyes in the back of his spotty old head.'

Tex laughed again. 'I know,' he said. 'All that glorious nosh going up to the Academy and I bet they don't appreciate it! Once when I was carrying a tray to the Winder I just let my face sort of fall into the plate and I ate a whole stuffed tomato!'

They both giggled.

'It's torture, putting the food in the lift, closing the door, seeing it disappear,' Tex said dreamily. 'Don't know how the Winder manages. If I –'

'Hey, Tex, you don't hate grubbins, do you?'

'What, molemen? No. Why?'

'Just wondered.'

'Brittel does, but he's a narrow-minded idiot,' Tex said with great certainty. 'And hates most things.'

'That's true,' Stormy said. 'He's always making nasty comments about them . . . I'm sure they're not all bad. He probably just wishes he could dig up gold and stuff, like they can.'

18

'I suppose they're a bit grubby,' Tex said. 'Don't know that I'd want to live underground; it'd make you smell. Too dark. And I wouldn't have their gold teeth, even if I were rich.'

Stormy tried to remember if the grubbin last night had had gold teeth. He'd had a lot of gaps, so maybe he had once. 'Brittel says grubbins shouldn't be allowed to live alongside humans. Says they steal and lie. He once told me his –'

Suddenly the bell started ringing, an urgent, sharp, harsh sound that shook the walls and rattled the windows in their frames.

Stormy froze. 'An alarm?' he whispered.

'Yeah, it's an alarm all right,' said another boy, joining them.

'I should think so!' Tex agreed, looking excited. 'Great.'

The boys rushed to the windows and peered out – all except for Stormy. He was too terrified to move.

'Something's up!' another boy said. 'I've just seen Mrs Cathcart running!'

The boys giggled. 'That's not running, it's rolling!'

'Last time I heard that bell, some twit up in the castle got burnt to a crisp by a flying horse,' Purbeck said.

'They think they're fireproof, those posh Academy boys,' Tex said.

'Wonder what's up this time?' another boy asked.

'I expect we'll find out soon,' Tex said.

Stormy straightened his bed covers quickly. His fingers were trembling . . . Had his thieving been discovered *already*?

* * *

Before breakfast the boys were lined up to listen to Mrs Cathcart, the housekeeper. She was so plump that her hands barely met around her squidgy middle. Having a squinty eye meant no one ever knew where, or at whom she was looking, so all the skivvies watched her intently, though their minds were on the pots of porridge slowly growing cold on the long tables behind them. Mrs Cathcart gave them the same old talk.

'You'd be scrabbling around in the filth of the village if it wasn't for the kitchen,' she said. 'You'd be dirty and hungry and lonely. The kitchen has saved you, and in exchange we ask only for hard work. Dedication. And loyalty.' She smoothed her blonde hair, tucking a short strand behind her ear.

Stormy gulped loudly.

'I've gathered you together to explain about the alarm you heard. There's been a break out. A convict has escaped from the dungeons!'

Stormy nearly toppled over.

A shiver rippled through the boys like wind through a field of nervous grass.

'He is a ruthless, violent creature. A *grubbin*! Not that I'm prejudiced or anything, but even if you only believe *some* of what you hear about them, you can't sleep easy in your bed . . . If we see him, we must not approach him. He's dangerous. He is a lifer, never *ever* to be set free, a

20

desperate creature. Report anything suspicious to me or Mr Otto, immediately!'

Stormy clenched his sweaty hands tightly together and looked straight ahead.

As Mrs Cathcart's stare went round the hall, it seemed to Stormy that one of her blue eyes lingered on him, watching him with special interest. He tried to make his eyes go glassy and vacant, like Purbeck's usually were. Oh, lordy! She *couldn't* know what he'd done! She couldn't!

Suddenly the door was flung open so violently that it crashed against the wall. The boys jumped. Mrs Cathcart squealed.

Otto! The long strands of his hair, usually neatly combed over his skull, hung down on one side of his big face. Sweat gleamed on his cheeks like olive oil. His cheeks were ripe tomatoes.

'Thief!' he cried. 'Robber!'

Stormy felt his stomach flip over and start to slide away towards his knees. His hand twitched with an automatic desire to own up. His feet even stepped forward involuntarily. *It was me! It was me!* But he said nothing.

'A robber in the kitchens?' Mrs Cathcart's arched eyebrows went even higher. 'Impossible! Are you suggesting one of my boys might have . . . Never.'

Otto stamped over to where she stood.

'My larder!' he cried. 'Someone has stolen food! Crumbs on the floor! Touched my muffins!'

21

Some of the boys giggled but were soon silenced by a look from Mrs Cathcart. 'Precisely what is missing, Mr Otto?' she asked.

'A raspberry muffin; an apple with a patch of orange-red on it, salami, one and a half inches of bread and – and my finest tweed coat!'

Mrs Cathcart tapped a plump finger against her chin thoughtfully.

'It sounds as if that escaped prisoner has paid *us* a visit. I'll ask the guards to investigate. Boys, you are dismissed! Watch out for anything unusual and report it immediately. Off you go to your porridge!'

Stormy's heart was thumping, arms trembling, knees knocking, but he could still walk. Slowly he made his way over to his table, and sat down next to Tex.

'You could eat anything from the kitchen now and Otto'd just think it had been the old grubbin thief!' Tex said, spooning up his porridge quickly. 'We should try.'

Stormy nodded weakly. He was safe for the moment – that was all he could think about.

'Funny you asking about grubbins this morning, isn't it?' Tex said, grabbing some bread. 'What wouldn't you do for a bit of butter, Stormy? And jam, eh?'

Stormy hardly heard him. He was remembering the two spitfyres skimming down the mountain in the twilight last night. Now he knew what they had been looking for.

*   *   *

22

Towards evening a mist came down and even the air in the kitchen became clammy. Stormy peered outside – swirling grey obliterated everything.

It seemed that everyone was waiting for something to happen, and at last it did. The kitchen door opened and a tall guard came in. His grey leather suit was beaded with moisture from the mist. The skivvies quietly laid down their knives and egg-beaters and inched towards him, hungry to hear news.

'Mind your dirty guard's feet on my clean floor!' Otto snapped.

The guard grinned. 'Same jolly Mr Otto we know and love,' he said. 'Thought you'd like to know that we've caught the culprit, Mr Otto. The food thief.' With a wink at the boys the guard helped himself to an iced chocolate bun from a heaped dish on the table.

'Oi, don't touch that!' Otto cried. 'Put that back immediately!'

'Delicious!' the guard said, taking a bite. 'Light and delicious! Mind, I prefer white chocolate myself.'

'Whatthedevil!' Otto yelled, and probably would have leapt on him if a second guard hadn't come in just then, carrying Otto's old green coat.

'Look what I've got!' he said, flinging the coat down and helping himself to a bun.

'My coat!' Otto cried. 'Oi! My buns!'

'Stingy, aren't you, Otto, even when we've done you a favour. We caught the villain and he was so desperate he was wearing *that*.' The second guard pointed to the coat.

'He's outside now; trembling and shivering like a little puppy. Says he wants to say he's sorry.'

'We aren't sorry,' the other guard said, picking a ripe pear out of the fruit bowl and polishing it on his sleeve. 'We never apologise for nothing.'

Otto gave him a cold stare before following them. The kitchen staff bunched behind him, straining to see.

The light spilled from the kitchen doorway on to a miserable sight. The grubbin hung like a limp rag between two pan-faced guards. His cheeks were smeared and blackened with grime and his trousers dirty and torn. He had lost not only a boot but also his leg irons.

'He says he'd like to apologise to you, Otto, in person,' the first guard said. He prodded the grubbin with his truncheon. 'Can't think why. We don't bother, little moleman – why'd you want to?'

'Don't listen to him!' Brittel snapped, stepping to the front of the onlookers and pointing a thin, stained finger at him. 'He's only doing it to get off more lightly. Dirty beggar! Nasty, wormy *grubbin*!'

The grubbin winced; his knees folded beneath him like paper and his head drooped heavily. His eyes were half closed and his chin shook as he spoke.

'Sorry, sir,' he muttered wheezily. 'Sorry for taking your coat and your food.' He forced open his eyes a little and peered at the kitchen staff intently, as if trying to pick out one particular face amongst the watching boys. His eyes met with Stormy's, and there was a flash of recognition on both sides. The grubbin quickly closed his eyes and

24

looked away. 'I had *no* help, sirs, *none*. It was all my own doing.'

'Of course he didn't have help, he didn't need it!' Brittel said. 'Stealing is in their blood!' He folded his arms across his narrow chest. 'It's natural for them, born to it.'

'We'll take him off now, then!' The guards hauled the convict up on his trembling legs. 'He's done his apology. Enough. Back to the dungeons with you.' And they dragged him away.

'What's the matter with you, Stormy?' Brittel said as they went back inside. 'Your face is a picture! You don't care what happens to a dirty old grubbin, do you?'

Stormy shook his head and added quietly, 'But he might be innocent. We don't know for sure.'

'Course we know!' Brittel said. 'Those little diggers are all bad. My father lost all his money because of them; cost him his life too, it did.'

'How's that, then?' Tex asked, playing for time, avoiding his kitchen duties.

'How's that? My father bought a mine off them; good deep one, supposed to be fresh, supposed to be full, only to find the grubbins had already cleared it out of precious stones and gold. Everything gone. Wasn't theirs to dig. They're thieves.'

'That's enough, Brittel!' Otto snapped, slamming the door to the yard. 'Back to work. All of you!' The boys scurried to their places.

'All very well,' Brittel muttered, 'but it was the ruin of my old man. Ruin.'

'I don't like mysteries,' Otto went on, ignoring him. 'Don't like wondering if my skivvies are honest or not. Glad to know the truth.'

Stormy had raced back to his place at the end of the table and picked up his knife again. *Honest?* The knife sliced his finger. 'Ouch!'

'Stormy?' Otto called out.

'Nothing, sir!'

Stormy sucked his bleeding finger and dived under the table as if he had dropped something.

He wasn't honest, but he was safe. He was safe! The grubbin had saved him! Hallelujah!

'But how did the robbing thieving villain get in?' Otto added, shaking his head. 'I don't know.'

Brittel pointed at Stormy.

'Ask that little grubbin-lover. He might know.'

Stormy kept silent. Avoiding Brittel's stare, he stood up and started chopping again. Now no one would ever know what he'd done.

5

Crash

A week passed; two, three, four. The winter nights drew in. It got colder and the first snow began to fall. The tiny stream that trickled down the side of the mountain froze. Ice formed in intricate lace patterns on the windowpanes. The compost heap with its crispy covering of snow turned into a beautiful white cake.

Stormy found himself often looking towards the tiny dungeon windows that were squashed beneath the castle and above the kitchens in the rock of the mountain, imagining the poor grubbin locked away in a miserable prison cell. What a horrible place to be.

He was on full-time compost duty now. Nipping down to the compost heap gave him a bit of fresh air and got him out from under Otto's critical gaze. It gave him a chance to look for spitfyres too; even just seeing one in the distance made him feel brighter. The sight of one would fuel his dreams for nights. Dreams where he had parents, who were spitfyre keepers, and Stormy, their beloved, handsome and brave son, had many wonderful adventures.

It was impossible; an impossible dream. He was a kitchen orphan and life was unfair; but still, if you couldn't dream, what could you do?

One chilly damp evening, Stormy wrapped a scarf round his neck and set off from the kitchen with the full bucket, whistling quietly. Luckily the sun hadn't quite gone, because coming down in the dark now, he was always looking over his shoulder nervously or staring hard into the murky places.

Suddenly a shadow fell over him; he stopped and looked up.

Two great dark shapes were right overhead. Two flying horses had swooped silently down and were hanging over him like two enormous birds.

Stormy's heart lurched painfully. The animals were *so* magnificent. *So* beautiful! They glided around, circling smoothly over him as if on an invisible wire.

'Hello!' Stormy yelled and waved. 'Hello!'

Neither sky-rider waved back. Goggles and helmets hid their faces. Stormy's own smile died. One rider signalled to his spitfyre, making it tip and bank to the side, then rise up vertically, until it seemed to balance on the tip of its hind legs. Stormy was frozen, watching in wonderment and awe. Suddenly its massive wings scooped backwards, thrust forwards, and with an enormous swoosh the compost heap flew up into the air.

The sky-rider laughed.

The powerful draught from the spitfyre's wings threw Stormy to the ground. Cabbage leaves, orange peel and bones swirled up and then fell back in a thick horrid rain.

A voice called, 'Thought you were a *grubbin*!'

The winged horse spun round. It opened its jaws and a blast of flames shot out and set light to the fragments of compost. Tiny balls of red scattered, starting miniature fires across the hillside.

Stormy's clothes were smoking. He rolled around on the ground, hitting out at the smouldering fabric. He was scorched all over, his eyes were stinging from the smoke and when he felt for his eyebrows they were much smaller than they had been before.

He could have gone up in flames. He could have been burnt to a frazzle, just on the rider's whim. His heart bumped.

There was a scream, a sudden crash and a wood-snapping sound. He spun round. The second spitfyre had smashed into a leafless plum tree. For a moment it was trapped, legs thrashing, wings flapping furiously. It neighed and cried out in fear. Then it fell, slammed into the vegetable patch, and somersaulted over the earth, throwing its rider off with a sickening crunch.

The black-suited sky-rider lay very still, eyes shut, but breathing. Stormy glanced to see he was OK, then ran over to the spitfyre, which was struggling quickly to its feet.

Here was a spitfyre, a real winged horse, only ten paces from him. He couldn't miss this chance . . . He edged towards it, grinning like an idiot, trembling with wonder and excitement. If he could just have a moment to study it . . . if he could just stand close and get a really good look at its wings and head and everything, he would die happy.

It was square on its feet now, shaking out its leathery wings and steadying itself. It was taller than a normal horse, its head towering above Stormy's on a strong neck. Wings grew from the creature's shoulders like some strange blue plant's stem might curve and grow from the soil, then billowed out into beautiful pale-blue fan shapes with a fine tracery of darker sinews and veins. It turned large sapphire eyes on him and puffed smoke from its nostrils in short, angry snorts; spitfyres' distant ancestors were dragons.

Stormy inched a step nearer.

The spitfyre tossed its head, flicking its dark blue mane from side to side, warning him to stay back. A tremor ran over its skin, rippling the short blue hair of its coat, making it shimmer violet, turquoise and midnight-blue. Warily, it pawed the ground with a blue hoof. Stormy drew closer, like iron filings to a magnet. He had read about spitfyres, had seen pictures of them, dreamed of them, but nothing had prepared him for the beauty or the wonder of the creature in the flesh.

He held out his hand.

'I won't hurt you,' he said. 'I'm your friend.' He saw

30

the expression soften in the spitfyre's eyes; it was listening and understanding. He could only use the same words he might with old Sponge or an ordinary horse.

'Good boy. Good boy. I just want to stroke you. Good chap. Well done.'

The winged horse lifted its head and continued to stare at him.

'You are so majestic,' Stormy said. 'You are wonderful, wonderful . . .'

Now he was almost close enough to reach out and put his hand on its neck. He raised his arm slowly, feeling the heat that oozed out from the animal as if it had a furnace inside it. 'You're fantastic,' he whispered. 'I think you're the most beautiful thing I've ever seen.' He reached towards the spitfyre and it lowered its head towards him, puffing out smoke gently. 'I just want to –'

'Bluey, stop! Hey!'

The winged horse jerked its head up and lurched backwards with a harsh throaty neigh. Stormy spun round. The sky-rider was scrambling to his feet, and tugging off his black helmet and goggles. Only it wasn't a he; it was a she. As the helmet came off, a long plait of dark hair, woven with white and red ribbon, snaked over her shoulder. She rubbed at her bruised head. She was tall and strong, and crossing the gap between them in three quick strides she jabbed a finger at Stormy.

'Don't you dare touch him, orphan boy! Bluey! Down!' she roared. 'Down!'

The glimmer of friendliness died in the spitfyre's eyes.

It belched out a cloud of black smoke and tossed its head, rattling and clinking the metal bridle.

'*Down!*' the sky-rider shouted.

The spitfyre folded its front legs and sank down onto the earth so that the girl could step up from a rock onto its back.

'What exactly did you think you were you doing, boy?'

She was the most perfect girl he'd ever seen – not that he'd seen very many – with dark glittering eyes, high round cheeks and a narrow nose which tilted up at the end. She was older and taller than him; and, he knew instantly, cleverer and smarter.

'I like spitfyres,' he said with a shrug.

Her dark eyes flashed furiously. 'What do you know of them? You're nothing. You can't touch a spitfyre!'

'I'm sorry. I was just –'

'You better just nothing. What are you, anyway? One of Brittel's orphans?'

'Yes,' Stormy lied straight away, immediately raising his status. 'I am.'

'Well, tell him from me he'd better watch out,' she said. 'Tell him to take care.'

'I will,' said Stormy. 'I will do that.'

'And no need to tell anyone else you saw us. All right?' She flashed a smile at him, showing very white and small teeth. 'Our secret?' She was putting on her helmet and goggles now, collecting up her reins. 'Can you keep a secret, orphan boy?'

He nodded, ready to lie down and die for her.

'When I speak to Brittel, who shall I say the message is from?' he called out as she turned her spitfyre towards the edge of the slope. She looked back over her shoulder.

'Araminta!'

She whispered something to her spitfyre, and they leapt over the mountain edge and seconds later were soaring away out of sight.

Stormy's grin stretched across his face. He made his way back to the kitchen in a dream. A spitfyre; he'd nearly touched a real, living and breathing, spitfyre. He almost had. *One day, I'll ride one*, he told himself. *I will. I will. Maybe with that wonderful Araminta.* He was so distracted that he almost tripped over Sponge in the kitchen yard.

The dog was standing perfectly still, watching something, its legs planted like four stiff pillars. He didn't budge when Stormy banged into him.

'Sponge? Did you follow me? What is it, old thing?'

Sponge was frozen, staring unblinking towards a shadowy patch by the kitchen door.

As Stormy drew closer, he saw what had glued Sponge to the spot – a large orange and black snake. A Zinger! Stormy knew that if the dog so much as moved a hair he was dead. Zingers were fast and there was no antidote for their poisonous bite.

Stormy approached carefully, hoping that Sponge wouldn't turn round. He didn't. He was mesmerised. The Zinger rose up and was weaving from side to side, ready to strike. Quickly Stormy reached for a garden spade. The snake saw him and turned its beady eyes on him. Its forked tongue flashed out and flickered.

'Yaah!' Stormy shouted, raising the spade. Instantly the snake dropped to the ground and shot towards him, a blur of colour, a zigzag like lightning slithering over the ground. 'Go, Sponge! Run!' He slashed out with the spade. The snake's darting mouth jabbed up at him but he leapt out of its way. As he jumped, he smacked the spade on the snake's head, stunning it. It bounced, flipping over like a skipping rope. Stormy spun round and hit it. And hit it. It didn't move again.

Sponge nuzzled his cold nose into Stormy's waiting hand and wagged his tail, then plodded towards the kitchen door, butting it open with his head calmly as if he confronted deadly snakes every day.

Otto was standing by the window. He must have seen what happened, but he gave no sign that he had. He just stroked the dog's head silently, and slipped him a morsel of food.

Stormy took up his place at the kitchen table again, his heart still booming and his breath jagged and fast. No one noticed the speckle of burns on his clothes and since almost no one except him went to the compost heap, he knew he could tidy that up later. Snakes and spitfyres all in one day! He imagined telling Tex about the Zinger, how he'd laugh. But he wouldn't tell him about the girl and the spitfyres. He wanted to keep the close encounter all to himself – it was too good to share.

'You!' Brittel had crept up behind him. 'I need sixty blue snails boiled up and winkled out of their shells. Now.'

It was one of the worst jobs and should have been done by the spitfyre staff, but Stormy had no choice. Snails it was. He started straight away. At least it was for the spitfyres. And at least he'd get a chance to give Brittel the message from that girl.

When he'd finished the snails he took them along the dark corridor to the spitfyre kitchen. Dotty, a boy with several large moles on his face, opened the door.

'What is it, Stormy? You look like you've wet your knickers.'

Stormy ignored him. 'I've got the snails for Brittel,' he said, showing Dotty the pail full of squiggles.

'Give 'em here, then.' Dotty held out a fat hand for them.

'I've got to give them straight to Brittel,' Stormy said. 'Right into his hands.'

'Sez who?'

'I have to,' Stormy said. 'I have a very important message for him.'

'Huh. Tell it me, can't you?'

'No. It's private.'

'Oh, hark at you, skivvy. Private? Get in, then.' He pushed Stormy inside roughly.

Stormy intended to take in every detail while he had this rare opportunity to look round the magical kitchen. Blue smoke swirled from the wood burning in the great range and green sparks flew up into the wide chimney.

The long table was covered in dishes and copper basins, glass jars and thick brown glass bottles. Along one wall there were rows of tiny shelves divided into small compartments and each contained minuscule glass bottles of coloured powders. It was like a paint palette – emerald-green, grass-green, lime-green, leaf-green. Blues. Reds. Every colour you could imagine all neatly arranged and labelled with their contents. Stormy longed to know what they were all for.

'Stormy to see you, boss,' Dotty said, leading Stormy over to where Brittel was weighing black shining grains, like seeds, in a pair of brass scales. It looked like magic to Stormy.

'Sez he's gotta message,' Dotty said.

Brittel looked at Stormy with loathing. 'And the message is?'

Stormy glanced at Dotty meaningfully.

'Off you go,' Brittel told Dotty.

'I have a message for you from Araminta,' Stormy said, lowering his voice.

Brittel dropped the ladle with a clatter and everyone in the kitchen turned round and stared at him.

'Back to your work!' Brittel shouted. 'Keep your voice down,' he added, gripping Stormy's arm tightly. 'What are you doing with a message from *her*?' he hissed.

Stormy felt his cheeks redden. He was going about this all wrong.

'I, she, I . . . She said just that you should take care,' he said. 'She said you should watch out.'

'Is this some sort of a wind-up? You playing a trick on me?' Brittel hissed at him. 'Where would *you* meet Araminta!'

'She said it was secret and not to tell anyone, but she was riding on a spitfyre and it crashed. By the compost heap.'

Brittel released his grip and pushed Stormy aside. 'All right. Very well. Forget you saw her; forget you heard what she said. Forget everything. Now go away. Get out of my kitchen!'

As if Stormy could forget seeing the spitfyres and seeing Araminta! Was he crazy? Still, he could keep a secret and he would.

That night Stormy settled down with his two books, both presents for good work over the years: *Spitfyre History* and *Spitfyre Myth and Legend*.

Reading about the Silver Sword Race was a favourite passage. It was held only every ten years. The Director of the Academy hid the special sword at a secret location that was only revealed on the day of the race. The names of the sky-riders who'd brought back the swords . . . Rowena Heath, Gregor Erskine, Wesley Grant – and 'Stormy' added in pencil – went into the Winners' Gallery.

Now Stormy also had the circus flyer to read. '*Dazzling feats of bravery!*' '*Daredevil death-defying acts!*' He tried to put himself in dark-haired Renaldo's place, tried to *be* him. The circus man glowed with pride; he looked as if any moment he would burst out of his skin with the joy of being the person he was. Beside him was a vast gold flying horse with glittery wings spread wide and flames shooting out of its mouth. Oh, if only!

Stormy slipped the handbill under his pillow, the images still burning on the back of his eyes.

6

Luck

A few days later, Mrs Cathcart called the skivvies together. Otto stood beside her, puffed up importantly like whisked eggwhite.

'I have an exciting announcement,' she said. 'Silence. Look this way. All eyes on me.' She waved a sheet of paper at them.

The boys were pretty certain that whatever the housekeeper had to say would not be very interesting.

'Are you listening?'

The boys shuffled guiltily.

'The Academy has a vacancy. Quite suddenly. A boy is needed to work in the servery and the stables,' Mrs Cathcart said, glancing at her piece of paper.

A groan went round the room, a groan that Mrs Cathcart – who had a fairytale view of spitfyres – interpreted as excitement. 'I know, I know,' she said, 'it is *thrilling*. You all want a chance to work up there, don't you?'

'She's bonkers,' Tex whispered to Stormy. 'I certainly don't!'

'I wouldn't mind,' a freckled boy called John said.

'More fun than here,' said another.

'Don't pick me,' one said. 'Pleeeeze.'

Going up to the Academy would mean leaving friends and only a few boys wanted to get any closer to a fire-breathing winged horse than they had to.

'Boys who go up there never come back,' Tex whispered again. 'Is she mad?'

One of the favourite topics for late-night horror stories was *what happened to the missing orphans?* Were they used as targets in firing practice? Were they thrown off the highest point of the castle so the birds could eat them? Did the Director eat them, sliced, on toast? Or were they boiled alive to make spitfyre fuel?

Nobody knew the answer – just that the boys didn't come back.

The boys' names were put into a wooden box for Mrs Cathcart to pick one. 'We must be fair,' she said. 'I know what a privilege it is to go *up* and work in the Academy and I would not like to put any boy above another.'

'Some privilege to have your hair singed off and skin toasted black,' Purbeck whispered, rubbing his big chin with glee.

The room had gone very still. Most boys were praying it *would* not be his name on the slip of paper she chose.

Stormy felt sick.

'Go on, Mrs Cathcart,' Otto said, 'let's not waste time. Work to be done in the kitchen.'

The housekeeper pushed her fat arm into the box and shuffled her hand about. Stormy pictured her sausage fingers flipping through the bits of paper like a fish swimming through weeds. He urged her fingers to find his name. He urged them to touch the word: S-T-O-R-M-Y. That wasn't hard, was it? *Keep going, fingers. Keep going. You'll find it. You have to. Can't you read?*

'Good luck,' Tex whispered to him.

Stormy nodded. He couldn't speak; he couldn't bear the thought of another boy getting this chance, and worst of all, getting this chance and not wanting it.

'Here we are,' Mrs Cathcart beamed, waving a slip of paper. 'Here's the lucky boy!'

She unfolded the paper and read out a name. Stormy couldn't hear anything because the noise in his ears was so tremendous; spitfyres were flying around his head, he could hear the shushing sound of their leathery wings and see the smoke puffing from their nostrils and –

'*Stormy!*'

All eyes turned to him. He stared back. Why were they looking at him?

Tex nudged him. 'You. It is *you*, fungus face!'

'Me what? *Me!*' It came out as a shout and the other boys tittered.

'Step forward, Stormy,' Otto shouted. 'Are you deaf?'

Tex and Purbeck gave him a push that catapulted him

towards Mrs Cathcart. He got in front of her and Otto somehow, and stood there like a fence post.

'Congratulations, Stormy,' Mrs Cathcart said.

Stormy did nothing, said nothing. He saw that Mrs Cathcart had lipstick on her teeth. Her left eye was wandering towards the window. It was suddenly hot.

Otto was staring at him hard. He looked as if someone had just opened the oven on his rising batter pudding.

'You'll do us proud, I'm sure,' Mrs Cathcart said.

'Ma'am,' was all he could manage.

Never before had he ever had any luck. Never. For the first time ever, he felt hopeful.

Later Mrs Cathcart squeezed Stormy into some Academy work clothes. A blue shirt with a button-up collar, the likes of which he had never worn before, a small dark blue jacket and trousers that stopped short of his matchstick ankles. It was all tight and constricting. The collar choked him: it reminded him of the grubbin's hands around his throat and he wondered how the poor man was now and if he were still a prisoner.

'There! My, you do look a picture, don't you?' Mrs Cathcart said, standing back and admiring her handiwork. 'I never noticed till now, Stormy, but you've lovely blue eyes. Irish ancestry, I expect. Don't worry, you'll be a fine young man when you manage to grow a bit, you really will.'

'Thank you,' Stormy said, who hadn't been worried about growing until that moment. The twinkle in Mrs Cathcart's eye was making him feel uneasy.

'You lucky boy! Aren't you so lucky?' She squeezed his cheek between her fingers.

He nodded. Yes. Yes. He felt like the Christmas goose they'd trussed up with a length of string. He could barely breathe, but he didn't care. He was going up Dragon Mountain. He was going to be *in* the Academy.

Stormy went to say goodbye to Otto.

'And who do you suppose is going to look after my compost heap?' Otto said, lightly beating a wooden spoon against Stormy's head.

'I am sorry, Otto, really I am, I –'

'*Sorry?*' He stopped his tapping. 'But this is what you wanted, *wanted most*, isn't it?' Otto asked him, strangely, weirdly concerned. 'Tell me it's what you wanted.'

'Yes,' Stormy said, a little perplexed.

'I thought so. I *knew* so. More even than moving you up to Brittel's kitchen? Tell me I was right about that?'

Surprised he should care, Stormy nodded.

'Well, you won't need me to do that now. You'll be up at the Academy, close to spitfyres *and* their food.' Otto stared at Stormy, shaking his head slowly. 'Sponge will miss you. You take care up there, now.'

Why was Otto being so nice? It made no sense. 'Yes, sir,' he said. 'Yes, I'll take care – are you quite all right, Otto?'

'Of course I am! Now, you be careful. Remember that Otto isn't so very far away . . . And remember, there'll

43

always be a place here for someone that can manage a compost heap like you, Stormy.'

Stormy grinned. His home wasn't the kitchen; he wasn't a skivvy. He was going to the Academy!

7

Academy

Stormy lingered just beyond the kitchen walls, savouring this odd sensation of aloneness. He turned away from the lane that led down to the village of Stollen, away from the kitchen buildings and, for the first time, headed up the stony path that spiralled towards the towering turrets of the Academy castle.

The path was narrow and rocky; unlucky carts had tipped right over the edge and tumbled down to the valley below. Few trees grew this high up; only some spindly sprigs of green showed amongst the pale rocks. The wind whipped around Dragon Mountain and moaned as it squeezed through tiny tunnels and gaps between the stones. Stormy hugged his jacket, feeling the air getting colder and colder the higher he went.

At the first bend in the path he paused to look down at the kitchens and dormitory buildings. It was strange seeing things from this angle, steep slate roofs all higgledy-piggledy, different shades of grey and purple; tiny windows he knew nothing about hidden in the eaves and tall crooked chimneys. He could even see the compost heap.

He followed the path round the mountainside until finally the massive wall of the castle reared up before him. Behind the wall, taller towers with pointed purple roofs rose into the sky.

The wooden gates were made of a dark wood, studded with metal spitfyres. Jagged metal barbs ran along the top, like the spikes along a dragon's tail. Stormy shifted his little bag of possessions into his left hand and pulled the bell rope. His heart went ding-donging like the bell.

Voices started up on the other side of the gate.

'What? Who's there?'

'Hello?'

'Who is it?'

'Someone at the door?'

It sounded as if there were several people talking in high-pitched voices.

'I'm Stormy, from the big kitchen down below. Come to work here.'

'Heaven help us!' a voice said.

'A new orphan!'

'Here in the Academy!'

There were scratching and scuttling noises from behind the gate, but it still didn't open.

'Hello?' Stormy said. 'Can you open the gate?'

'Just about to do it.'

'Please,' Stormy said. 'Could you –'

'Go on, then!'

'Out of the way!'

'Here goes!'

The bolt was drawn back noisily and a small door within the vast gate opened. Stormy stepped through cautiously. 'Hello . . .'

Two littles were wrestling with each other on the other side. They were the size of five-year-old children, but their wrinkled skin showed they were much older. They both wore red trousers with braces and green checked jerkins.

'You didn't do it properly!'

'*You* couldn't open a paper bag!'

One little ran off and instantly the other followed. They disappeared into the child-sized gatehouse and slammed the door shut with a loud bang.

There were littles who lived in Stollen, and they seemed usually to be wise and jolly creatures. He wished the littles hadn't disappeared; they might have helped him.

Stormy had stepped into a very large courtyard paved with massive creamy stone slabs, worn smooth by hundreds of years of feet. It was surrounded on all sides by high walls. To his left, in the corner, there was a small tower and standing at its base, either side of an iron door, were two guards. Between them was a flight of steps leading down – to the dungeons, he guessed. The guards did not move.

Directly in front of him was a tall, thin, grey house with rows of identical pointed blank windows. He walked towards the forbidding place. He felt himself being watched, but saw no one.

Not knowing what else to do, he went up the steps to the door. The door handle and door knocker were both shaped like spitfyres. Stormy knocked tentatively.

After a while, a girl of about his age opened the door. She was thin, dressed in a droopy blue gown and a grey apron and looked as if she never got enough food or sleep. She was busy tidying up her long dark hair, rolling it into an untidy knot.

'I'm sorry,' he began, 'I don't know where to go. The littles at the gate just –'

'You shouldn't come to *this* door,' the girl whispered. She smiled shyly. 'This is the *Director's* house. This is out of bounds for you – for the workers – unless invited, of course.'

Stormy felt his cheeks fire up hotly. He stumbled backwards down the short flight of steps. 'Sorry. Sorry, I didn't know . . .'

'Don't worry. No one saw you. You need that door there.' She pointed to her left to a narrow arched doorway. 'The servery.' She was already closing the big door on him.

'Thank you, Miss –'

'Maud.' She grinned suddenly and her whole face brightened. 'Just Maud, but you can call me Miss Maud if you like . . . no, not really, just joking. Good luck,' she added, closing the door. 'Take care.'

Encouraged by that smile, Stormy went towards the door she'd pointed to. *I'm really close to the spitfyres right now. I'm going to live and breathe spitfyres . . . I'm lucky, I am so lucky.*

But in truth he felt very small just then, surrounded by the giant walls and very ignorant of the Academy's ways. As he looked up he saw a group of students pressing their faces up against the glass of one of the windows, waving and shouting at him. He couldn't hear a thing but he could see that they were laughing at him. He tugged at his too-short sleeves and flattened down his hair.

At last he reached the servery door and knocked on it quietly, so quietly that no one heard him.

Stormy didn't even hear the knock himself.

8

Spitfyre Keeper

Receiving no answer to his knock, Stormy went in. Passing along a narrow corridor, he came to a sort of kitchen with a table, oven and shelves of pots; he guessed it was the servery.

It was empty.

Perhaps he shouldn't have come in like that, but he couldn't stand out in the courtyard being laughed at.

He put his bag down on the floor and looked around.

There were four tall windows on the opposite side of the room that overlooked a wide terrace on the mountain edge. The windows were greasy with fingerprints and dusty. The old stove looked like it hadn't been used for years; the copper pans on the dresser were tarnished. The floor seemed to have been coated with old jam.

A figure passed the windows and came towards the door. Stormy prepared himself – perhaps this would be his new boss?

The door opened and the man creaked towards him.

Despite his nerves, Stormy had the wit to think that the noise was odd, that stone floors didn't creak.

The man was a walking skeleton. His head was skull-like with sunken eyes and cheeks; his skin was grey. Huge hands hung like stone crabs from his long arms. All his features were large; his nose was long and drooping, with black nostrils like tunnels. His ears stuck out like cupboard doors and his eyebrows were thick and black. Around his neck he wore a heavy chain with a key on it.

He creaked over to Stormy. It wasn't the floor that was making the noise, but the man's right leg, which dragged along the floor as if it held a hidden weight and, as he lifted it, there was the sound of wood on wood, bending.

'The new skivvy?' he said slowly.

'Yes, I'm Stormy, sir.'

The tall man shook his head. 'No, no, we don't do *sir* here.' He sighed. 'I'm Al. Stable boss; keeper of the winged horses.'

'*Spitfyre keeper!*' Stormy said reverently.

Al lowered himself stiffly to a chair at the table, manhandling his right leg into place. 'I do my job, Stormy; I keep the spitfyres. That's all I do here, my job. Nothing else.' He toyed with some crumbs on the table. 'Do *your* job, Stormy, and ask no questions and you'll be happy as a . . .' he looked at Stormy from beneath his heavy brows, 'whatever's happy, I don't know. Yes?'

'Yes, sir. I mean yes, Al.'

'Good. I brought you a list of servery and stable duties,' Al said. 'Did you know Ollie? He had your job, before –'

he hesitated, 'before he left. He never did quite get the hang of it. He came up from Otto's kitchen too. Like Smithers and Freddie . . .'

'I remember Ollie,' Stormy said. 'We called him Oily. He used to write poetry and we teased him. He had long dark hair, didn't he?'

'Dark, yes. Poetry, yes. He was useless. Simply no other way to describe him.'

'I won't be, I promise.' Stormy quickly scanned his list of duties. The word SPITFYRE appeared a lot – reading it made his pulse race. 'I love flying horses,' he said.

Al frowned; his whole face sank into a heavy, lined expression. '*Love* spitfyres? Ah, Stormy once upon a time . . .' His voice faded away.

'All my life I've dreamed about working with winged horses,' Stormy said.

Al gave him a pitying look. 'I've worked with them for years and years. How will you feel after you've cleaned out thirteen mucky pens every day? Fed and watered the hungry bad-tempered beasts, eh? Spitfyres! Come. I'll show you where you sleep. You're sharing with Ralf. You two work the West-side spitfyres. Troy and Roy do the East side.'

'East? West?'

'Depending on their need for light, Stormy, and for heat. The hottest side is the West. Late sun. East side is for morning spitfyres; they don't need to get so warm. Put it down to their dragon blood.'

Stormy felt a little thrill ripple through his bones; he was learning important things already.

A flat-sounding bell rang suddenly and Stormy jumped. 'What's that?'

Al smiled slowly. 'That's the dumb waiter.' He nodded encouragingly as he saw understanding dawn in Stormy's eyes. 'Yes, the lift, Stormy, from *your* kitchen.'

Stormy pictured the enormous lift coming up from hundreds of feet below, as the Winder cranked the handle. It was passing through the ceiling of Otto's kitchen, through walls and floors, rumbling and creaking up through the shaft cut into the stone of the mountain, through the dungeons and up to the Academy. He'd never even *dreamed* of seeing it from this side: the UP side.

The kitchen cupboards rattled and shook as the lift came nearer. There was a rumbling movement deep under their feet. A sound like a small dog whining sang up through the ground.

'Cogs and wheels,' Al said, shaking his head as if he could hardly believe there were such extraordinary things. 'Levers and pulleys, eh?'

With a final jolt that shook the dishes on the dresser, the lift wheezed to a halt. Al opened a cupboard door to a container full of food; plates of cold meats that only Otto could have arranged, with slices of salami swirling out in overlapping spirals interspersed with fancily cut gherkins and sprigs of parsley and chives. There were salads of baby tomatoes and fresh herbs and a mountain of warm fresh bread rolls.

Al wheeled out two trolleys from a side room and wiped his long skinny forearms over them, scattering little black objects that looked suspiciously like mouse droppings.

'That'll do,' he said.

The lift had brought up with it the scent of Otto's kitchen. Stormy pictured the bustling room below – Sponge, Otto and Tex, everything he knew. It wasn't homesickness yet, just a sharp reminder.

Al nodded at the food. 'Professional stuff, that. Gordon Blur as we say up here. Great!' He peeled off a slice of pink ham, rolled it into a tube and handed it to Stormy. 'Here.'

Stormy shook his head violently. 'No, no!'

Al shrugged and picked up a tomato, wrapped salami round it and offered that to him. 'No? Can't I tempt you? It's delicious.'

Stormy gulped. 'Mr Al, sir, don't you know you can't do that? I mean, sorry, but if you did that down there, Otto'd have your head sliced off, easy as the top off a boiled egg.'

Al shrugged. 'Well, we're not down there where Otto can see, are we, Stormy, my friend?' he said. 'Go on, help yourself, boy!'

Al was carefully placing the food on a plate and looking at it, not eating it.

Help yourself? It had to be a trick or a test. If he did eat something, no doubt he'd be sent straight back, labelled a thief or even locked away in the dungeons. He shook his head. 'No thank you, Al, no.'

'Your loss, young man.' Al piled olives and onions and

cucumber slices onto his plate. 'There'll be plenty more – that's starters.'

Perhaps it wasn't a trick, but still Stormy wouldn't touch a morsel until it was his proper mealtime. Lordy, imagine if Otto had seen what Al did? He'd have a fit! It was too horrible to think about.

'Now, let's go find Ralf,' said Al.

A green lizard scuttled across the floor, picked up a morsel of food and vanished with it into a mouse hole in the wall.

'You've got green lizards,' Stormy said.

'But not those nasty orange ones,' Al said.

'And mice,' Stormy added, picking up his bag and following Al out.

'I like mice,' Al said.

He led Stormy out onto a wide stone-flagged terrace. A low wall was all that separated them from the sheer drop to the valley below. Black hills, covered in pine trees, ringed them in; chains of rugged, pointed summits reaching far away into the distance. The highest peaks were capped with blue-white snow.

'It's great being up so high,' Stormy said. 'In the kitchen we always looked up – well, you could look down, but there was only the forest and Stollen to look at.'

'Long way down,' Al said slowly. 'Long and winding path.'

'It goes right by our kitchen window,' Stormy told him.

'I knew that. Yes, I knew that. I've never been down, not since I came here,' he said.

It seemed strange to Stormy that someone who obviously didn't like it here never took the chance to get out.

They had come to a narrow flight of stone steps cut into the wall of the castle. Slowly Al eased himself up the steps and, stooping down, he hammered on the small door. 'Ralf! Visitor for you.'

He nudged Stormy inside and shut the door behind him. 'See you later.'

9

Ralf

A very pale boy was sitting on the edge of one of the two beds in the low-ceilinged room. He stared up at Stormy from below a long fringe of dull brown hair.

Stormy nodded towards the other bed in the room. 'For me?'

'Can't see who else it would be for,' Ralf said. 'It *was* Ollie's.'

Stormy dropped his bag onto the bed. 'I've never had my own bed before!' He sat on it and bounced up and down. 'Brilliant!'

'Sleep on the floorboards down there, then?'

'No, a bunk bed, and every time my mate Tex turned over, the whole thing wobbled. What happened to Ollie?'

'Mind your own business.'

Stormy waved the paper with his list of duties on it cheerfully. 'What's the worst job?'

'Anything involving Academy students,' Ralf said at last. 'Then spitfyres, then everything else. It's all worst.'

'Al seems OK,' Stormy said, 'a bit glum. Least he doesn't whack with spoons – does he? . . . I love spitfyres.'

'You know a lot about them, do you?' said Ralf.

Stormy stared at the floor. He didn't know a lot about spitfyres, of course he didn't, he only knew what he'd read. He wanted to tell Ralf how wonderful coming up to the Academy was, how lucky he felt. 'I've always wanted to be with spitfyres,' he said. 'I might come from a sky-rider family, you never know. It could be in my blood, couldn't it? I know it's not likely, because spitfyre masters are always rich and powerful and I am just an orphan – but I was found wrapped in a red wool blanket, not just the usual bit of sacking. Mrs Cathcart told me.'

Ralf stared blankly at the wall. '*Red wool?* Really? And do you have a peculiar birthmark too? Something that looks like a spitfyre or a dragon's wing?'

A spark of hope flared up inside Stormy's chest. 'Well, not that I –'

Then he saw Ralf was sniggering; he was mocking him.

'No? That's what happens in books,' Ralf said. 'Isn't it?'

'All right,' Stormy said, his voice cracking, 'but I . . .' How could he explain his feeling for a creature he'd never actually touched? He couldn't understand it himself, this *need,* this physical *want* to be with a spitfyre. 'Well, I'll see, won't I?' he added lamely.

'Huh,' Ralf said. 'My dad worked here when I was a kid. But he died,' he said gloomily. 'Then I got stuck doing his job and I don't like it. Don't like any animals really, they're not natural. But I'm sure it was different before – or maybe that was just because I had my dad. Dad liked them. Was good with them.'

'What about the Director?'

'Oh, the Director!' Ralf said. 'You can't fault him, but . . .' His voice faded. 'You'll see.'

Stormy looked at the timetable. 'What do we do first?' he said brightly.

Ralf sighed. 'Do you have to be so enthusiastic? You'll see soon enough.' He swung himself off the bed. 'Let's go.'

Stormy paused at the top of the narrow stone steps to look round at the mountains. There was so much air up here. He felt the place was full of possibilities. Nothing Ralf said would change that.

He listened hopefully; except for the distant cries of some large birds circling above it was quiet.

'Where *are* the spitfyres?' he asked, as they made their way back to the servery.

'Round the bend! Hah, joke!' Ralf didn't laugh. 'Some *are* round the bend. You'll see them soon enough.'

Al was sitting with his bad leg propped up on a chair. He was eyeing a tomato that he'd speared on the end of his knife. 'How does Otto grow these tomatoes?' he said. 'They're so tiny; sweet as cherries.' He rolled another gently up and down the table. 'Ralf, oblige with the starters, please?'

Ralf scowled. 'You might have taken them along, Al,' he said, rushing out with the trolleys.

Al went on staring at his tomato. 'Main course coming any minute . . . Now.'

The bell rang and rumbling noises started up. As the lift came closer and closer, the scent of the warm food filled the air. Stormy's mouth watered. When he opened the dumb waiter and saw the hot crusty pies, sausages and mashed potatoes and honey-coated roast carrots, he almost keeled over with hunger.

Ralf came back and helped Stormy to unload the food onto the trolleys.

'There we go,' Al said, without moving from his seat. He leaned over and spiked a sausage and broke off a bit of piecrust. 'That looks good, doesn't it?' He laid the bits on the table and began to shift them around with the tip of his finger, making a pattern. 'Otto knows how to cook, I must say he does, the rogue.'

'Right, Stormy,' Ralf said when the trolleys were loaded up. 'Follow me. Do what I do.'

They went down a long corridor and stopped at a blue door. A bald man wearing a black uniform opened it immediately. Without a word or look, he took the trolleys and thrust them through swing doors into the dining room beyond.

When the doors opened a burst of noise erupted – shouting, laughing and the clink of cutlery. Stormy caught a magical glimpse of brightness; lights shone, silverware glittered. He saw, in that instant, covered tables, the red and green of the Academy uniform, smiling faces, paintings on the walls, vases of flowers, mirrors . . . and then the door swung shut and it was gone.

He wondered if Araminta was there. Or the sky-rider

who'd messed up his compost heap, but there was no second look; Ralf was already heading back.

'That's it, then,' Ralf said, clapping his hands together. 'Lunch duty done and dusted.'

'And *our* lunch?' Stormy's breakfast porridge was a long time ago.

Ralf laughed. 'You should've grabbed some when it came up. Now you'll have to wait for the leftovers.'

'Leftovers?'

'That's right. That's what we eat.' He saw Stormy's startled expression and laughed. 'It's not so bad, just a bit cold. Hey, leave the trolley and let me show you this.'

Ralf nipped off down a side corridor and pushed open a big door.

'No one's around, they're all stuffing their faces. This is the Gallery.' He pulled Stormy inside. 'The Silver Swords. Look! I don't care for spitfyres, but aren't *they* something?'

'The Silver Swords?' Stormy repeated. 'Oh, my . . .'

The room was long and narrow and down one side were seven large swords. Each sword was wobbly and misshapen, strangely undefined, as if it hadn't been quite finished. Above each sword was a name on a placard.

'I've read about the race,' Stormy said.

'Yeah? It's next year. They're talking about it already. It's the highest trophy of all. I wish I had a sword . . . Come on, let's go get a breather.'

They went out and sat on the low stone wall. It was icy cold and Stormy shivered. Ralf took out a mouth organ and began playing it softly. The sad notes seemed to be caught by the breeze and dragged away towards the mountains.

Stormy peered down at the barred dungeon windows and below that the roofs of the kitchen, and beyond that the village and down into the distant valley and the town of Stollenback, a smudge in the distance. 'Miles and miles to the bottom,' he said.

Ralf shuddered. His mouth suddenly trembled and the notes wavered and died.

'Ollie.' He held his mouth organ against his chest and stared down into the valley. 'Ollie had an accident,' he said quietly.

Stormy stared at Ralf, then at the emptiness below.

'Here?'

Ralf nodded, turned away and walked slowly back to his room.

10

Araminta

Al was still sitting at the table when Stormy went back in. He'd pushed the scraps of food around and around until they'd formed a flying thing – a bird or a spitfyre; it was hard to tell which. Stormy wondered if Al ever ate anything.

'Lift,' Al said, nodding towards it.

Stormy went to the lift.

'Cake,' Al said.

Stormy collected an enormous iced cake studded with nuts and cherries and placed it gently on the table.

'Cake,' Stormy agreed.

'For the Director's house,' Al said. 'You take it.'

'Me?' said Stormy in horror, looking at the vast cake beneath its pristine dome.

'You. It's an Otto special, for the Director. He and his darling daughter, they like cake. I think they'd like to eat cake for the rest of their lives. Just cake. Soft and creamy and no chewing. Funny, I don't like cake. I like something to gnaw on. Bones and crusty bread.'

'Can Ralf show me?' Stormy was thinking of those sneering boys and girls at the window.

'No need. It's the tall building. Lots of windows. You'll have seen it when you came in. Buck up, lad.'

Stormy felt panic rise up and lodge heavily like a brick in his chest. But he couldn't not do it, the first job he was given. *Buck up*.

He walked carefully across the empty courtyard without glancing at the students' windows. The courtyard seemed to have expanded and the Director's house looked tiny and distant. The walk took years. He was sure he was being watched. It made him walk like somebody else, like someone who hadn't done much walking and had to think about how to do it. He glared at the cake, willing it not to touch the sides of its glass dome.

Maud opened the door.

'Hello,' Stormy said. 'It's me again.'

For an instant her face lit up and a dimple appeared in her left cheek. 'Hello, you again. How are you getting on?' She looked away shyly and dug her hands into the pockets of her apron. 'How's it going?'

'It's fine. Great. I love it.'

'Good.' She smiled and the dimple appeared again. 'You're brave. I'd hate it – not the spitfyres, but everything else . . . How about Al? He's a good man, don't be put off by his gloominess.'

'Cool. He's cool. He sent me to bring this,' Stormy said, lifting the cake up a little.

64

'Really? I thought you must just like carrying it about,' Maud said with a giggle.

Stormy reddened. 'No, I –'

'Did you cook it?'

'Oh no, I couldn't . . . well, I probably could because I do know how, but we're not allowed to, down in Otto's kitchen.'

'I see,' Maud said sternly. 'But do you know how to *eat* cake?'

'Of course I do. Oh . . .'

She was teasing him and he couldn't look at her. He let his gaze wander instead down the brightly lit corridor beyond. There were paintings on the red walls and glass chandeliers, mirrors and ornate gold tables. He'd never seen anything like it, or even dreamed such things could exist.

'Hey! Mind the cake!' Maud held out her hands. 'You'd better give that to me before you drop it.'

But before Stormy could pass it to her, a girl strode down the corridor towards them. She moved with the force of a hot wind. Her eyes were cold. She was beautifully dressed in a yellow satin skirt and a white blouse. He felt his knees give a little; Araminta. The girl who'd crashed her spitfyre.

She shoved Maud aside carelessly. 'Who's this? Who are you talking to, Maud?'

'He's the new boy to help Al. He's –' Maud began.

'I think he can speak, can't he?' Araminta stared down at Stormy scornfully. She obviously did not recognise him at all. 'You can speak, can't you? Well, can't you?'

He was disappointed that she didn't remember him, but it was also dawning on him that she wasn't just a sky-rider, she was important. She lived in the Director's house.

'I help in the servery, but really I'm to help the spitfyre keeper with the flying horses,' he exaggerated. Why had he done that? She wasn't interested in him anyway.

'What are you doing here, then?'

'Delivering Otto's cake,' he said, showing her the cake. 'I've brought a cake. It's a cake for the Director. It's from Otto.' Now he was talking rubbish.

Araminta tossed her head so her long black plait flicked over her shoulder. She was staring at him with the same oddly disturbing look that Mrs Cathcart had given him when she had dressed him in his new work clothes – as if he was something tasty to eat. Or maybe she *did* remember him?

'Follow me. Bring the cake,' she said.

Stormy glanced nervously at Maud, sure he shouldn't be going inside, but she had taken a duster from her apron pocket and was rubbing furiously at the brass fingerplate. He stepped into the hall.

'Don't bring the cake! Give it to the maid!'

He wished she'd make her mind up who was to bring what. Quickly he passed the cake to Maud and followed Araminta, entranced by the glossy rope of dark hair swinging from side to side across her back. The tiny fraction of her face he could see showed her skin was as smooth and pale as a porcelain doll.

'This is the Director's study,' Araminta said, leading him into a room. 'You must never, never come in here.'

Stormy began to back out.

'What are you doing? Come in!' she snapped.

He went in and stood beside a round table in the centre of the room. There were books on it, a decanter of golden liquid, glasses, a box of cigars, and a massive glass paperweight in the shape of the Academy castle.

The walls of the study were lined with shelves of books and stuffed heads of deer and wolves. The deer looked petrified and the wolves looked fierce and Stormy thought how unfair it was to leave the poor deer being forever frightened.

Mastering the Skies, Aerodynamics for Animal Flyers, The Science of Spitfyres, Spitfyre Folklore, Training for Spitfyre Sky-riders, Flying Horses Forever – the titles of the books sent a thrilling shiver up his spine.

'So, you replace Ollie?' Araminta said. 'I suppose you're surprised I know a servery worker, aren't you?'

Stormy shook his head, then nodded; she was so confusing.

'The silly boy made a name for himself . . . You have a good head for heights, have you?'

He wished she wouldn't stare at him so.

'Yes, miss.'

'The other boy did not.'

'Didn't he, miss?' He pretended to know nothing of Ollie's fate because it seemed safer.

She flicked her hair. 'Don't answer back!' She glared at

him. 'Well, what do you think? Will you make a name for yourself? Answer me!'

'I'm not clever,' Stormy said. 'I've never had the chance. But if I had the chance, if I could read all these books, or –'

She shook her pretty head. 'No chance of that, kitchen boy!'

The swirly patterns on the green and gold carpet swirled some more. 'No, miss.'

'I'm the Director's daughter,' she said. 'I give orders here. I can do whatever I like.' She watched him closely, waiting for him to answer.

'Yes, miss.' *The Director's daughter? Oh, my!*

'And you must always do as I say,' she added.

'Yes, miss.' Stormy nodded. Unable to return her stare he looked round at the fascinating things in the room, coming to a stop at a painting of a young man. 'Is that the Director there?' he blurted, pointing at the picture.

'Which one, you totally rude boy?'

There were *two* almost identical paintings of two young men on the walls facing each other. They both wore their hair long, curling close round their faces.

'Either.'

'You are very nosey for a kitchen boy,' she said. 'One is my father and one is his brother. I never met my uncle. He's dead.'

'Oh, I'm sorry.'

'Don't be. It happened ages and ages ago and he left all his money to Daddy so actually it was pretty lucky. If you

68

have to share something you end up with less of it, which isn't good. Don't you agree?'

Stormy had always shared everything – his bunk, his clothes, and his food. But still he nodded.

Suddenly there was a knock at the door and Maud came in. 'Did you ring? Tsk tsk,' she added, eyeing the table. 'I am sorry.' She began dusting the table vigorously. 'I'm so sorry, didn't I polish this mahogany to your liking, miss? I could –'

'No. I did not ring! Maud, you've got bells in your skull instead of brains. How dare you interrupt us? Go away.'

'Yes, miss.' Maud gave Stormy a quick cheeky grin, so fleeting he wasn't sure it had been there at all, and backed out. 'I can't imagine what I was thinking,' she muttered with a smile as she closed the door.

'Maud has been with us since she was a baby. An orphan, like you,' Araminta said. 'Daddy treats her as part of the family; he is a very kind and generous man. My mother died, you know. Just three years and eight months ago. I think I'm forgetting her a little already. Daddy has forgotten her completely. Ah well . . .'

Stormy hardly heard her. What if Araminta and the Director had adopted *him* when he was a baby, instead of Otto and Mrs Cathcart taking him in at the orphanage? How different his life would have turned out then.

'You'll love it here,' she went on. 'My father is a great man. He has big ideas. He's building the Academy into something stupendous. Its reputation is growing and soon –' She hesitated. 'Soon our spitfyres will rule the world!'

Stormy nodded, fired by her enthusiasm. 'Yes, yes, I'm sure they will,' he said. *Our spitfyres. Our* spitfyres!

'Well, you'd better go,' Araminta said, smiling at him sweetly. 'I'm sorry, you must have lots of horrid dirty menial jobs to do.'

Stormy turned to leave, but she suddenly stopped him. 'Wait. Do you think I'm very beautiful?'

'Yes. I did when I first saw you,' he said, honestly. 'When you crashed the spitfyre and –'

She went very still. '*I* crashed the spitfyre? When did I crash . . . It was *you*!'

'Yes. By the compost heap. And you asked me to give a message to Brittel. I didn't tell anyone else, honestly.'

Her eyes flashed dangerously. 'Good. My father doesn't allow me to fly, boy – he would be angry if he found out. Don't speak of it to anyone, do you understand? If you do, I will make things very difficult for you. I can, you know, and I will.'

Then she was pointing at the door and he was going towards it. Stumbling and knocking into the furniture, he made it to the corridor. He felt as if he'd been turned upside down and shaken. He wiped his sweaty palms down his trousers as he tottered towards the front door.

The fresh air was like nectar. He breathed it in deeply and ran down the steps two at a time. He forced himself to walk across the yard slowly, as if his cheeks *weren't* on fire. He had never met anyone as bewildering as Araminta.

11
Spitfyres

The servery was deserted. Stormy stared at the trolleys of half-empty dishes and bowls of untouched perfect, delicious Otto food.

All that grub and he didn't feel hungry. Araminta had troubled him. He put aside a little pie on a dish and laid a cloth over it. Maybe later . . . The rest of the food he would have to tip into the rubbish buckets. He hated the thought of throwing it away and decided to put it off for now. He began to wash the dishes, wipe down the table and sweep the floor.

Still no one came.

He started to clean the forlorn room. The small stove hadn't been used for about a hundred years. Old grease had dried in rivulets like candle wax and was as thick as his fingers and black with age. He chiselled it off with a blade. He rubbed and scratched and scrubbed, hoping he could scour Araminta's cutting words from his mind.

He kept expecting someone to shout at him or to deliver

a whack from a number six spoon, but there was no one to do either. He was alone. Below, in Otto's kitchen, in the dormitory, the dining hall, you were never alone. Stormy stopped working and listened to the clock ticking and the birds outside calling. He didn't like this peace. He felt the vast openness of the outside all around him; freedom – he didn't like that either. He missed the smells of the linen cloths drying by the stove, the warm bread, and garlic frying. Cakes. Hot apple pie. And he missed smelly Sponge leaning against his leg.

As he wiped his wet hands down his trousers, his fingers caught on a length of white ribbon dangling from his pocket. *White ribbon?* Perhaps it had always been in the pocket of the too-short blue trousers and he hadn't noticed it before. Perhaps Mrs Cathcart put it there for some odd womanly reason. He stuffed it back in quickly at the sound of Al's squeaky leg.

Ralf came in behind Al.

'Hell's bells,' Al said, stopping mid-stride and looking slowly round at the sparkling kitchen. 'Look at this, Ralf.' Al sat down stiffly at the kitchen table, wiping his palm over the clean surface.

Ralf whistled.

Stormy handed Al the list to remind him of some of the duties – cleaning being one of them. He fancied he smelled sherry trifle all of a sudden, and the smell came from Al.

'Haven't I done it right?'

Al took the list from Stormy and scrumpled it up and

chucked it on the floor. 'I never said *follow* it, did I?' Stormy felt his heart flip; he was in trouble . . .

'It's all right,' Al grunted. 'If you must. I'd rather you didn't. Oh, I don't care –'

'Dinner time,' Ralf interrupted as a buzzer sounded. 'That's the spitfyre food.'

Stormy followed him to a stone-floored pantry adjoining the servery. It smelled like the compost heap. All that hard work down below, all that cleanliness, and then this . . .

The dumb waiter rattled its way towards them. The walls shook and the sound of screeching wheels filled the room.

'You know spitfyres are really rated down in Otto's kitchen,' Stormy said tentatively, knocking a cockroach from its perch by the lift. 'I mean, they *worship* them, almost.'

'Oh, yeah?' Ralf said.

'Brittel cooks special recipes – they've taken years to develop. They make the food behind locked doors.'

'Is that so?' Ralf said blankly.

'Each spitfyre gets a special blend of –'

'All the same to Al what they get,' Ralf said, 'so it's all the same to me.'

'You know it's a bit dirty up here,' Stormy said. 'Otto teaches us to have pride in –'

'We don't do pride here! And spitfyres don't know about clean,' Ralf said. 'Spitfyres never come in here,' he added with a chuckle.

Stormy hated himself for sounding prissy, but hated the

dirt even more. Now Otto's ranting and raving about keeping order, about cleaning and scrubbing didn't seem so fanatical.

Ralf opened the metal doors of the huge dumb waiter. Inside were buckets labelled 1 – 13. Stormy lifted the lid off one; the smell was awful. He slammed it back on and reeled backwards. 'What's in there?'

'Don't like to think,' Ralf said.

Holding his breath, Stormy inched the lid off and had a closer look. 'Oysters, beetles, primroses,' he said, 'some green stuff, chopped potatoes, I think, and carrots, and some sort of long wiggly thing . . . Rather the spitfyres than me!'

They loaded the food onto the two 'dragon-wagons', as Ralf called the larger trolleys, and wheeled them back along the corridor and out of the servery onto the terrace.

By now it was almost dark and Al brought out some lanterns. The light glinted on the specks of ice caught in the cracks and crevasses of the walls. The air was sharp and very cold but Stormy hardly noticed.

The spitfyres at last!

The castle walls towered upwards on their left, disappearing into the dark sky. Windows were tiny yellow squares of light that seemed to float magically in nothingness. On the right of the terrace was space, a drop of thousands of feet to the valley below. Far, far away a few lights glimmered in Stollen and way beyond that, more lights in a cluster, which was Stollenback.

Stormy hugged the wall nervously.

Al leaned on the dragon-wagon as he pushed it along. He didn't speak. It was as if just walking and pushing were hard enough. His lame leg swung stiffly and hit the ground with a dull *thud, thud.*

A string of caves cut into the rock beneath the castle came into view. Large animals moved inside them, and every now and then a shower of flame and sparks illuminated them.

Stormy tingled from head to foot.

'Dragon caves,' Al said. 'Used to be dragons here. Now it's stables for the spitfyres, you see.'

'I see. And no terrace wall,' Stormy added, even more aware of the drop on their right.

Al laughed darkly. 'Spitfyres don't want anything in their way.'

Of course; he had so much to learn.

He could smell the spitfyres now; the dirty hay, and a most peculiar scent of sulphur and newly burnt wood. And he could hear shuffling, snorting, hooves clacking on the stone, snorts and bellowing cries.

His pulse was racing madly.

Ralf brought out some overalls and rubber boots for Stormy from a storeroom. 'They're filthy beasts!' he said, wiping his hands and throwing down a bucket. 'Put them on, they're fireproof, or were . . .'

Stormy reluctantly dragged on the stiff overalls; they were stained and smelled like a cheesy old dishcloth.

'Here. Take this.' Ralf passed him a three-pronged wooden device that looked as if it was used to turn the laundry; only this was lighter with a longer handle. 'It's your thork.'

'Do I need a – a *thork*?'

'You do,' Al said, leaning heavily on the dragon-wagon. 'First thing you should know is that when you step into a spitfyre's den you are stepping into its home. They don't like it.'

'I don't suppose they would –'

'But they must back off. You are master and they *must* let you in. Some will let you get closer than others before they start backing off; they've got different boundaries. That's why we hold out the thork as we go in.'

'Better they burn or bite a thork than your arm,' Ralf said grimly.

'And it's no good me telling you what the limit is with any spitfyre because it's different for each, and for each keeper,' Al said. 'Once the spitfyre's backed up and isn't too cross about losing its space, you go in. Do the necessary.'

Stormy nodded.

'In the morning, that's fresh straw down. Fresh water. Food in the trough. Got that? Night's just food and water.'

'Yes. I understand,' Stormy said.

'We muck out proper when they go fly,' Ralf told him.

Stormy wasn't bothered about the duties. Any idiot could do that – he just wanted to get close to see the spitfyres clearly.

'On we go, then.'

The wagons rattled noisily. The lantern lights wavered

and wobbled as gusts of wind got into them. The food was growing cold.

'Number one,' Ralf said.

They were at the first cave. Al arranged the lanterns so they had light to work by.

Stormy was right next to a real flying horse.

It was a massive creature of silvery grey – the size of a shire horse with feet like dinner plates and legs like small trees. The sheer size of it took his breath away. The pulsating power and heat coming from it made him giddy.

The spitfyre was puffing smoke and shifting restlessly around its cave. Its bat-like wings were folded against its side, but they twitched and stirred, as if they were going to unfurl at any moment. There was a fierceness about it, as if it wanted to escape and fly away, like a dog on the end of a leash. It was both scary and thrilling.

'Oh, Al! Oh, Ralf!' Stormy cried. 'Look at it!'

Ralf huffed. 'Don't know what you're so excited about. Work with flying horses as long as I have, then, well . . . It's just a spitfyre – a horse with a bit of lizard thrown in. Here, I'll do him and show you how. Number one's Star Squad – a bit wild, a bit special.'

Ralf held up the thork and pushed his way into the cave, jabbing the pronged thing at the creature and shouting. The spitfyre's eyes rolled, showing the whites, and it snorted crossly. It reared up on its hind legs and blew out a cloud of pungent smoke, but Ralf dodged the dangerous hooves and quickly did his work. 'Food!' he called out. 'See here, water!'

He ran out, wiping the sweat off his face with his sleeve. 'Done.'

'You're brave!' Stormy said.

'Thanks,' Ralf said with a grin.

'What's the Star Squad?' Stormy asked Al. 'I've never heard of it.'

'The elite,' Al said, leaning on the wagon. 'Strongest. Biggest. Best.'

'They go on secret missions,' Ralf said. 'Do special work for the Director. Now, you do the next one. Number two's OK, I promise.' He handed Stormy the nearest bucket of food.

'But –' Stormy looked at the bucket. 'It's for number five!'

'Who cares?' Al said. 'Otto won't see, or Brittel, will they? We do Star Squad careful since we must, but the rest get what they get.'

Stormy hesitated. Cleaning the kitchen had been a mistake . . . He mustn't make another, he must do as he was told. He didn't want to be sent back to Otto. He took the bucket.

The spitfyre in the second cave was silvery-pink with shining coral-coloured wings. It was watching them closely, not face on, but like a bird, cocking its head on one side and staring with one gleaming dark eye. What an eye! It was as big as an eagle's egg and it swivelled in its socket, showing the yellow-white around it. Its purple hooves pawed the ground as if it was going to leap at any moment. A chain clinked and rattled on one of its hind legs. Stormy had never imagined that. He'd thought they would be free to come and go, flying out into the wide sky whenever they wanted.

Nobody, nothing was free if a spitfyre wasn't.

Stormy took off the lid. The food was red and orange with freshly chopped strong-smelling herbs sprinkled over it which made his nose sting.

'Go on, then,' Al said. 'Don't be scared. Thork at the ready. Get in before the daft thing goes crazy with hunger.'

Stormy squared his shoulders, ready to go in. 'What's its name?' he asked.

'We don't bother with names,' Ralf said.

'Too much effort,' Al said.

But a name would help so much, Stormy thought, facing the massive spitfyre. I'd really like to call it something, *anything* . . . He was so terrified that he was trembling from head to foot as he inched forward, holding his wooden thork up in front of him, nudging the air with it tentatively as if trying to ward off a gnat.

The whole of the cave seemed to be filled with the body of the spitfyre. Heat radiated from it like a boiler. Stormy felt a sweat break out all over his skin. The pink spitfyre puffed out a gust of hot breath, smoky, with a whiff of sulphur that made him cough.

He held up the food bucket and the spitfyre sniffed noisily at it.

'Hello,' Stormy said quietly, 'I've got your dinner. I hope you like it. Brittel made it – it looks lovely.'

'It'll be a bit wary of you to start with,' Ralf shouted

from the cave entrance. 'They've a suspicious nature, spit-fyres. And that one does bite, so keep it pushed back.'

The spitfyre grumbled, jabbed its head at Stormy and sent out a cloud of ash, but nothing worse. Stormy edged towards the food trough with the bucket.

'Don't mind me,' he whispered. 'I'm just nobody.'

He must have been too slow, or the spitfyre was too bad-tempered or too hungry, because suddenly it snorted violently and a stream of fire shot towards him.

'Mind yourself!' Ralf cried. 'Oi! Watch out!'

The flames narrowly missed Stormy's feet. With a yelp he dropped the bucket and ran. The spitfyre bellowed deeply, dived on the food and began to eat it greedily.

'Ha, ha!' Ralf laughed. 'That was something! Number two doesn't like you!'

'But . . . but I didn't mean him any harm,' Stormy cried, deeply hurt. He felt as limp as a rag, sapped of all energy and *so* disappointed.

'The Star Squad can be tricky, like you saw, but number two wasn't *so* bad, was it? Not really? Buck up and try number four,' Al told him. 'The Squad's a difficult lot, but they're best at flying and best at –'

'Best at being beasts,' Ralf said.

'Number one, three, five and seven are Squad,' Al went on. 'You need to watch them. There's a couple on the East side too. Get special things.'

'Special what?' he asked.

'Just things,' Ralf said. 'Number four's OK. He's gentle, you'll see.'

80

The green spitfyre in the fourth cave was smaller and didn't spit at him. It had emerald scales around its hooves and a fine blue and turquoise tail.

'Hello,' Stormy whispered. 'I wonder what your name is, lovely one? Dinner's here.'

The spitfyre shifted out of the way, squashing itself against the wall, keeping its eyes on the food bucket. He put the food into the trough and filled up the water. As the green spitfyre came over to eat, Stormy laid his hand on its neck and stroked it. There! He'd touched one at last.

He went out beaming. He could do this. He would do this. He was going to be the best spitfyre keeper's third assistant ever.

'That's better,' Al said. 'That's good.'

'Scared?' Ralf called to him.

'A bit.'

'You're bound to be; it's your first time,' said Al. 'OK. We'll work our way along. You just do the yellow one in nine and the old one in ten and we'll do the others.'

'OK.' Stormy nodded.

He was surprised to find the caves were so smelly; the straw wasn't fresh and the troughs weren't clean. Otto's rubbish bin was positively spic and span compared to these caves.

Both the spitfyres he tended had sores where their shackles rubbed. Were the stables ever really clean? Since Al didn't seem to care about himself, why would he care for the flying horses? Brittel had made their food so carefully for them. It wasn't difficult to match bucket number six with spitfyre number six. That wouldn't be hard. He'd do that, and find out their names. Once he knew their names he'd be able to manage them better. A name was part of a spitfyre's identity; it was their very essence. A sky-rider needed it to understand his animal, to get it to co-operate and work.

He took as long over the yellow spitfyre in the ninth cave and old grey one in ten as Ralf and Al took to do all the others. The grey spitfyre was arthritic and its wings were crumpled and short. It peered at him with bloodshot eyes and when he patted it, its insides rumbled like a volcano and orange smoke gushed out of its nose. Stormy took this as being a good omen.

They came to the last stable; it was cut at a right angle into the cliff, so the spitfyre inside was hidden.

'Thirteen,' Ralf said. 'Terrible.'

'Why?'

'Oh . . . ' Ralf glanced back towards Al and went on in a lowered voice, 'Even *he* won't go in there. We just chuck in the food. This one's dangerous. It's eaten students, bones and all.'

Stormy swallowed. 'Don't be daft,' he said nervously. 'You're just trying to scare me, aren't you?'

But when he saw that Al was standing back by the dragon-wagon, a strained, faraway expression on his lined face, he wasn't sure.

Ralf swapped his thork for a long forked metal pole. 'Use this,' he said.

Stormy was shaking as he put the bucket of food down at the cave entrance and pushed it inside with the pole. Something moved in the deep shadows, but he saw nothing more than a sparking flash. The smell was awful.

'Don't you ever go in? How do you know how it is?' Stormy asked. 'Is it all right?' he asked Al.

Al wiped his mouth as if he had a bad taste in it. 'That spitfyre is not rideable,' Al said. 'Not tameable. Not anythingable. Best left alone and forgot.'

12
The Director

Stormy went back to the servery with just the empty buckets and rattling wagons to keep him company. He'd need to wash everything, and tidy, and he still had to throw out that leftover food. The servery was empty, but Stormy thought he heard a quick scuttling noise as he went in. He was sure someone had been there – and some of the leftover food had gone. He pictured an army of mice sneaking in and stealing it, but that couldn't be.

While he scrubbed the buckets clean he thought about the dirty caves, the cobwebs as big as bed sheets, filthy wet straw, bones and eggshell ground into the floor, overgrown hooves on the spitfyres and patches of sore skin. Tangled manes and tails. *Not if I was in charge*, he thought. *Not if I was spitfyre keeper – then it would be neat and clean and smart.* He'd loosen the shackles or do away with them entirely. He'd wash the spitfyres' coats and brush their manes and tails and oil their wings to keep them supple . . . He'd be their friend. Even the Star Squad would like him – *specially* the Star Squad. He'd learn how to talk to them . . . He'd write a book about them . . . He'd become famous . . . He'd . . . Why didn't *Al* care? *He* didn't seem bothered about anything, not spitfyres or people or food or anything . . . If only . . .

'Oi! You don't need to *wash* those!' Ralf yelled, coming in. 'That's only spitfyre stuff. Stop! You'll drive Al bonkers.'

Stormy took the crumpled list of duties out of his pocket. 'It says to wash the buckets,' he said. 'Send them down clean. Keep order. It's my job. Anyway, I like cleaning.'

'I don't,' Ralf said. 'Neither does Al. So just stop it.'

That night Stormy lay awake in bed and listened to the silence. Ralf had turned his back on him and appeared to be asleep. He almost missed the snoring and whimpering, the shudder and wobble of the old bunk bed when Tex tossed around beneath him. He had to remind himself how lucky he was to be here in the Academy, working with spitfyres.

He felt for the white ribbon which he'd slipped under his pillow, a silent reminder of Mrs C and the kitchen. He supposed it had been a kind thing for her to do.

There wasn't enough light to read his books, so he pulled out the old circus flyer and stared at the dim pictures of the Great Renaldo instead, trying to imagine life in a circus. And he thought about the spitfyres. Tomorrow he'd see them in daylight. Tomorrow he would start getting to know them. Tomorrow he'd start learning everything he could. He was

85

so excited he thought he'd never sleep, but at last he did, with the circus programme clutched in his hands.

He woke once. A noise like thunder rumbled through the air. He guessed it was a storm approaching and waited for lightning or rain, but when none came he realised it had been the roar of a spitfyre. Which one was it? he wondered sleepily. Ah, what did it matter? It was a spitfyre, a lovely, wonderful, beautiful winged horse . . . unless perhaps it was that bad one in the thirteenth cave? Was it that one, that no one went in to see and was best forgotten? Poor thing. And Stormy fell asleep feeling sad.

The next day Stormy woke early as usual. Ralf was still sleeping.

All night he had been plagued by dreams about the spitfyre in the thirteenth cave. Was it really so dangerous? Was it even a spitfyre? What if it was something entirely different, like a dragon? What if it was ill and needed help?

Shaking only a little, he sneaked out of the bedroom and made his way to the caves. No one had told him he couldn't go there on his own.

The spitfyres were all dozing in the cool of the morning. One or two looked up at him briefly but without interest as he went past.

He hated the thought of an animal being a prisoner in the dark cave and no one seeing it, of it seeing no one and nothing. *I'll just take a quick look – I just have to see for myself.*

He stood outside cave thirteen for a few minutes, getting

his breath back and just listening. There wasn't a sound from inside. Nothing. Stupidly, he hadn't brought a thork or a lantern, but he hadn't got time to go back and find them. He took a big breath, squared his shoulders and stepped inside.

A fold of rock blocked the entrance. He inched slowly round it.

The smell hit him like a brick. It stung his nose and made his eyes water. He coughed and choked and almost turned back, but went on, pinching his nostrils tight. He let his eyes adjust to the gloom and stopped again. A little daylight came in behind him, and soon shapes began to emerge from the shadows. He could hear wheezy breathing.

He took another step. He could see it now. It *was* a spitfyre.

It was lying on its side, its legs outstretched, a tattered wing draped limply over the ground like a bit of curtain. It was too dark to see what colour its coat was, or its wings. It was thin and bony and so still that if it hadn't wheezed so, it might have been dead.

'Hello,' Stormy said.

The spitfyre jerked up off the floor and turned its head to him, letting out a loud croaky neigh, an angry warning bark. Stormy jumped, banged his back on the rock, cried out in pain and quickly fled outside.

Back on the terrace he stood with his hands over his boom-booming heart. He walked back to the servery slowly.

Maybe the spitfyre was mad, maybe it was wild, but

still, it was wrong to keep any animal like that. It was horrible and wrong.

Al and Ralf were having breakfast together in the servery.

'Where have you been?' Ralf asked him as he came in.

Stormy shrugged. 'Walking,' he said, hoping they couldn't tell he was lying.

'Don't wander around on your own,' Ralf said. 'Some of those spitfyres are dangerous.'

'They can't be,' said Stormy. 'They're chained up.'

'Chains can be broke,' Al said.

Stormy piled his plate with croissants and jam, fresh strawberries and peaches. The sad spitfyre wasn't his problem, it really wasn't, but . . .

'The spitfyre in cave thirteen,' Stormy heard himself say. 'I was just wondering . . .'

'Don't,' Al said. 'That's my business. Interfering will get you into trouble.'

Stormy stared down at his plate, trying to get the image of the sick spitfyre out of his head. 'I just . . .'

Ralf scowled discouragingly at him. Al fixed him with a stare. 'No one is allowed to go near it. Understand? It is forbidden. You will lose your job if you go near it.'

'But –'

'The Director is addressing the students in the courtyard,' Al went on, carefully buttering two pieces of toast and spreading them with a thick layer of jam. 'He likes an audience for the medal presentation, so you two had better come and swell the numbers.' He cut the toast into smaller and smaller squares and laid them on the table. 'Let's go.' Al left the toast and took a swig from a dark bottle. 'Come on.'

They left the uneaten breakfast food piled on the side to deal with later.

The massive courtyard was full of students wearing the smart red and green Academy uniform. The youngest ones looked about twelve while the bigger students, Stormy guessed, were about sixteen. Nervously he took his place beside Al and Ralf just by the servery door and hoped no one would notice him.

Staff wearing crisp dark suits stood watching by the Director's tall house. Ralf pointed some of them out. 'Mr Jacobs, Mrs Lister, Mr Bones,' he said. 'The other teachers keep themselves to themselves. Those three are pretty decent compared to the rest.'

Mr Jacobs was large and bald. Mrs Lister was grey-haired. Mr Bones peered short-sightedly through big black-rimmed glasses.

'The *rest*? The staff or students?' Stormy asked.

'The students. Waste of space, students. Don't do anything useful. Don't ride, most of them,' Ralf said. 'Some learn about spitfyres, about digestion and reproduction, that sort of thing. I can't think of anything more boring, but still . . . Some study their history. Others do spitfyre psychology or behaviour. Some even try and teach them tricks.'

'I want to be a sky-rider,' Stormy blurted, and immediately wished he hadn't.

'Hah!' Ralf said. 'Dream on! That's only for the rich kids. Where'd *you* get a spitfyre? Costs a fortune to keep one here, you know.'

The door of the Director's house opened and Araminta appeared. In a flash Stormy saw again the wickedness of her beautiful smile, her sparkling eyes when she'd warned him to keep quiet. He felt quite weak looking at her, but he couldn't take his eyes off her either.

She stood on the top step holding up her hand to shield her eyes from the sun, staring around the packed courtyard as if looking for someone.

If only she were searching for me! Stormy thought; and then . . . *I hope she isn't searching for me!*

He felt a dig in the side. 'What?' he said, almost falling over.

'Your mouth's hanging open,' Ralf said. 'Idiot! Look, here he comes!'

The Director!

He was so short! Tiny, even. Stormy had expected someone tall and dashing. Disappointment washed over him coldly. But the Director was broad across the shoulders, and he held his head proudly, like a sea admiral on the deck of his boat, surveying the ocean. The muscles strained against the fabric of his shiny, well-cut suit. His tanned, lined face looked kind, yet strong and stern, instantly making Stormy want to win his approval. His short hair was white and crisp as paper, sticking up sharply in two peaks either side of a bald patch, like swan's wings. His fatherly gaze swept the courtyard, the fingers of one hand tapping his other hand thoughtfully. Stormy's first negative impression changed. Now he wished the Director would glance his way and notice him; wished he wasn't just a servery boy.

The students silently got themselves into rows.

Four tall grey-suited guards stood to attention on the far side of the courtyard.

An air of expectancy hung over everything.

A small table had been placed on the wide top step and Maud was carefully arranging trophies and medals on it. The Director began to speak quietly to the students, so quietly that Stormy had to strain to hear him. He was pleased with their exam results. He was delighted with their flying skills. Funding for the Academy depended on getting good results, he said and encouraging new students to enrol.

'. . . My Star Squad in particular,' he went on, 'has shown outstanding bravery and dedication in their work. I'm only sorry that since it is highly secret, I cannot tell you about it!'

Everyone laughed.

'Next year will be the year of the Silver Sword Race . . .'

The students bubbled with excitement.

'. . . Some of you will be thinking about taking part in this great race and starting preparation even now. I'm proud to say, there is one student here whose father actually won it, twenty years ago!'

A name was spoken back and forth amongst them.

'Yes, that's right, Hector's father, Wesley Grant! And it

91

is fitting that I am awarding Hector this medal, one of the finest the Academy offers, for his sky-riding talents. The Cardoman Cross!'

Everyone clapped. The lines of students parted and one tall, well-built student detached himself from the others. His frizzy dark hair was brushed back off his large, high forehead and tied in a ponytail. A large square chin jutted out below a short, rather girlish nose. He had small, deep-set eyes, like circles of green bottle glass. When he reached the top step and stared down on the other students, he smiled confidently, looking suddenly warrior-like.

'Wow,' Stormy whispered, smoothing his own hair back into a short bunch at the nape of his neck and pulling himself up as tall as he would go.

'Wow my bum!' Ralf snapped.

'What's wrong? He's a champion. He won a prize.'

Ralf's eyes narrowed. '*Prize? So?* Can't he still be a creep? I hate him. The Director's paid double by Hector's family,' he went on quietly, 'because other spitfyre Academies are too scared to have him – insurance and all that. He's a liability. If he hurt himself there'd be hell to pay. He'll win the Silver Sword, but you can be sure it'll be by cheating.'

Stormy winced. He didn't want to hear anything bad about a sky-rider.

'But even Hector's money doesn't account for how rich the Director is,' Ralf went on, unusually talkative. 'He's got pots of money.'

Hector collected the medal from Araminta and held it up for everyone to see. The students clapped enthusiastically and then the ceremony was over.

The two littles whom Stormy had met when he first arrived came out of the gatehouse and began tumbling and cartwheeling through the crowd as it dispersed.

The Director walked down the steps and in amongst the students, talking to them, patting them fondly. His size didn't seem to matter – he was a miniature powerhouse and the students responded warmly to him. Each one he spoke to glowed with pride.

Stormy had found himself clapping. As if somehow he was part of the assembly, as if *he* was being honoured with a medal. When Al called him to go back into the servery he had to shake himself out of a dream where he was being thumped on the shoulder and handed a large golden cup. He felt as if he'd been in the Academy for years, not just one day. The time in Otto's kitchen was fading. He *would* be a sky-rider. It might seem impossible now, but he knew he could do it. If he worked hard for Al, if he got to know the spitfyres, if he found a million gold coins, if . . . surely, surely . . .

'Who's this young man?'

Stormy felt a rough punch on his arm and crossly turned to Ralf.

'What, Ralf?'

The Director and Araminta had materialised in front of him with Hector just behind, his green eyes focused far away, as if he was bored.

'This is the new help from Otto's kitchen, sir,' Al said with a little nod. 'His name's Stormy.'

'Hello, Stormy,' Araminta said.

His ears went hot.

'Are you enjoying working with our spitfyres?' her father asked. The Director was talking to *him*! To *him*!

The Director's eyes were piercing; the whites were bright and as white as his hair. It was impossible not to meet his gaze, impossible to hold it, impossible not to look back again . .

Stormy nodded dumbly.

The Director put his hand on Stormy's shoulder and squeezed it gently. Stormy shivered. He felt as if a god had touched him. 'We are delighted to give orphans such an opportunity. I'm so pleased to have you here, Stormy. You look like a fine young man. Is he working hard, Al? Doing as he's told? No interfering? Obedient?'

'I would say he is, Director.'

They stared at each other meaningfully, then the Director patted Stormy again and walked off. Hector turned to follow him but stopped when he saw that Araminta meant to speak to Stormy.

'Well, skivvy,' she said, in a much less friendly tone than before, 'glad you know when to keep quiet. Now, speak up, what have you been doing?'

'I –'

'Daddy likes you. He thinks you've got potential, I could tell. That means a lot, so make sure you live up to his expectations.'

Stormy gulped.

Araminta turned to go, then added, 'There's something hanging out of your pocket!'

He looked down and found a length of ribbon dangling there. Quickly he pushed it back in. 'Sorry. Thank you –'

But she had gone.

13
Yellow Powder

Stormy stared enviously at the students as they filed through the main Academy doors at the end of the ceremony and disappeared. He felt like a rat scuttling to its burrow as he slipped back into the servery.

His cheeks were still hot from talking with Araminta. That stupid ribbon – he thought he'd left it under his pillow. He looked at it crossly, and then was surprised to see it was a different piece of ribbon all together. It was shorter, which meant the first bit couldn't have been from Mrs Cathcart after all!

He stuffed it back into his pocket . . . Could they possibly be from Araminta? He remembered when he'd first seen her, at the compost heap, and how she'd had white ribbons woven into her hair. His cheeks burned afresh. But why would she give them to him, and what did they mean?

'I'll rest a bit,' Al said, sinking down at the table and propping his lame leg up on a chair. He began lining up the cold uneaten toast from earlier across the table. 'I'm tired.'

'All right, Al,' Ralf said.

Most, or nearly all the half-eaten plates and dishes of food had gone.

'Did you chuck any leftovers out?' Stormy asked.

'What, me? Not likely,' Ralf said.

'Someone has.'

'*You* probably, and you've forgotten, Mr Clearer-upper.'

'I didn't –' insisted Stormy.

'Hush, you two. I'm tired,' Al said again, playing despondently with the key around his neck. 'Leave me and go do the shift.'

'OK.' Ralf shrugged at Stormy. 'Al's down today,' he whispered on their way to the food lift. 'Best let him be. He gets very down. Notice he always wears black?'

'What's wrong with him?' Stormy asked.

'Don't know . . . Everything,' Ralf said. 'Come on.'

Roy and Troy, the twin brothers who looked after the East-side flying horses, joined them at the lift. They were identical, with pink faces and straight hair, cut so it hung down on either side of their narrow faces like curtains.

'I'll never tell you apart,' Stormy said.

'I've got the earring,' Troy said. 'I'm Troy.'

'I haven't,' Roy said. 'That makes me Roy.'

The food for the East-side spitfyres came up first and the twins hauled it off, chatting together.

The thirteen West-side caves were still in shadow. There was a faint dusting of snow on the paving stones.

97

'There'll be sun shining down on the East side,' Stormy said wistfully.

'Yes, but ours will be cold,' Ralf reminded him. 'Best when they're cold. Quieter, less trouble.'

They picked up buckets, brooms and a hose from the storeroom and put on the same dirty overalls from the night before.

'That stupid old medal ceremony's made us late. Students'll be here soon. Come to see their dear little spitfyre darlings and they'll get in our way. We've got all their muck to clean up.'

Stormy knew from his books that spitfyres were naturally clean animals. If they had a choice they would never soil their cave; but they had no choice.

'There's other jobs we're supposed to do,' Ralf said, 'but we don't bother.' He saw Stormy's look of surprise. 'It's just got that way; it's not my fault. Al wants it that way. I don't think he likes spitfyres, not really.'

'Then why does he have this job?'

Ralf shrugged. 'Al doesn't care, so I don't care. It's much easier not to bother, Stormy.'

'We should do it properly,' Stormy said. '*I'll* do it properly.' He yanked the dragon-wagon out of Ralf's grasp and hurried ahead with it.

'Hang on, hang on,' Ralf came after him. 'You can't do it alone.'

'Course I can!' Stormy said.

But the sight of the silver spitfyre in the daylight, huge and fierce and hungry, brought him to a halt.

'Here, calm down, Stormy!' Ralf rushed up. 'You can't do it all. And, look, there's a bit of extra for number one,' he said. He took a small glass bottle from his pocket and uncorked it. 'Magic dust,' he said, sprinkling the yellow powder on the food. 'And then this.' He took two ladles of food from the bucket next to it and added it. 'Number one's Star Squad, don't forget,' he said.

'What's the powder for?' Stormy asked.

'Haven't a clue,' Ralf said. 'Orders, that's all. In you go, if you dare.'

Holding his thork in front of him Stormy crept into the first cave, sidling in alongside the spitfyre's hot body. 'Hello. Don't burn me,' he whispered. 'This is lovely stuff – snails, herbs and mashed squib-beetle.'

The spitfyre didn't like him. It shook its head and sparks sprayed from its nostrils, showering round Stormy. He quickly stamped out a small fire that sprang alight in the hay.

'Gently does it! I'm your friend. I won't hurt you!' But the spitfyre gnashed its teeth and pushed at him, and he had to run or be crushed against the rock. At least he'd done it. Done it and not got hurt.

More confident now, he went into the next cave and fed and watered that spitfyre almost casually. By the time he came out from the fourth cave, Ralf was adding a fine dusting of yellow power to its food, ready for him to take in to number five.

'Hello, spitfyre number five, how are you today?' Stormy asked it as he went in. 'Here's your breakfast. It looks nice.

Eat it up. Specially made for you by Otto, Brittel and his merry men.'

When they came to the thirteenth cave, a wave of sadness washed over him so he felt quite sick. The spitfyre had looked so ill and so feeble earlier, and he wasn't allowed to help it.

'Wait!' cried Ralf, as Stormy picked up the bucket of food and prepared to go in. 'Use the pole!'

'Oh, I don't need it.' He assumed Ralf didn't know how ill the spitfyre was. Having seen it earlier he was certain that it was too weak to hurt him. And he wanted to show how daring he was.

He took the bucket of food into the dark, smelly cave. He didn't get past the fold of rock before the spitfyre's roaring and spitting sent him scurrying back outside. His heart was booming. He felt foolish.

'I told you it was dangerous!' Ralf yelled.

'But –'

'It's Al's problem,' Ralf said, looking embarrassed. 'It belongs to him. Makes *me* shove the food in. It's been here years and years. I don't think it's ever been out of that cave, not so as I can remember.'

'*Never* out of its cave?' Stormy cried.

'Al had an accident; you've seen how he limps? That's something to do with number thirteen.'

14

Hector

They made their way back up to the top of the terrace. The blue spitfyre in cave five lunged at them crossly as they went past, making Stormy shout out in surprise. Then number one shot flames at them so they had to leap in the air.

Ralf laughed. Stormy tried to laugh, but felt the heat through his overalls.

'What's up with them?' he said.

'Nothing. Ignore them,' Ralf said. 'Some students teach them to do that.'

The Star Squad spitfyres were the most jittery. They were the ones pulling on their chains and bellowing; the ones blowing out flames.

'Are they always like this?' said Stormy. 'Are they all right? I wonder –'

They turned at the sound of voices and saw a group of students coming towards them.

'Damn,' Ralf said, thumping his fist against the dragon-wagon.

Hector led the group. He was wearing a tight-fitting dark suit and long boots which, with a stab of envy, Stormy recognised, was the Academy riding outfit. It showed off Hector's well-toned muscular body to its very best. He was play-fighting with another boy, pushing and shoving and pretending to hit him, and they were both laughing. Stormy put his head down and tried to merge into the scenery as he and Ralf headed back to the servery. He knew what a pathetic figure he made in his too-small jacket and big boots. He knew his hair was tangled and too long. He probably had food stains on his jacket front too.

'Whoa! Hi there, Ralf!' Hector called and he held up his hand so the band of students he was with bumped into each other as they suddenly stopped. 'Who's the new friend, Ralf?'

Ralf nudged Stormy in the ribs.

'Stormy,' Stormy said.

Hector nodded slowly, as if he was thinking about it. 'That's an interesting name. Are you? Are you Stormy?'

'No,' Stormy said. 'I don't get into rages, if that's what you mean. It was because –'

Hector held up his hand. 'Nah! Too much information. You must have come up to replace Ollie? Ollie was such a sensitive chap,' he said, gazing over the valley. 'A really *nice* boy. Did you hear what happened to him?'

'Not now, Hector,' said the boy he'd been play-fighting with. He was small with large brown eyes and very straight black eyebrows and hair.

Hector spun round and glared at him. 'Ollie had an

accident, Bentley, what's wrong with talking about that?' He faced Stormy again. 'I don't know why people won't talk about it. Still, I'm glad we've got a new boy to help, because although Ollie was a dear chap, he was about as much use as a one-handed grubbin when it came to spitfyre care. He was scared of them. You aren't scared, are you?'

'No,' Stormy said, standing a little taller, jutting out his chin. 'Not me.'

'Good, that's good.' Hector nodded towards the caves. 'Come with me!'

Stormy glanced at Ralf and then followed Hector to the first cave. Of course this Star Squad spitfyre, the biggest and scariest, was bound to be Hector's. And since they'd fed it, the spitfyre had become electrified – Stormy was glad he didn't have to go into its cave now. It was tugging at its chains and snorting. The silver scales around its muzzle actually seemed to have lit up and were glowing with heat. It fixed its eyes on Hector expectantly, almost lovingly, and began to puff and bellow so narrow orange flames flickered from its nostrils.

'This is Sparkit,' Hector said.

Sparkit. Stormy thrilled to his name. It was perfect. *Sparkit.*

'What a monster, eh?' Hector said with pride. 'I hope he behaves for you. You'll look after him, won't you?'

'Oh, yes, I will,' Stormy said.

'You'll need to take extra care of him. He's very special, worth a great deal of money. Unlock him, would you?'

'Bridle him first, Hector,' Bentley said with a nervous laugh. 'You know the rules.'

'What rules? Sparkit's fine. In you go, new boy.'

'I don't have a key.'

Ralf tossed him a bundle of keys.

'Now you do,' Hector said. 'In you go.' Stormy's knees buckled. 'Don't be scared.'

Stormy glanced at Ralf, who was looking oddly pale and strained. Perhaps Ralf was a little jealous of the attention Stormy was getting, or perhaps he was scared for him.

Stormy grabbed a thork and, holding it up protectively, he crept in, determined to do well, determined not to let his nerves spoil this moment. The spitfyre rolled his eyes, arched his neck and snapped his jaws, spitting out tiny balls of fire at him. Stormy dodged, feeling a blast of hot air follow him round the cave. He could hear the students chuckling behind him, and that made him hotter and more determined to do things right. He went on, creeping behind the spitfyre towards the darkness and the chinking chain. The great bulk of the creature, hot and pulsating, seemed to fill the cave. He was much hotter and jumpier than he had been when Stormy first fed him.

There was only a thin space between the spitfyre and the wall, and one careless side-step from him, or one *intentional* side-step from the bad-tempered spitfyre, would crush him against the rock. This animal oozed aggression. He did not want Stormy in there. Without turning his head towards him, only rolling his eye so he could keep

104

track of him, the spitfyre was squeezing him against the rock.

Stormy picked up the heavy chain carefully, letting his hands inch along it until he reached the metal cuff. He was so close to the spitfyre he could see the individual silvery hairs of his coat and the pulsating veins that ran below the pale skin of his belly. The smell of cordite and burnt matches filled the air.

He fumbled through the keys, looking for the right one. Sweat was pouring off him and dripping into his eyes. His fingers slipped and fumbled. He found himself squashed against the hard uneven wall, furiously fitting one key after the other into the lock.

'How you doing?' Hector yelled.

'Good, good!'

At last he had the right key. Carefully he turned it. Carefully he unlocked the leg iron and lifted it off.

Sensing he was free, the spitfyre puffed out short, excited breaths, and some tension that had been there evaporated, only to be replaced by another sensation – as it got ready to move outside – of thrilled *expectation*.

The grubbin convict must have felt like this, Stormy suddenly thought, when *he'd* got his leg iron off. Poor grubbin. Nothing should ever be chained up.

The spitfyre danced out, hooves noisy and sharp on the stone. On the terrace he appeared as a black feature-less winged shape against the brighter, lighter sky. He unfurled his wings like new leaves opening for the first time and shook them energetically. The sun blazed through the membranes, showing the sinewy spokes like an umbrella.

Bentley shouted something about his bridle, but Stormy could only stand and stare in awe. Fantastic, just utterly fantastic!

The massive spitfyre began to circle and paw the ground, anxious to go.

'You forgot my gear!' Hector yelled. 'My gear!'

Stormy looked round quickly. There was a large empty stone basin at the back of the cave, where in the olden days the dragon's treasure trove would have been. No *gear*.

'Hurry up!'

'Coming!'

He scanned the cave. Hanging on the wall near the entrance were goggles, a helmet and reins. Stormy seized them quickly and took them out. 'Here you are.'

Sparkit had swelled in size. He was prancing about, shifting and sidestepping, eager to go.

'Sparkit! Bridle!' Hector said, and the spitfyre reluctantly lowered his head so Hector could fit the reins and bridle on. There was no bit to go in his mouth; Stormy knew that winged horses did not submit to anything being placed in their mouths. Ralf held the reins while Hector fitted his helmet and goggles on, and then he stepped up on the mounting block and swung himself onto the spitfyre's back.

The students shifted out of the way quickly, knocking into each other in their hurry to make space.

'Sparkit! Fly!' Hector commanded, and leaning forward he whispered instructions into the spitfyre's ear. 'Fly!'

With a loud swish, Sparkit flung out his wings to full extension and flapped them once slowly, experimentally, then again, harder and faster until dust blew up.

'Fly!' The spitfyre lurched forward, neck outstretched.

A great wave of air ripped round the onlookers so they fell back against the wall. Stormy was incapable of moving or speaking. Blood pounded inside his head. It was so beautiful!

'Fly!'

Spitfyre and rider leapt into the void like an enormous bird. One moment Sparkit was hanging in the air, wings spread, next he was dropping like a stone, plummeting into the valley.

'No!' Stormy yelled, rushing to the edge, totally sick with horror, his face frozen into a ghastly grimace. They had fallen thousands of feet . . . they'd be dead . . . or so hurt . . . why wasn't anyone doing anything?

'No!'

He ran, was almost at the edge, when with a sudden loud whoosh, the air heaved and the spitfyre soared back up into view. Stormy toppled. The spitfyre flew up and up and away.

Bentley and the others clapped and cheered.

'He always does that,' Ralf said, picking up his thork. 'He's one big show-off.'

Stormy stared after the disappearing spitfyre. Slowly he got up. Total horror was slowly replaced with a dull admiration . . . And for the first time in his life, he felt completely and totally overcome with a terrible envy, and it hurt.

He helped several other students with their spitfyres, asking the names of their animals as he did so. It wouldn't take him long to learn them; it wouldn't be hard.

The red spitfyre in eight with the topaz eyes and the long yellow mane was Kopernicus. The emerald-green spit- fyre was called Daygo, and of course the blue spitfyre was called Bluey. It belonged to Bentley.

The last time he had been this close to Bluey was when he'd crashed into the garden of Otto's kitchen, and then Araminta had been riding him. He wondered if Bentley knew that she had borrowed his spitfyre. Probably not, and he certainly wasn't going to tell him.

'My, he's frisky!' Bentley said, trying to rein Bluey in. 'What's up with him?' But he didn't wait to hear if there was an answer and soon he was swirling up into the sky, blue merged into blue, and he was gone.

The spitfyres are wasted on these students, Stormy thought, watching as one by one the spitfyres left the terrace. He imagined what it would be like to sit astride one and feel the thrust and pulse of the powerful wings. To glide through the air, miles above the ground and go anywhere he wanted . . . He sighed. Life was so unfair.

15

Cosmo

Later, Stormy thought over his feelings. Envy. He wanted everything that Hector had. And more. But it wasn't the riding, the outfit, the power; it was because he loved these creatures and he thought he would be a good sky-rider, a nicer one than Hector, a more caring one than Bentley.

He was sure that the Great Renaldo loved his spitfyres; you could tell he did from his pictures. He cut a brilliant figure in his red trousers, white boots and twirly moustache. Stormy put the flyer into his pocket. Perhaps some of the Great Renaldo's skill would seep into him and help him. Stormy would get the food lifts cleaned up and do something about the spitfyres getting the right food. That would help.

Al was in the servery, sitting at the table, staring out through the open door onto the terrace. Cherries, slices of pineapple and apple had been fashioned on the table top into a lopsided face.

'Hello!' Stormy said. 'Is the food good?'

There was that sherry trifle smell oozing out of Al again, but no trifle.

'Otto's food's too good to eat,' Al said, twiddling a cherry eye. 'Would be wasted on me.'

If Al hadn't been *eating* trifle but he smelled of sherry, maybe he'd been drinking it? Maybe he drank a lot of it? Maybe that accounted for his weird behaviour . . .

'What's that in your back pocket?' Al tugged at the white ribbon in Stormy's trouser pocket.

As Al pulled the ribbon, the circus flyer came out too and fell on the floor. Before Stormy could get it, Al had stamped his foot down on it.

'What's this?' He bent to pick the handbill up and almost toppled over.

He *was* drunk.

'It's just something about a circus,' Stormy said, putting out his hand for it.

'My giddy aunt flipping Sally!' Al whispered. 'Where did you find this?'

He was smoothing the sheet out on the table and staring at it. For the first time dabs of colour emerged slowly in his cheeks, almost as if he was thawing.

'Cosmo's Circus.' Al was shaking his head slowly. 'Look, look at him there!' He pointed to the young man with the moustache. 'Don't you recognise him?'

Stormy shook his head. As if? How could *he* recognise a man in a circus when he knew no one and had been nowhere?

'It's *me*, you lummuck. Me!' Al grinned at Stormy's

110

surprised expression. He rubbed his big hands over his face, feeling along his upper lip as if searching for his lost moustache. 'It was a long time ago,' he added.

'*You!*' Stormy grabbed the paper and stared at the young man. 'You were *death-defying*! The high spot of the show! *You* were the Great Renaldo?'

Al sighed. 'Ah ha,' he said.

Stormy waited for more and when Al didn't speak, he went on, 'You look amazing in the picture.' He sat down, encouraging Al to talk more. 'Awesome.'

'Huh.'

'What happened? Why didn't you stay at the circus?'

'Forget it, Stormy.' Al's face suddenly went hard.

'Please. Oh please!' Stormy fixed him with a pleading stare. 'I'm really interested. Please tell me, Al.'

'I'm too drunk. Oh, what the heck, who cares? What does it matter? I was born into the circus,' he said, leaning back in his chair and staring into the distance. 'My father was a circus man; he worked with rare animals, seaquins, unicorns and serpents, that sort of thing. He was good.' Al smiled slowly; his look was dreamy. 'I can see Pa now,' he said, 'stroking those bad-tempered seaquins, never a thought for their evil beaks! They didn't interest me. But when the circus got a spitfyre, oh, then things were different. I loved it. I had a way with it too, though I didn't realise it at the time. The circus bought more of them; they were popular with the crowd. I became their friend; I could stroke their noses and pour ideas in their little ears and they understood me –'

111

'A spitfyre whisperer!'

Al nodded. 'The spitfyre trainer was harsh and used a whip. He'd had every finger burnt and was scorched almost bald! Cosmo was glad to replace him.'

He stopped and stared out of the window, his face settling back gloomily into its normal scowl. While Stormy waited for him to continue, he tried to see some of that young man, that spitfyre whisperer and lover, in Al's stony face.

He couldn't.

'My father died; it was a giant python that did it – wrapped itself too tightly round his neck. That left me on my own and in charge of all five spitfyres. It was like living on a tightrope; balancing on the edge of life and death all the time, but I wasn't scared. I lived and slept with my spitfyres, I tried to get right inside their heads to understand them . . . I thought I could do anything. You understand that, I know you do, Stormy. You love spitfyres in that way, in that special way . . .'

Stormy nodded.

'But Cosmo was so demanding, he wanted so much from the spitfyres and me. Faster! Jump higher! More daring!'

'What did Cosmo make you do?'

But Al hadn't heard him. 'Spitfyres are ancient beasts. Complicated. They have feelings and you can push them too hard. Push them back with the thork until they bluster and spit and spark at you. The audience liked that, Cosmo liked it, but it means nothing; they get annoyed and then they jump out of the way, *bounce* away.'

112

'But they could just burn you,' Stormy said. 'How come they didn't shoot flames at you?'

'Cosmo cheated,' Al said quietly. 'He fed them non-flammable food before the shows. They couldn't do more than make smoke.'

'Go on,' Stormy urged. 'You were saying how the spit-fyres pretend to attack but then bounce away.'

Al sighed. 'They didn't really want to fight. I used their names; I was their friend. But for the audience it looked good – bounce them up onto a table or even up onto the sides of the cage . . . And then there was the Spin . . .'

'*Spin?*'

Al nodded. 'The Spin,' he repeated heavily. Cosmo wanted me to do it –'

'Hello!' Ralf came in, slamming the door behind him. 'What are you two up to?' He pointed to the clock. 'Dinner time!'

Al shuddered and came back to the present with a jolt.

'The *Spin*,' Stormy urged him. 'Go on.'

Al shook his head. 'I knew I wouldn't like talking about it, Stormy. Leave me be. It hurts to talk about it. The Spin was the end.'

It wasn't the right moment, Stormy knew it, but he had to ask. 'I want to look after your spitfyre,' he said.

Al stood up, knocking over his chair. He slammed his fist on the table, suddenly alert.

'NO!' he roared. 'No one goes near that spitfyre. It is forbidden, Stormy. Forbidden!'

113

16
Maud

Al drank all week long. He drank until his voice slurred and then he drank some more until his chin dipped onto his chest and he fell asleep.

Stormy went to bed worrying about spitfyre thirteen and woke worrying about it. How could he help it when he was forbidden to go near it and both Al and Ralf were watching him so closely?

So he bided his time. He polished the old copper pans and he cleaned the windows in the servery. He cleaned up the food lifts, scrubbed the stone-flagged floor and blocked up as many mouse holes as he could find. He sorted out drawers and cupboards and rearranged them, putting everything in order. Now Otto's ways – the cleaning and organising and routines – didn't seem so harsh or worthless after all. And all the time he thought about the lonely spitfyre in the last cave.

'Waste of time,' Al said, looking at the sparkling windows.

'It's a dump. Keep it a dump,' Ralf said.

It was the same with the stables. Each time one of the caves was left empty while the spitfyre was out flying, Stormy went in and cleaned it. As he got braver he even took the gentler spitfyres out of their caves, tied them up outside and then cleaned. He scraped off the thickly encrusted dirt and brushed away cobwebs from the cave walls. The nose-burning smell of spitfyre urine began to fade. He noticed that the animals soiled their caves less once they were clean, and would wait for him to let them out.

Now he knew each spitfyre's name and nature.

The unpredictable Sparkit was in number one. Snapdragon – who would try and nip him when his back was turned – in two. The buttercup-yellow Westerlie in three, then the beautiful emerald-green Daygo in number four. Bluey in five. Then there was a fat pink spitfyre with very small frilly wings who went by the name of Lacewing. Next came Polaris, another Star Squad spitfyre whose coat was brown or green depending on where the light hit it; it had extraordinary eyes with golden irises. Kopernicus, in eight, had a dull red coat, like old velvet, and violet-coloured scales around its hooves and nose. In nine there was an orangey-yellow spitfyre called Cloudfree. She was gentle, with a crooked ear, and damaged wings so she couldn't fly. Spikelet in the tenth cave was an old spitfyre who was rarely taken out. The girl who owned it said it was just there because all her family had ridden it and now they didn't know what else to do with it.

Eleven and twelve were both black spitfyres with slate-grey wings. They looked identical, except Smokey in the eleventh cave was bad-tempered and stamped its hooves on Stormy's feet when he tried to go inside and clean, and Kyte, in number eleven, was sweet-natured and gentle. Kyte had coal-black eyes and a long nose with a white star between his eyes.

And then there was the spitfyre in the last stable. Thirteen. The spitfyre with no name and fur so dirty the colour of its coat could only be guessed at.

Al had forbidden Stormy to enter the cave, but Stormy had no intention of obeying him. He ignored the warnings he got from Ralf and each day he inched round the rock in cave thirteen with the spitfyre's food and put it close enough for the flying horse to reach it. Every time he went in he was afraid that the poor thing might be dead, but each day it was still breathing, and although he couldn't help it, he hoped it could hear his voice gently coaxing it to eat and saying encouraging things.

One day when Al was dead drunk and Ralf had been sent on an errand by a teacher, Stormy took the opportunity for a longer, proper look at the sick spitfyre.

Holding a half-shuttered lantern so it wouldn't blind the poor creature, he inched his way inside the cave. He felt sure the spitfyre had got used to him a little now. He called out softly, warning the spitfyre that he was coming, and it did not immediately spit. He must have scared it the first time, by bursting in like that.

'Hello. It's me!'

The spitfyre dragged its head from the floor; its eyes were clogged with sticky yellow gunk. It was all bones; its shoulders and hips stuck up through its skin like tent poles. Stormy gulped.

'Poor thing, poor thing,' he whispered, going nearer. 'It's only me. You know me, Stormy. I bring the food. It's all right.'

The spitfyre threw out a broken whinny sound and half sat up. Stormy didn't budge. He swore. He swore again. The creature was just blustering out of fear, that was all. Al shouldn't let this be – it just wasn't right. He had to do something before it wasn't there at all. He had to do more to help it.

'It's just me. Don't be scared. Is it the light? I can dim the light more.'

His lantern wobbled, sending scary shadows and shapes skittering over the walls. He steadied himself, determined not to let the spitfyre force him out.

It was weak and sank back onto the ground, watching him warily through its half-open eyes.

'Shh, shh,' Stormy said, softly. 'Don't be scared. I won't hurt you.'

It was smaller than all the other spitfyres. Its short ragged mane stuck up like a crest. Its tail was thin and matted. Some of its left ear was missing. It was impossible to see what sort of a state its wings were in.

'Don't be scared,' he said again. 'I'm a friend.'

A puff of foul-smelling tarry smoke was the spitfyre's reply.

117

Stormy stepped closer and immediately it tensed, baring its yellow teeth and tossing its head in warning. It tried to fan out its wings, but it was too feeble and all they did was flutter weakly.

'It's all right, it's OK,' he said soothingly. 'I don't want to hurt you. I want to make you better. I want to help.'

The place stank. It was piled with dirty straw and empty buckets and all sorts of rubbish – bones and rind and eggshell. The goggles and reins on the wall hadn't been touched for years and were thick with greasy dust and cobwebs.

Stormy sank to his knees and shuffled closer, keeping eye contact all the time, murmuring encouraging sounds. 'Good thing, good spitfyre. I won't hurt you. There, there.'

He touched it. The spitfyre let out a squeal and Stormy snatched his hand back, his heart racing. After a moment he put his hand on its neck again. 'I won't be scared of you,' he said as calmly as he could. He reached his hand to it. 'I want to be your friend,' he said. 'I must find out your name; I want to help you.'

The spitfyre flopped back onto the floor, no longer fighting. 'You haven't eaten your food. There, there's your food, just by you. See, I won't hurt you. I'm going to get you cleaned up and your wings mended and . . . I'm going to help you somehow. I'll come back. I promise. I'll come back and help you get better.'

That look in its eyes – it wasn't malicious or truly fierce, it was the same look that the stray cats had when they came begging for food at the kitchen door. They spat and

118

hissed like anything, but their eyes were full of fear. If he never did anything else in his life, he vowed, if he never managed to be brave or daring or to ride a spitfyre, at least he would help this animal. Nothing was going to stop him. Nothing.

'Where have you been?' Al was limping around the servery, one hand on the table, the other holding an unopened bottle of wine. 'What have you been up to?'

Stormy turned away so Al couldn't see the look in his eyes which might betray him. 'Nothing,' he lied.

'I want you to take the Director this bottle of elderflower champagne. It's from Otto,' Al told him. 'Go.'

He went.

The two guards standing outside the dungeons seemed to never move and never change. Perhaps they even slept standing up. Was the grubbin Stormy helped locked up down there now, beneath their very feet?

Just as he was about to knock on the door, it opened. The Director stepped out and they nearly collided.

'Oh, sorry, sir, sorry!' Stormy yelped, tripping back down the steps. He thrust the bottle at the Director. 'I was bringing this!'

The Director stared at Stormy for a while, as if he was trying to identify him.

'I'm Stormy, sir, from the servery.'

'Ah yes. Come over here, Stormy, come this way.'

Alarmed, Stormy allowed the Director to lead him to the east side of the courtyard, near the tower and the two guards. He stopped by the wall and pointed out over the valley to the distant blue hills.

'What do you think of that, then?' he asked Stormy.

Stormy had never in his whole life been asked to give his opinion on anything. Skivvies weren't supposed to have thoughts. He gulped nervously. This was his moment to think of something original and clever and he couldn't think of a single thing.

'Of what, sir?'

'The hills. Those mountains. The valley. Those places are full of hidden treasures, gold and silver and jewels.'

'Really?'

'And we need them clean and free of . . . free of *bad* people. Don't we? Wouldn't you like to be master of all you can see?'

'I've never really thought about it,' Stormy admitted.

The Director put his hand on his shoulder. 'You should, Stormy, you really should. Dreams can come true. When I was a lad, Stormy, I had dreams. I didn't have the best of beginnings, as you haven't, but I did something about it. I changed my life. I moved on. I shook off those shackles that bound me to that other life . . . I am the Director of the Academy, the best spitfyre Academy in the world.'

'Yes, sir. That's wonderful, sir.'

'And you will change your life too, won't you?'

'Yes. Yes, I hope so.'

'Good.'

Stormy thrust the bottle into the Director's hands, explained again what it was, and ran back to the servery.

120

He felt immensely proud that he had been singled out and spoken to. Next time though, he vowed he'd make a better job of it.

They were doling out the morning feeds when Ralf stopped, leaned on his thork and stared hard at Stormy.

'Look,' he said, 'I've got to tell you, for your own sake – Al doesn't like what you're doing.'

Stormy froze. 'What? What am I doing?'

'Cleaning. Tidying. Interfering with his spitfyre. You know.'

Stormy relaxed and grinned. 'How could he not, you idiot? It looks so much better. The spitfyres are happier. It hardly stinks at all – you have to agree it hardly stinks.'

'Sure, but –'

'I know their names too. I've learnt them all. They're easier to manage when you use them.'

Ralf sighed. 'I just wish you wouldn't . . .'

'Don't be daft. I want the Director to see how well I'm doing. He might give me a better job.'

'Oh, *Stormy*! This place . . . It's run this way because it's run the way *they* want it run, Al and the Director. Don't interfere, that's all I'm saying – and keep away from thirteen.'

'I can't keep away! But look, Ralf, you don't need to know about it.' Stormy had promised thirteen that he would help, and nothing would make him break that promise. 'Just ignore me.'

Ralf made a snorting noise of disapproval and went on

with his chores. When he took the small bottle of yellow powder from his pocket and sprinkled it over the food, Stormy couldn't help himself from commenting.

'If that stuff's so good, why not give it to all the spitfyres?' he asked.

'I just do what I'm told,' Ralf said.

'Is it the Director's orders or Al's?'

'Don't ask so many questions. I don't care.'

'It's just, well, I even wondered . . . ' Stormy looked up at number five, Bluey, with its mean sapphire eyes, '. . . could it actually make them a bit more fierce?'

'How do you mean?'

'The Star Squad spitfyres. I can see they're the fittest and the finest, but . . . haven't you noticed? After they've eaten, they're angry and sort of wild.'

'Stormy, you are nothing but a servery helper,' Ralf said. 'You are not a spitfyre expert. Forget about it.'

But Stormy couldn't do that.

The courtyard was empty – although you never knew whether you were being watched or not with all the overlooking windows. Stormy went quickly back towards the servery, keeping close to the wall.

He heard laughter and shouting and a group of students spilled out of a doorway. Quickly he nipped into the nearest passageway.

He was next to an open window. It was a classroom of some sort, and on the wall was a large portrait. The name at the bottom said: WESLEY GRANT. WINNER OF THE

SILVER SWORD. He was a plumper, older version of Hector. The Director had said something about him at the medal ceremony. Stormy felt a pain in his chest – a mixture of envy, pride and admiration. Lucky Hector! Sky-rider, rich and a famous father. It wasn't fair.

Suddenly the classroom door burst open and a group of students came in. Stormy ducked down and he would have crept away, but a few seconds later he heard the Director's voice too and he froze, listening.

'. . . and the Star Squad will have the greatest sky-riders the world has ever known,' he went on. 'We are already reaping the rewards of all your efforts, ploughing the money back into the Academy. Your training has been highly successful and I'm proud of you all. Proud of what you've accomplished. It's a pity we must keep our activities so secret, but I can't see any way round that at the moment. Not everyone will understand what we are doing. Not everyone will share our ideals, but that doesn't matter. It doesn't matter at all.'

'I like it being secret,' someone said. 'It makes it more fun.'

The others laughed.

'Quite, quite,' the Director said. 'Why should the *unchosen* be in on our secret? But when they experience the New World we're forming, when they feel the purity of it; then they will understand. Now, tonight's little exercise is this . . .'

But before Stormy could hear another word the window was slammed shut.

The noise of the window shutting rattled his bones. It closed him out and made him feel more of an outsider than ever.

He dragged himself out of the passageway into the deserted courtyard, wondering at what he'd heard. Although he longed to be 'chosen', there had been something chilling about the Director's speech. He couldn't quite put his finger on it. What was wrong with the old world? Maybe things weren't wonderful for him, but the students were fine; they had everything already. What more could they want?

He was so distracted that he didn't see Maud and almost walked right into her.

'I'm so sorry!' he cried out.

Maud laughed. She was carrying a pie which Stormy had nearly sent flying.

'You are determined to get a pudding on the floor, aren't you?' she said. 'You were in a dream.'

'I was. I am. Too much to think about. Actually,' he said, blushing, 'I was hoping I might see you.'

Maud grinned. 'Here I am.'

'Where are you going? Can we talk?'

'I'm taking this to the gatehouse. It's a treat for the littles. They love popapple pie.'

'I'll come with you.' Stormy knocked on the gatehouse door for her.

'Who's there?' came a shout.

'What's that?'

'Who's that knocking on the door?'

124

'You can't come in! You can't come in!'

'It's Stormy and Maud,' called out Stormy.

The door opened a crack and a little gnarled face, wrinkled like a walnut, looked out.

'What d'you want?'

'To give you something,' Stormy said.

'Don't believe you. Why should you? You just want to see some freak things, don't you? We're not freaks, you know. You want to see tiny chairs. Teeny-tiny doll-sized beds and tincy-wincy china. Is that it?'

'Don't be so silly, Mr Small,' Maud said, pushing forward. 'As if we would! I've got pie for you.'

The door opened wider.

'Well, why didn't you say so,' said the tiny person, holding out his hands.

Stormy glimpsed a room choc-a-bloc with things. Not an inch of bare wall showed – they were covered with paintings of ponies, spitfyres and littles. Two sets of shelves were lined with large official-looking books. A desk was open, showing stacks of papers and pots of pens.

'Is there room for that pie in there?' Stormy said, pretending to hold it back.

'Cheeky!' Mr Small said, and grabbed the popapple pie. 'Thank you, Maudie.'

The door slammed shut.

'Come and sit here,' Maud said, pointing to a bench in the courtyard. 'It's not in sight of the Director's house.' She looked embarrassed. 'Araminta likes to know where I am and what I'm doing and –'

'Al and Ralf are the same. But Araminta said you were part of the family.'

'Well, I wouldn't say that, exactly,' Maud flicked her apron. 'Would you?'

Stormy grinned. 'No. But it must be fine living in that grand place though. I'd love it.'

'Stormy, if you only –'

'Oh, Maud! You're the only person I can talk to here. Can I tell you something?' And before she could answer, he told her everything. How he was cleaning things up, that there was a sick spitfyre he wanted to help, how he had overheard the Director, how Ralf gave the Star Squad yellow powder that he thought made them fierce. 'You should see Sparkit after he's had the stuff,' he said. 'He's scary. So it can't be a good thing, can it? I don't think Al knows . . . You know, down in the kitchen I never thought about much. I never questioned anything! I wish I had now. I don't know what to do.'

Maud began wrapping her apron strings round and round her finger. 'Other helpers have asked that sort of question. Ollie asked a *lot* of questions,' she said. 'He asked about the Star Squad. He wanted to know what they were training for. It's not a good idea to ask questions and interfere.'

'But don't you think I ought to tell the Director what's going on?'

'Oh no, don't do that!' Maud cried. She grabbed his arm. 'He is – well, he is the Director and he's very busy and . . . I think he can be pretty tough, you know.'

126

'But he seems so kind and clever.'

'*Seems*,' Maud said grimly.

Stormy was surprised at the hardness in her voice. 'But Maud, he wouldn't harm the spitfyres, would he? Not the Director,' he went on. 'I wonder what he meant about the New World? It did make me feel a bit . . . *cold*, somehow.'

'Oh, I've heard the New World stuff before,' Maud said. 'That doesn't worry me, it's just talk, just talk to get his Star Squad to work harder, but that poor thing in thirteen, that worries me.'

'Me too. Al has forbidden me to do anything. I don't want to lose my job, but it's so poorly . . .'

Someone shouted and Maud glanced towards the house nervously. 'I'd better go. Listen, Stormy; Ollie complained about Hector, he wanted things done differently . . . He was worried too, and . . .'

'What do you mean? Why did he complain about Hector? Isn't Hector a star? Hasn't he the best spitfyre?'

'Yes, and yes, but you don't really like him, do you?'

Stormy bit his lip. He didn't. He wanted to, but he didn't.

'You see, Stormy,' Maud said, 'Ollie didn't just fall off the cliff . . .'

He looked at her imploringly, hoping she *wasn't* going to say what he was beginning to suspect . . . He did not want to hear it. He didn't want to hear anything bad about the Academy.

'Oh, Stormy, it was awful!' Her voice cracked,

remembering. 'Hector was flying back to the terrace and Ollie was crouched down . . . I don't know what he was doing – mucking around, being silly – and suddenly Hector spotted him and went for him! His spitfyre did an amazing sort of twist in the air, grabbed Ollie in its teeth and picked him up! It was terrible. Awful! And Ollie screamed and then, then, the spitfyre flew out over the hill and just let go . . .'

'*Let go?*'

'Yes. Opened its mouth. Let go. And he fell. And fell. And fell. We never saw him again.' She paused. 'It was recorded as an accident, but it was no such thing. I don't think he was the first to go like that, either. I've heard things, that's why I don't trust them. I don't trust anyone here apart from the littles.'

Maud's eyes were brimming with tears.

At last Stormy said, 'Did anyone else see it?'

'Only Ralf – he was Ralf's special friend. But you see, we don't count. No one would listen to us.'

'Are you sure you saw it clearly?' Stormy said. 'I mean, Ollie might have teased Sparkit, or maybe it was a game that went wrong . . .'

Maud shrugged. 'Does it really matter? It was terrible, and Ollie is dead.'

17

The Spin

As Stormy made his way back to the servery he thought about what Maud had told him. Ollie wasn't the first skivvy to disappear from the Academy. The orphans had always joked about the missing boys, Freddie and the others, and perhaps they had asked questions too . . .

Al wasn't in the servery and Stormy scrubbed at the dirty dishes, trying to put his thoughts in order.

When Ralf appeared, Stormy couldn't help asking him about the accident. 'Is it true Hector's spitfyre killed Ollie?'

Ralf went bright red, then deathly white. He nodded.

'Ollie hadn't got a chance.' He swallowed and rubbed at his eyes. 'Ollie was a good guy, Stormy. He was a good friend. A really good friend.'

'Hector must have tried to stop his spitfyre, though.'

'D'you think so?' Ralf said. 'Didn't look like he tried that hard to me. Mind you, those Star Squad spitfyres have minds of their own.'

'Will you help me, Ralf?'

'Do what?'

'Anything. Anything to find out what's wrong here, because something is wrong. Help me stop Al drinking. Improve the conditions for the spitfyres?'

Ralf shrugged. 'Stormy, it's not possible. Don't try. Don't end up having an *"accident"*. Don't. It's not worth it.'

'It is worth it! The spitfyres are worth it.' Stormy surprised himself by shouting. 'I can't do nothing. I'm going to . . . At least let's all use their names, and give them the right food.'

He ransacked the drawers in the servery until he found some old card labels. PLATES. CUPS. PANS. They must have been stuck on the cupboards when the servery had a bit of order. He turned them over and wrote on the back of them in large, clear letters: Sparkit, Snapdragon, Westerlie, Daygo, Bluey, Lacewing, Polaris, Kopernicus, Cloudfree, Spikelet, Smokey and Kyte.

Ralf shook his head. 'Al won't like it,' he warned him. 'He doesn't like things smart and sorted and all neat. He likes it all undone.'

'What about the Director? He'll appreciate it.'

Ralf shuddered. 'I have an idea it's not *names* that the Director doesn't like.'

'Al spends so much time in his room he probably won't even notice the cards,' Stormy said. 'But I think if we use the names all the time, the spitfyres will be easier to control. And maybe you could stop giving them that stuff in the little bottle. The yellow powder.'

'Huh,' Ralf grunted.

'And I'm going to ask Al about his spitfyre again. He can't just neglect it. It's cruel.'

'Hark at you ruling the spitfyre stables now!' Ralf made a rude face and shook his head. 'Al won't like any of it – and here he comes! Take care, Stormy! Seriously.'

Al weaved in, glugging from a tall dark bottle labelled *Super-Strong Robber's Rum*. So it was rum, not sherry, but then all alcohol smelled the same to Stormy.

'Wass goin' on?' Al's voice was slurred. His wooden leg crashed hard against the table and he fell onto a chair.

'He's just making some nice labels for the dear little spitfyres,' Ralf said in a sickly childish voice. 'I'm off. I don't want any part of it.' He went out and Stormy heard him playing his mouth organ outside.

'Stormy?' Al looked surprised. 'Stormy, Ralf says you're making labels. *Labels?* Wha's labels?' He swivelled round and tried to make eye contact, but his eyes lost their focus. He blinked. 'Stor . . . ?'

'Yes. I'm –'

'Labels. Writing things down. Matching things up . . . Don't! Don't do it.' Al tipped up the bottle and drank. 'You put this thing with that thing and you make something bigger. Worse. Stormy. I like you. You're my friend. Stop with the labels.'

'I am your friend. I'm helping, that's all – since you're not doing anything,' he added. 'And things aren't right here.'

'I can't do anything. I can't. How can I? I'm sick of life. Sick of everything.'

'I went into stable thirteen,' Stormy told him. And when Al looked blank he repeated, 'Cave *thirteen*, Al – where *your* spitfyre is.'

Al choked on his drink and shot upright, coughing.

'I don't have a spifft, flying spiff, spitfyre!'

'OK, but you used to,' Stormy said. He took a big breath. 'I've been visiting her. I had to!' he added quickly when Al lurched towards him angrily. 'It's on my list of duties,' he added.

Al sank back into his seat with a groan. '*Duties*,' he muttered. 'Who cares about them?'

'And it clearly says that I have to go in and change the water and take in the food to every single spitfyre. So I must. If I didn't I wouldn't be doing my job properly, would I? Might get sacked,' he added with a forced brightness.

Al groaned again.

'Please, Al, tell me what happened. Maybe I'll be able to help, or understand if you explained. You were about to tell me, before, about the circus –'

'Don't know anything about a circus.'

'Cosmo's Circus,' Stormy pushed on. 'You were going to tell me about the Spin.'

'*Spin?*' Al looked bewildered. 'Did I tell you all that? Did I? I don't like talking about it.' He lifted his bad leg up to rest on the chair and rubbed his knee. 'It makes me ache, deep into my marrow. Why did I tell you?'

'Because you know I love spitfyres like you do – like you *did*. Go on, tell me about the Spin, tell me.'

Al drank from his bottle again and rubbed his big hands over his face. He sighed.

'The Spin. That was what did it for me. Cosmo had seen the stunt done in some far-off foreign land, somewhere hot and junglish, I s'pect, and was impressed. Most impressed. He didn't care that it was done with a different type of spitfyre, a foreign spitfyre; he wanted it in *his* circus . . . He kept on and on at me to try it. He knew it would bring in the punters. He knew he'd make money on it.'

'What is it, exactly?' Stormy asked, a tingle of excitement rippling up his back.

'What's the Spin?' Al swayed, and for a moment Stormy thought he was going to keel over. His hand was shaking. His eyes had a faraway look. 'Spitfyres are moody. Delicate. Dangerous. They obey because we own them and then we name them. They can't ignore their name, Stormy; a name has a special hold on them. You speak it and they obey. It's just one of those weird things, so weird really, weird as weird as weird . . .'

'Don't fall asleep,' said Stormy. 'Come on! So what happened?'

Al hit himself on the forehead with the flat of his palm. 'They got out of control,' he snapped and quickly took another drink. He sat up straight, suddenly lucid.

'Picture this,' he went on. 'A great round tent with a pointed roof, but today the roof is wide open and I can see the stars through it, silvery sparks in the dark, dark sky . . . Cosmo has sent the littles out into town with

133

pamphlets so everyone knows I'm going to try the big number, the *Spin*. The tent is full, they're jammed in like sardines: there isn't an empty seat to be had. Everywhere you look there is a sea of excited faces, and they're laughing and clapping and yatter-yatter-yattering. *He's going to do the Spin. He's going to do the Spin.* There is a metal cage inside the ring; it's got thick bars but it's open at the top because the spitfyres are flying tonight.

'The littles let the three best spitfyres into the ring where I'm waiting for them, waiting in my finest clothes, all spruce and bulging muscles, glistening skin. But although I look the part, I've had a drink, Stormy; maybe more than one . . . maybe more than two or three or four . . . and when I look at those three magnificent spitfyres I see six of them, and they're all swaying and lurching, their teeth ready to bite, hooves ready to strike.

'I pull myself together. I can do this. There's Cosmo watching me. I wave. It's all right, Cosmo! No worries, boss!

'I start the programme. Gently at first, I tell myself, it's supposed to be gentle at first, but I can't be gentle. I can't. I lunge out at Donata with my thork and a whip. Poor creature, she doesn't understand and she snorts and bounces, trying to work out what I want. You can see, any idiot can see that I'm doing it wrong. She gets more and more upset. I *want* her to be upset. I want her to look fierce so the audience will think I'm brave. They'll admire me if I'm brave. They'll love me! Then I go at Firefly and get him shaking, spitting and smoking, trying to scorch

134

me, and thank God he's eaten non-combustible stuff or I'd be charcoal right now. I've got all three up on the pedestals with such a lot of flapping and tail swishing. I've done it thousands of times before with much less fuss and bother, only tonight I *want* the fuss and bother. It suits me.

'Cosmo is looking worried. Good. Good.

'I get out my whip and smack the ground. They hate it. They flinch and wince. But they jump. They bounce off their pedestals and onto the sides of the cage. You should hear their clattering hooves on the metal! What a racket! This is it, this is the first part of the Spin, and I can hear the audience clapping and *oohing* and *ahhing*. Such fools! Fools.

'I crack the whip again and again. The spitfyres don't want to run but I'm calling their names and asking it of them, again and again, and they begin to move faster. They start to strike off the sides of the cage now, leaping from one spot to another, so fast they are just a blur. They are moving as one, like a snake – all their colours meld together so it looks, yes, like a giant serpent is in here with me. And I think now, now! I shout at them. SPIN! They tuck their wings in close to their sides and go spiralling, spiralling upwards, spinning like weird magical tops towards the sky. There is nothing more beautiful, nothing . . . I can hear the audience screaming and clapping but as if they are far away, as if I'm in a dream. I've performed the impossible Spin but it's all a cheat, I'm just a cheat, and then –'

Al stopped. His eyes had become horribly glass-like, staring, cold and sad. He took a long swig from the bottle and set it down gently.

'And then Firefly spins not upwards as he should, but *out*. He corkscrews over the top of the cage and into the audience.

'Firefly is a big spitfyre. He's strong. Magnificent. He's roaring and smoking. The crowd scatter. They scream. Donata's out too. The Spin is too much for her, she's dizzy, can't walk, she knocks into people, tramples them. She is crazy with fear; it's not her fault. She gallops out through the door. Firefly follows. Mayhem. Madness. Screams. And they fly away. They leave me, my dear, dear spitfyres. Up and away and vanish.

'The cage door is open now and Cosmo is coming inside to me . . . and so is . . . this other person, oh, this other person so dear to my heart, so much in my thoughts . . . I talk to the last spitfyre – she's my best spitfyre, my most talented, most beautiful, most trusting – I try and calm her . . . I don't know what I say, but she turns on them, she is so upset and she rears up and with one swipe of those polished, diamond-sharp hooves, she strikes this person to the floor. Dead.' He swiped his own arm across the table, knocking off his bottle with a crash. 'Dead! Dead. Terrible!

'Mayra. It is my Mayra who is lying there all broken and with her eyes shut as if asleep. She looks asleep. And then the spitfyre turns on me, she turns on her master.' Al smiled wryly. 'She was crazy with fear and loathing and

136

. . . Listen.' He leaned over and tapped his lower leg; it sounded like an old dry log. 'One bite and she takes it right off,' he said. '*Snap!*'

Al slowly toppled over onto the table. 'That spitfyre was number thirteen,' he wept. 'Thirteen. I wish she'd killed me.'

18

Tell-tale

Stormy walked out onto the terrace. There was no sign of Ralf. He breathed in the fresh cold air and tried to unclench his fists and unlock his tight jaw. Poor Al. Poor Mayra – his wife? Sister? And poor thirteen.

He glanced up at the white and black mountain peaks carved sharply against the clear blue. It was so beautiful. Bluey was making elegant figures of eight in the sky. He watched enviously, wishing it was he on the back of the spitfyre but knowing that was impossible. Still, how beautiful, how glorious, something to aspire to.

He looked along the terrace towards cave thirteen. Why hadn't Al destroyed the poor thing, or sold it, sent it away? Anything rather than commit it to a long drawn-out prison sentence like this. It was horrid. The two of them were locked in some terrible stand-off and it would end up killing them both.

He glanced down at the new name labels in his hands. Of course Al and Ralf knew the spitfyres' names. They chose not to use them – that way the spitfyres remained just 'animals' to them. But if he didn't do something soon number thirteen would be dead and the Star Squad would be out of control.

What if the Director knew what Sparkit had done to Ollie? Would he investigate the yellow powder then? He knew that Ralf was giving it to the spitfyres, but why? Could it be in revenge for what happened to Ollie? What if he told the Director about thirteen? About how very sick it was? He couldn't. He couldn't go straight to the Director, he just didn't dare, and ever since he'd overheard the talk about the New World he was making, Stormy had found the Director more daunting. Maud couldn't help, didn't think he should interfere . . . What about . . . He pictured Araminta and how pleasant she had been the last time at the medal ceremony. She was flouncy, difficult, but – he smiled at the idea – she'd be impressed that he was trying to help; it would prove he was a capable lad. Prove he had potential. Yes, he would go and tell Araminta. The idea made his heart start thudding horribly loud and hard, but he had to do it.

He went that afternoon.

Maud opened the door. Stormy tripped backwards down the steps. He wasn't prepared to see her, and hadn't thought about anything other than how he would phrase what he had to say to Araminta, and now here was Maud. Instinctively he knew that she wouldn't want him to do this.

'Hello again!' she said. 'The littles ate the popapple tart

all in one sitting! Aren't they funny?' Then she saw his expression. 'What is it? Why have you come?'

'I need to see Araminta.'

Maud's smile crumpled into a worried frown. She pushed the door against him. 'She's busy. Honestly, Stormy, I don't think –'

But Stormy hardly even heard her. He had truth and honesty on his side. He was a spitfyre lover and had given himself the role of spitfyre rescuer, and nothing was going to stop him. He would speak to Araminta. He would.

'Who is that? Maud, who's there?' Araminta yanked open the door. 'Oh, it's the dear little kitchen boy with the blue eyes! I suppose you couldn't keep away? Let him in, Maud; let him in. He can't help being charmed by his superiors.'

'I wondered if I could talk to you for a minute,' Stormy said, still standing on the step.

'You wondered if you could talk to me? Come in my house and talk to *me*?' She looked pained.

Stormy's brain began to jumble up. Araminta was so confusing. 'Please. Yes.'

'Make sure you don't put any dirty marks on anything.' Araminta opened the door and stood back. 'Come on.'

'Don't trust her, Stormy, don't!' Maud whispered to him as she shut the door behind him. 'Be careful.'

But Stormy's head was buzzing with pride and importance. He could only think of the spitfyres. He was going to help them and Araminta would think he was clever

140

and . . . He squared his shoulders and tucked his hands in his pockets so he couldn't leave grubby fingerprints on anything and followed Araminta into the house.

She led him into her father's study. Maud lingered. 'Go away, Maud, dearest girl. Go and get on with your mopping.'

'Yes, miss.' Maud left, closing the door behind her.

'Now.' Araminta turned her brilliant eyes on Stormy. 'Tell me what it is.'

Stormy felt his feet and his heart sinking into the thick soft carpet. The room smelled of beeswax and lavender and a wave of nausea slipped over him like oil.

Araminta was making his courage evaporate. 'Well, er, the thing is, I don't think the spitfyres are being looked after properly,' he said. 'I don't think Al is doing his job.'

'What's this?' Araminta smoothed her ribboned plait across her shoulder. 'You are a servery boy, just barely learnt the ropes, and you come here to tell tales on your betters?'

'It's not like that –'

'Isn't it?' Araminta said. 'Come on then, let's hear what you have to say. Give me the gory details.' She sat down in a chair by the table and folded her arms. 'Speak.'

'I like Al. I don't want to get him into trouble, he's a good man, but he hardly even visits the spitfyres. He –'

'Oh, you can't fool me. You hate Al; you want his job. You don't have to pretend you like him!'

'I do though, I do!' protested Stormy. 'But I love the spitfyres more and they can't speak, they can't say what

141

they need. He isn't feeding them their proper meals. They've got sore legs . . . *And* I think Ralf is poisoning them.'

'*Poisoning* them? That's a good one! You're wasted in the servery, boy. You should be writing stories.'

Stormy blushed, but went on, 'I think he's giving them some sort of poison, or it might be a drug –' He held his breath. 'At least I *think* so,' he added lamely. Suddenly it sounded so feeble. The yellow powder was probably a vitamin.

'Poison? Drugs?' Araminta laughed. 'You are so inventive, Stormy. Where can an orphan like you get such a wild imagination?'

Stormy opened his mouth but no words came out. Did she believe him or not? It was so hard to tell. He had felt as if he'd made a logical leap, thinking, when he heard about Ollie, that Ralf might pay Hector and others back by poisoning the spitfyres. But now he wasn't so sure.

'Well, how do they do it?' Araminta went on. 'Where do the drugs come from? What are they like?'

'Yellow –'

'Yellow! My favourite colour!'

'And Ralf adds it to their food. Just the spitfyres' food. I'm not sure because –'

'*You think? You're not sure?*' she said in a singsong voice. She suddenly smiled at him. 'Al doesn't know you've come here?'

Stormy shook his head.

'Good. I've heard enough. I'm bored. Go on, go now.'

'But you will tell the Director?'

Araminta wound her plait round her fingers. 'We'll see. Off you go. This is just between us for now. Don't mention it to anyone else.'

Stormy was so frightened at what he'd done that he didn't dare go straight back to the servery. He couldn't face Al and Ralf now he'd betrayed them. He slipped along the edge of the courtyard and pressed himself into a corner and stayed there just trying to calm his pounding heart. I did the right thing, he kept on telling himself. I did. It's for the spitfyres, so they'll be better treated. That's all. But he wasn't sure. Maybe he'd gone to Araminta because he *did* want to get Al into trouble, like she'd said. He *did* want Al to leave. He wanted Al to disappear and leave the spitfyres for him to look after; he wanted to be the Academy spitfyre keeper – wasn't that the truth?

He made it back to his part of the castle, but crept around, afraid of meeting anyone. He had shopped his friends. He was a snitch.

He felt sick.

There was no sign of Ralf or Al. He would go to cave thirteen. He knew it was risky, but he had to do it.

He set off.

Feeling something in his pocket, he reached in and pulled out another length of white ribbon. It was the third piece. What did it mean? Could it really be Araminta putting them there? Was it her way of showing him she liked him – secretly – the way in olden days maids had given knights their hankies before dragon tournaments?

Stormy lit a lantern and took it into the cave.

'Hello! I'm here!' The spitfyre – he knew it was a female now – was lying down with her legs tucked beneath her. She turned towards him, blinking in the light. Plumes of smoke, like grey clouds, puffed from her nostrils. She must have been alone, in silence and darkness for so long – for how long? He guessed it was years. This was why he'd betrayed Al, to try and save *this* spitfyre.

'I've done nothing. I said I'd help you and I haven't. I'm so useless, but I *am* going to help you,' he told her, kneeling down to look into her eyes. 'I'm your friend. I'm an orphan, a lonely thing, just like you. We'll work together. We'll be friends.'

She didn't spit at him. She didn't bellow and neigh.

She was watching him intently, puffing, blinking, head tilted to one side.

'Let me come closer. Let me be your friend.' He shuffled nearer, holding out his hand in front of him, whispering softly. 'I won't hurt you. I promise. I want to be your friend. There, there.'

He ran his palm over her neck, smoothing the thin coat of purplish hair, feeling the bumpy roughness of scabs and scars beneath his fingers. All the time he stared into her eyes, watching for a change in them, a warning she might suddenly turn on him, but all he saw there was great sadness and fear. After a few minutes he felt the spitfyre relax a little and a tension went from her. She stopped puffing and exhaled more slowly, the smoke lessening.

'I'm going to help you get better,' Stormy said, never

stopping his caressing. 'I think I can. Good food and fresh water, love and care, these will make you better. That's what I'm going to give you. That's what I'm going to do. I promise.'

A sudden clinking sound of a bottle rolling over the stones outside made the spitfyre tense sharply; sparks flew from her nostrils, she snatched up her head and a rumbling growl sounded in her belly.

Stormy ran outside.

It was Al. He waved an empty rum bottle at Stormy. 'What are you doing? Get out of there! Get out!'

Al teetered across the terrace in a figure of eight, almost tripping over his own wooden leg.

'S'my spitfyre!' Al roared drunkenly. 'She's my flying horse! G'away from her! I told you not to!'

'I wasn't doing any harm, Al. She's lonely.' Stormy's voice wavered. 'She needs help. She'll die if –'

'Shurrup!' Al yelled. 'Shurrup! G'away or I'll kill you! I'll kill you dead. Deader than deader than dead . . .'

Now Stormy realised just how much Al hated his spitfyre. He wanted to destroy her; he might destroy other spitfyres too.

Al had to be stopped.

Telling Araminta about him had been the right thing to do.

19

Shock

Stormy woke suddenly that night, catching the tail end of a scream hurtling through the air like a solid object. It was followed by a quiet with such an edge to it, he thought it must have been a dream. He sat up and looked over at Ralf. He was very still, too still to be asleep.

'Did you hear that, Ralf?'

'Go back to sleep,' Ralf muttered. 'It's nothing.'

It was a freezing night and much easier not to go and investigate. Stormy turned over and tried to sleep but now he was awake his brain was busy . . . Had Araminta spoken to the Director yet? How was the spitfyre in thirteen? What was its name? Why was Al so pig-headed? Why . . .

He slept at last.

Next morning it was cold and overcast and snow began to fall; great thick blobs of white that soon covered everything.

'See anything last night?' Ralf asked him, looking out of the window and pulling on an extra jumper.

'No,' Stormy said and immediately wished he'd had the courage to get up and investigate that noise. If he had, he was sure there would have been something to see.

'Good,' Ralf answered.

Stormy thought Al looked odd the following morning. He always looked odd, he reminded himself, but now he seemed especially sad. There were inky shadows beneath his eyes and a purple tinge to his unshaven chin.

'Just getting the hang of things, aren't you, Stormy?' Al said, not as if he was pleased, more as if he was sorry.

'Yes, I think so,' Stormy said, puzzled.

The bell went and they began to unload the lift. These days Stormy helped himself to the food while it was still warm: hot croissants with melting butter, steaming fruit buns. It was delicious and he hardly felt guilty at all, but he still didn't fancy Otto finding out.

At lunchtime, Al lent a hand getting the dishes onto the trolley, which was unusual.

'Give that gravy a stir, won't you?' he suggested, passing a large jug to Stormy. Stormy placed the jug carefully on the sideboard and stirred it with a long spoon. Suddenly there was a terrible crash behind him and he jumped.

'Sorry!' Ralf cried. Splinters of white plate were scattered all over the stone floor.

'I'll get a dustpan and brush,' Stormy said, immediately going to the cupboard.

'He's a good lad, see. He volunteers,' Al said gloomily. 'See that, Ralf? See him volunteer to help?'

147

Stormy heard Ralf say, 'Sure, he's just *perfect*!' There was a heavy pause and then Ralf said, 'Oh, Al, what?' He giggled and Al laughed and for some reason that Stormy could not fathom, he felt his blood run icy cold. They were laughing at him, he was sure.

When he came back there was a strange atmosphere in the room. Something had passed between the other two, something that excluded Stormy. He felt it strongly and hated that it made him feel so lonely. They both turned round and stared at him.

While Stormy cleared up the mess Al and Ralf watched him and when he glanced up at them, their expressions were stony. His hands were suddenly slick with sweat and he swallowed loudly. He guessed what it might be; their furtiveness, their laughter. They'd been talking about him. Had they found out he'd told on them? Then they knew he was a sneak. Now they would hate him.

But it was much worse than that.

In the middle of the afternoon while the snow fell thick and fast and Stormy was alone in the servery polishing the few bits of old silver, Al limped in noisily.

'You're to come with me,' he said. His face was set in a frown; the deep creases on either side of his mouth were sharper and blacker than ever, like cracks in rock.

'What is it?'

'Can't say. Just come with me.'

Stormy washed his hands and followed Al out across the yard to the Director's house, watching Al's wooden leg drag a clear path through the snow like a tiny plough. It creaked like a boat on the sea. By the time they'd reached the front door Stormy's knees were weak and his heart was thudding fast and hard.

Maud did not look at him as she let them in. She didn't even give him a secretive twinkling smile. The Director was waiting for them in his room.

'But surely this is the boy who was doing so well!' the Director said, patting Stormy on the shoulder, dusting off the snow. 'The boy you told me was using his intuition and working hard.'

Al shrugged and shook his head. 'It is. It was.'

Stormy looked anxiously from Al to the the Director; this wasn't how things were supposed to go.

'However,' the Director glared at Stormy, 'if what you say is correct, Al . . .' He was gently working at his white hair so it stood up from his bald head, contemplating what to say. 'We had an incident at lunch time,' the Director said. 'It was most unpleasant and unsavoury. There was a mouse in the jug of gravy. A mouse! Fortunately it was my dear Araminta who found it as she poured gravy over her potatoes, and not a fee-paying student.'

'But –' Stormy cried.

'Don't interrupt!' The Director's face was as hard to read as a slab of marble. 'I spoke to Al, didn't I, Al? And he confirmed that there was no mouse in the gravy when it arrived in the lift. He had stirred it himself and told me it was lump free and mouse free. It was only after *you* had touched it, Stormy, that the mouse could have entered the vessel.'

'But I never –'

'Be quiet. Since you were a boy who showed so much promise, it is especially disappointing. Araminta herself had picked you out as a likely lad, one who would rise.'

Stormy's knees were jelly; this couldn't be happening.

'But . . . No, this is about the yellow powder!' Stormy said. 'They know I told. Al doesn't really even like the spitfyres! Ask Ralf. He knows. And thirteen . . .'

The Director shook his head calmly. 'That is perfect nonsense. And I have spoken to Ralf, of course. He denies adding anything to their food. Why would the keeper or his assistant harm his own spitfyres? I fear you have made things up to suit yourself, Stormy. Apparently it is well known within the Academy that you want to have Al's job, but you cannot ever rise by cheating or practising underhand behaviour . . . You are relieved of your duties as from now.'

Stormy could not speak. He stared at them both blankly.

'That means you're fired,' Al said quietly. 'O.U.T. means out you go.'

Stormy and Al went back to the servery in silence. The moment the door was closed Stormy turned on him.

'You did this! You and Ralf! I know you put that mouse in the jug. I heard you laughing. Why? Why did you spoil everything for me?'

Al sank down wearily. 'It's a funny old world, Stormy.'

'Is that all you can say? And what about the yellow powder? Why do you let Ralf do that? You must know it's –'

'Stormy, it's over,' Al interrupted.

'But, but . . . You know how much this place means to me! You know how I love it. I love the spitfyres. I'm getting to know them, I'm good with them. Al, why did you do it?'

Al would not meet his eye. He reached for his bottle. 'It's a rum world, Stormy, and rum's the answer to all our problems.' He took a long draught from the bottle.

'But it's not fair! I don't want to leave.' Stormy was close to tears.

'You don't have any choice, old thing.'

'I'll refuse. I'll fight. I'll . . . Is there no way I can stay? Please? Please say there is. Tell the Director what really happened, he'll believe you. Oh, please, Al, don't do this to me!'

'It's over,' Al said. 'Over.'

'But I won't see the spitfyres again. Thirteen – I so wanted to –'

'All over,' Al said quietly. 'Pack your things and go. I've sent word. You're the first orphan ever to be sent back. The first. That's something. Try explaining that to Otto,' he added with a small laugh.

Stormy went out into the snow. He rubbed his fists in his bleary eyes. What an idiot he was! He'd mucked everything up and lost his only chance to better himself. He was being sent back to the kitchen. *Down* to the kitchen. *Down* to Otto.

He shuffled to the edge of the terrace and stared down into the void. The cold air froze his tears and swept round him, swirling up the snowflakes so they almost blinded him. Better to fall off here, he thought, better to simply tip over the edge and disappear into the blackness than endure Otto and all those boys sniggering and laughing at him. He could not face the orphanage again, he could not!

A low bellow startled him and he swung round. A dull light was coming from cave thirteen. How was that possible? Stormy ran towards it and went inside. There was an orangey light drifting around the roof of the cave, a floating pool of mysterious colour. It could only come from the spitfyre.

She was staring towards the doorway as if she had been expecting him.

'It's me, it's only me,' Stormy sobbed. He stood there in the pale orange light, wanting to put his arms around her, but not daring to. 'I'm going. I have to leave.'

For the first time the spitfyre wasn't eyeing him doubtfully, but looking at him, looking right at him, eye to eye. She swished her tail. She whinnied softly. She knew him. She recognised him and was greeting him for the first time – and the last.

'Goodbye,' Stormy said. 'Goodbye.'

PART TWO

20

Time

When Stormy thought back on that day – and he often did – he thought of it as a day of fog; a day so clouded by events he couldn't see or think or feel properly. It was the day his dreams died. The day his life was put on hold.

He never doubted that Al and Ralf had set him up. The muffled sniggers he'd heard when he went to get the dustpan and brush for the broken plate would haunt him forever. But why had they done it? *Why?* And how was the yellow powder involved?

'Was it just because I cleaned stuff up?' he asked Tex for the hundredth time. 'Was it because I told Araminta what was going on? Did Ralf have something against me?'

'Sorry, mate, I don't know,' Tex said.

'I don't understand what went wrong.'

'If I was you I'd just forget all about it,' Tex said. 'You're home. It's great to have you back. We missed you.'

Occasionally, up in the castle, Stormy had thought about Tex and Purbeck and the rest, but mostly he hadn't.

Everything about the Academy had totally absorbed him because it was about spitfyres and he *was* spitfyres, he was, right to his very core.

It had been horrible going back. Everything had been horrible. The walk down the steep hill back to the kitchen had been the worst walk of his life. The path was cold and slippery with slushy snow and he had felt more alone than ever before in his life. He almost walked on past the kitchen gates to the grubby village of Stollen below, but what could he do there with no money and no hope? Instead he had gone straight to explain things to Mrs Cathcart, but Mrs Cathcart wasn't interested in his explanations.

She wouldn't listen to him.

She would not even look at him.

'This has never happened before, Stormy,' she said, addressing the rack of ornaments in her room. 'We are appalled.'

'I'm sorry.' Stormy hung his head.

'A boy has never been returned like this, like baggage. Like an unwanted parcel.'

'I'm sorry,' he said again.

'I just can't understand it. Why would you want to frighten the students with a dead mouse? Why would you do that? It can't have been a mistake or an accident; a mouse is far too big for that. You're lucky they didn't lock you up in the dungeons. I will send up another boy immediately, but this time I will choose him myself. A boy I can trust . . .' She turned round. 'And you looked so lovely in your uniform, Stormy . . .' she added, dabbing at her eyes.

He went slowly up to the dormitory, ignoring the whispers and sidelong glances from other boys. Another skivvy had taken the bunk above Tex. The mattresses looked narrow and hard. He put his bag in the corner and went to the kitchen, not knowing what else he could do.

Brittel saw him and called out to the others.

'Look what the cat's dragged in,' he sneered. 'We thought those spitfyres would recognise a worm when they saw one and gobble you up.'

Sponge waddled up to him, wagging his tail, and Stormy had to swallow hard to dislodge the lump that rose in his throat when the old dog, pleased to see him, licked his hand.

When Otto saw him he immediately threw a size five spoon at him. 'Stormy! Good to have you back, you little carrot cake!' he cried. 'The compost missed you!'

'Thank you,' Stormy mumbled.

'How many ounces of suet in a sponge for six?' Otto roared. 'Don't tell me you've forgotten. What's the best flour for pancakes? How many *mice* in an apple pie?' Everyone laughed.

Tex pulled him into a corner. 'Get an apron on quick,' he said. 'Blend in. They'll soon forget.'

And he was right. Within half an hour Stormy might never have been away. He slipped into the routine again quickly. He watched the potatoes being lovingly mashed to within an inch of their lives; the carrots sprinkled with chopped parsley, the sauce being sieved and stirred until it gleamed like molten gold. He sniffed the wonderful scents longingly; a meagre helping of porridge and soup and bread were all he'd ever eat now. But those two up there would eat what they wanted. He'd like to tell Otto what went on up in the Academy, how his food was mistreated and wasted, but he wouldn't. He would never tell tales on anyone ever again.

When a call came down to the kitchen for Purbeck to go and see Mrs Cathcart, everyone knew who had been chosen to replace Stormy at the Academy.

Purbeck took off his apron slowly, watching Stormy all the time. He didn't want to go; and he knew how important the job was to Stormy.

'Sorry, mate,' he whispered as he passed him.

'But shall I tell him what I know?' Stormy whispered to Tex.

Tex shook his head. 'He'll learn for himself.'

And Purbeck didn't care about spitfyres, so perhaps it would be all right for him. He would do exactly what Al ordered him to do without question.

Mindlessly, Stormy scraped and peeled and chopped. It was hot and steamy and everything seemed dreadfully normal and dull. He had a terrible premonition that he would glance up at the window and see Araminta's haughty face staring in at him. She would be so proud and so beautiful and he would have pastry mixture up to his elbows or worse. It was unbearable. Dreadful.

He couldn't work out how his life had been turned upside down so quickly and so enormously.

'I've thrown away my one and only chance,' he whispered to Tex. 'I'm finished.'

Tex grinned back. 'Nah, you'll soon get over it.'

That night he went over it again and again with Tex. 'I didn't do anything wrong, Tex, I didn't. I was doing well. I was helping. I was having such a good time. I was going to help the spitfyres.'

Tex could only shrug and pat his arm in sympathy. 'Least you came back, mate,' he said. 'No one else has achieved that!'

Stormy now slept in a bottom bunk that shook and rattled as John, the boy above, snored. He hated looking up at the mattress, which seemed to sink lower and lower the more he stared at it, until he thought he would suffocate. He lay awake for a long time thinking about the spitfyres, thinking about Hector and Araminta and the space that he had left behind which Purbeck was now going to fill.

He took the three white ribbons from beneath his pillow and held them tightly in his hand. They evoked such clear memories of the Academy. Araminta must have liked him to give him these odd tokens, if it was she and not Al or Ralf playing silly tricks on him.

Nobody seemed to care about the yellow powder and what it was doing to the spitfyres. Stormy rolled over and stared at the wall. How had it all gone so terribly wrong?

The days slipped one into another like water filling a hollow. Stormy could not stop time passing. He could not change anything.

At first, he always had an audience greedy for stories

about the Academy and the spitfyres, but as the days went by he talked less, finding he wanted to keep it to himself and that way keep it safe; keep it *his*.

He didn't tell a soul about the sick spitfyre. He could hardly bear to think about her, knowing she would think he'd abandoned her. If only he'd been braver. If only . . . well, he planned to change. Even here in the kitchen, he was going to be different.

He couldn't stand looking at his useless face in the mirror. He hated himself, and just about everyone else too.

He shrank further and further into himself. The quieter and more inward-looking he became, the fewer people wanted to be with him. In the end even Tex got fed up with him.

'You were only up there at the Academy for a while – you talk about it like it was a lifetime!' Tex said.

And that's how it felt to Stormy. A lifetime. An absorbing, exciting, strange, yet complete lifetime. And he was now committed to spending the rest of his life, a life years and years long, in the steamy old kitchen being shouted at by Otto and without a spitfyre in sight.

Something had changed between him and Otto. He often found the cook staring at him questioningly, and although he still shouted at him and threw things at him, Stormy knew it wasn't done maliciously.

One day Otto took him aside to talk to him.

'So, tell me, how is Al?' Otto asked.

'Do you know him? I never thought . . .' It was a relief

to speak to someone who knew people 'up there'. Stormy felt something quietly pop inside him, like a cork from a bottle, setting him free. Now the Academy could be real again, just as it, and all the people and spitfyres inside it, had been beginning to take on an unreal, dreamlike quality.

'Oh, Al! Al isn't happy,' Stormy told him. 'He drinks a lot. He's miserable.'

'He drinks? He drinks a lot, does he? He was always one for the bottle.'

'I think his past makes him unhappy.'

'Whose doesn't?'

'He –' Stormy stopped. No, it would be a mistake to tell Otto too much. 'He said you were a fine cook.'

'Did he? You're a good boy, Stormy. I'm putting you in charge of knife sharpening, as from today. OK?'

'Thank you, Otto. Yes. Deal.' There, already things were moving. He was going to be different, better, stronger.

So Stormy became the knife sharpener and every day he took all the knives out into a back larder where he could work alone, honing the blades on a stone wheel that he turned with a foot pedal. It was useful for getting rid of his bad temper. He pounded the pedal furiously, making the wheel hiss and the knife blade spark and smoke against the stone. The smoke and sparks reminded him of the flying horses.

The kitchen had never had sharper blades.

Time passed quickly like this: days into weeks, into months and then a year.

In all that year a day never passed without Stormy being

tormented by thoughts of Al's spitfyre. And there was nothing he could do about it, that was the worst. He couldn't avoid settling back into his old life in the orphanage and the kitchen, but he never quite settled back into his old friendship with the other skivvies. They called him a snob.

'You're no fun, Stormy. You've changed.'

Stormy wasn't happy. He knew he'd been wronged and he wished there was a way to put things right and clear his name. Sometimes he dreamed that he was walking up the steps to meet the Director and receive a prize. 'We mistreated you, Stormy. You are a hero. I want you to enter the Silver Sword Race. You're sure to win.'

And the Director shook his hand and everything was wonderful.

21

Break-out

Stormy was perhaps the first to hear the alarm ringing from the Academy that morning, because these days he was usually the first to wake.

Soon all the other boys awoke too and rushed to the windows, chattering. Instantly he was transported back to the time, over a year ago now, that the alarm had rung to announce the escape of the grubbin convict he had helped.

He got up quickly, dressed and was first in line for his porridge.

By the time he was down in the kitchen working his shift, the Academy guards had arrived and were searching for an escaped convict; he watched their tall figures criss-cross the windows. Tex said he'd seen a swarm of spitfyres searching the hillside. Stormy wished he could go out and see them; although every sighting of a spitfyre caused him anguish, he craved a glimpse of them.

In the middle of the morning, just as the Academy lunch

was ready to be sent up, two damp, muddy guards strode arrogantly into the kitchen.

'Morning, Otto! Morning, boys!' said the first guard. 'Did a convict drop by for breakfast this morning, by chance?'

'Of course not!' Otto snapped. He quickly swished away the plate of cheese scones that were cooling on a wire grid on the table before the guards could touch them. 'Hands off!'

'Well.' The guard held up a rusty pair of pincers. 'D'you recognise these?'

Stormy's insides caved in: *he* recognised them.

'Those are mine!' Otto roared. 'They've been missing for ages! Where did you find them?'

Stormy remembered very clearly that cold night he had taken the pincers out to the grubbin. He remembered his terror, the freezing air, how the little man quaked with cold and how he, Stormy, had quaked with fear.

'Found them down by the compost heap. Believe they've been used for cutting . . .'

'*These*,' said the second guard, brandishing a pair of leg irons from behind his back as if he were doing a magic trick. He rattled them noisily. 'Are these yours too, Mr Otto?' he asked.

'No. Of course they aren't.'

'It is most weird,' the first guard said. 'We found the pincers down by the compost heap, but these here leg irons were hanging on the apple tree just outside that door.' He nodded to the kitchen door behind him. 'And if you look closely, you can see that there is an old cut, mended, and a new cut, done just recent, I would think.'

'You're talking in riddles. Say what you mean, can't you?' Otto said.

'I'm saying that this convict that's escaped is the same as the one that escaped before and took your coat, and he used the pincers last time he escaped and hid 'em and then used them again this time he escaped,' the guard said. 'At least, I think that's what I'm saying. You've got me confused.'

'And why would he hang the blooming shackles outside my door?' Otto bellowed.

'Now we was wondering that too,' the guard said. 'Any ideas?' He cast his eye over the crowded kitchen. 'Anyone?'

Stormy did have an idea: his grubbin had hidden the pincers in case he ever got free from the prison again, and now he had *got* free and he'd used them again to cut his chains a second time and he wanted Stormy to know it too.

Getting no answers from the skivvies, the guards left at last and the kitchen returned to normal.

'Always did wonder where those pincers had gone,' Otto said to Brittel. 'I saw they were missing, but it was long after the convict business. I never linked the two together. Thought it might be Purbeck that had taken them – just in case he ever got that big head of his stuck somewhere again.'

'Wonder what this dirty grubbin has done,' Brittel said. 'Probably on the steal, or worse, maybe come to murder us in our beds. Inbred, they are, and it makes for bad blood. Shouldn't be allowed to live amongst us humans, in my opinion.'

Otto looked at him sharply. 'No one asked for your opinion. I don't like that sort of language here. A grubbin is a living thing, just like us all, even if they do prefer the dark and the underground. Don't you go jumping to conclusions just because they don't live like us.'

Brittel sneered. 'I'd prefer to pass my time with a slimy worm,' he said, nodding at Stormy. 'Though don't know if I'd notice the difference!' He wiped his stained fingers down his apron. 'Disgusting.'

'Heavens, Brittel! How much of my precious saffron are you putting in the spitfyre food?' Otto said, pointing at Brittel's fingers. 'Or are you washing in the stuff?'

'That's turmeric and sulphur,' Brittel said huffily. 'Good for their ignition. Gets the sparks flying.'

Otto gave him a dark look.

'Well, don't be too generous. It's expensive.'

Sponge followed Stormy into the back larder and lay down on a mat beside him while he began on the pile of knives. 'You're a good old dog,' he told Sponge, stroking his grizzled head and fondling his ears.

He took up the first knife and set the wheel spinning. The noise filled the small room.

'Fancy that grubbin putting his leg iron in the tree, Sponge.' Thud, thud went the dog's tail on the floor. 'Why would he do that, d'you think? Did he mean *me* to see it,

Sponge?' Thud, thud. 'A sort of *remember me* or a *thank you*. What do you think?'

Sponge, dozing, rolled over onto his side with a groan and stretched out his legs stiffly.

'I wish you could tell me something interesting, Sponge. Wish you could tell me what's going on up at the Academy. What Al's up to. How thirteen is doing. You've no idea how I long to be back there.'

'*Stormy!*'

Stormy jumped. '*Otto!*' His foot slipped off the pedal and banged on the floor, waking Sponge.

Otto looked round the room. 'Who were you talking to?'

'Just Sponge.'

'Sponge is as deaf as a post,' Otto said.

'Makes him a very good listener,' Stormy said, picking up another knife.

Otto stood there, nodding at him for a while, rubbing his big hands over his potato nose and watching the spinning stone. Stormy began to dread what might be coming next. He couldn't have been more surprised when Otto said, 'It was me that got you that place up in the servery.'

Stormy dropped the knife with a clatter and stared round-eyed at Otto.

'I fixed it,' Otto went on. 'Those names in the box? Every single paper had yours on it. Mrs Cathcart never checked – why would she? I knew you wanted the chance.' He sighed. 'Now I'm wondering if I did you any favours . . . You liked it up there, didn't you?' He nodded to the ceiling. 'At the Academy?'

167

'Yes. I did. Did you really do that? Thank you, Otto. I never thought – not for a moment,' Stormy said. 'Really, thank you.' He quickly took up the next knife and wiped the blade down his trousers. 'Thank you.'

'You saved my half-baked Sponge from that snake, and you are a good worker. It was the least I could do. The least . . . Did Al ever mention me?' Otto asked.

'I told you he said you were a good cook – a fine cook. That was all.'

'I was the chef for Cosmo's Circus,' Otto said, 'just for a while.'

Stormy dropped the knife again, this time narrowly missing Sponge's nose.

'*You* were in the circus?' He let the wheel slow and stop.

Otto nodded. 'Cosmo liked exotic food and I provided it.' Otto perched his large behind on a wooden bench. 'I quite enjoyed circus life – until the accident. Did he tell you about Mayra?'

Stormy nodded. 'A little.'

'Mayra was my sister, did he tell you that?'

Stormy shook his head.

'She ran away. At last I tracked her down working in the circus. I went to bring her back, but she wouldn't come, absolutely refused to, so I stayed too.' Otto picked up one of the knives, a great thick-bladed, wooden-handled thing, and began to twist it round and round in his big hands. 'That Renaldo calls himself Al now. He drank those days too. He ate like a pig and I fed him like a pig.'

'Why?'

Otto shrugged. 'I hoped if he got fat my sister would stop loving him . . .' He paused for a moment. 'Al used to sleep with his spitfyres, eat with them, discuss politics with them . . . but not on the day of the accident, he didn't. Didn't see them at all. Not once. I *know*,' Otto added, seeing Stormy about to question him, 'because I made it my business to know. On the day of the accident someone had told him Mayra was leaving him for Cosmo. He abandoned his spitfyres – didn't even feed them and got totally drunk.'

'He did admit he was drunk the night of the Spin.'

Otto nodded his great head and rubbed his big nose. 'It was all his fault.' He stepped round his sleeping dog and twirled the stone knife grinder round slowly, thoughtfully. 'The spitfyres were crazy without Al's care and attention. Mayra was killed instantly. The spitfyre didn't have bad thoughts towards *her*, I'm sure, but it was confused. I lost my sister, my dear little Mayra.'

'I'm really sorry, Otto,' said Stormy quietly.

'That's why Al dare not come down from up there,' Otto said. 'I watch the path. I know who passes here. My Sponge watches too.'

He picked up a knife and set it against the stone wheel and let it turn gently. The noise was hideous and Sponge woke with a start and blinked up at Otto.

'Al dare not come near me.'

22

Mr Topter

One morning a few weeks after the escape of the grubbin, Mrs Cathcart spun into the hot kitchen like a tornado. 'Otto! Stormy!' she shrieked, whirling around as she looked for them. 'Come quickly! Come!'

Otto frowned at her and slowly wiped his hands down his apron. 'Woman! Stop your screaming! And shut that door!' he said in his deep voice. 'You'll deflate my soufflés!

'But, but, there's a man to see Stormy!' she cried. 'You won't believe what he says. Come quickly both of you, please.'

Otto slowly turned to the silently watching kitchen staff. 'Brittel. Jones. You're in charge. No slacking. No wasting time. No touching. I will be back and I know how much there is of everything. Stormy, come with us.' He pushed Stormy out ahead of him. 'Brittel's up to something; using my kitchen for it too,' he said quietly, half to himself. 'Got to keep an eye on him.'

'Brittel?'

'Yes, got to watch him, watch him like a hawk,' Otto muttered as they went up the stairs.

Mrs Cathcart led them to her office, where a stranger was sitting on the edge of her small armchair. He was middle-aged, ugly as a pug, with tiny bright eyes behind minuscule glasses.

'Is this the one?' he said, pointing at Stormy.

Mrs Cathcart ushered Stormy forward. 'Yes, this is Stormy. Stormy, this is Mr Topter. He's a lawyer. He's come all the way from Stollenback.'

'Hello, sir,' Stormy said, holding out his hand.

Mr Topter shook his hand vigorously. 'Good morning to you, young man. Good morning. I am about to change your life!'

Stormy looked to Mrs Cathcart, then to Otto, who shrugged.

'Are you, sir?' he said without much interest, as it seemed highly unlikely.

'I am, young man. Mrs Cathcart, I think you'd better sit down before you fall down.'

'Thank you, thank you.' Mrs Cathcart wobbled to a chair and sank onto it gratefully, fanning herself with an old greetings card.

'I won't beat about the bush. As of a few days ago, this boy now has good prospects. High hopes.'

'High hopes?' Stormy repeated, thinking if there was one thing that he did not have it was hopes, high or otherwise.

Mr Topter nodded. 'Let's just double-check here. As I

171

have explained already to Mrs Cathcart, I have come to see a certain orphan boy from the kitchen, a skivvy called Stormy. That boy is you, isn't it? You most certainly are an orphan, aren't you, and you are called Stormy?'

Stormy nodded.

'Phew. Mustn't get the wrong one, and one orphan is so much like another these days. Now, orphan, you have a benefactor.'

'What's one of those?' asked Stormy.

'Someone who wants to help you, Stormy. Someone who wants you to have what you want most in life.'

'I don't think that's possible,' Stormy said.

'Well, well, we'll come to that,' the squashed-faced man said, seeing Stormy was confused. 'This benefactor is your friend –'

'I don't have any friends. Well, not outside the kitchen and the orphanage.'

'Nonsense. This person is your friend. I will refer to him as "he", but please understand that doesn't necessarily mean that he is a he; it is for convenience alone and it could just as easily be a female I am talking of. Do you understand? This person, *he* wants you to have hope; hope is something he did *not* always have. He wants you to have some hope and expectations in life to make up for your poor start with no parents to love and cherish you. He wishes for you to have the good life you might have had – indeed perhaps that *he* might have had and did not have. Opportunities and success and . . . and everything! I cannot tell you anything at all about his identity, and

172

this is most important, boy. Your benefactor insists on remaining anonymous – unknown to you or any other living soul except myself. Even if you have suspicions as to his name or face, you are to keep those suspicions to yourself. Now, your benefactor's wish is for you to have everything, I repeat, *everything*, you desire, so . . .

'. . . You, Stormy,' went on Mr Topter, 'have a place at the Academy. You are to be a sky-rider!'

Stormy staggered back into the solid bulk of Otto. 'Steady, lad, steady,' Otto said, placing his ham-like hand on his shoulder.

Stormy squeaked wordlessly. It wasn't true. It couldn't be true; someone had discovered his dreams and was now holding them out for him to touch, making them real, but they couldn't be. It was impossibly cruel.

'It's true, Stormy, it's true!' Mrs Cathcart cried, folding him against her soft chest. 'You're to be a sky-rider. You're to go up to the Academy as a *pupil*! A *scholar*!'

Stormy disentangled himself from Mrs Cathcart before he suffocated. Otto shrugged and held out his empty hands as if to say it was nothing to do with him this time.

'But I'm just a skivvy. I'm just Stormy. It can't happen – can it?' Nobody's dreams came true. Nobody's.

'I wish you could tell us a bit about his benefactor,' Mrs Cathcart said, wiping her eyes. 'I want to shake his hand. I want to hug him and kiss his cheeks – or hers!'

'I don't know anyone rich,' Stormy said. 'The only person . . .' And he stopped. The only person he could think of who might do this, who had the power to do

173

this, who might care about him at all, was the Director. He was rich. Powerful. He had been sorry to let him go. He'd said he had potential . . .

Suddenly he found himself grinning from ear to ear.

'So, you will take this offer, orphan? You do wish to ride the horses with wings?' Mr Topter asked.

'Yes. Oh yes!' he cried.

'Sign here, then.' Mr Topter pushed some papers over the desk and handed Stormy a pen. 'You'll need a uniform and then you'll need some books and pocket money. I'll leave Mrs Cathcart to look after all those trifles.'

'Thank you.' Stormy was dazed, and all he could do was grin.

'I'll be on my way, then. My employer, your benefactor, will be glad to hear his offer makes you happy.'

Stormy nodded. 'I am. It does! I am. Please thank him. Her.'

Mrs Cathcart showed Mr Topter out, chatting happily with him.

But Otto was frowning. Over the last few months Stormy felt they'd become friends, and he was surprised and disappointed that Otto wasn't pleased for him.

'Well, Stormy, you have another chance,' Otto said. 'You'll be back up at the Academy, back with Al.'

'Yes.' Stormy nodded. 'Al doesn't eat your food, or hardly touches it,' he said quietly, hoping it would please Otto to know this. 'He cuts it up into tiny little pieces. Sometimes he throws it to the birds.'

A half-smile twitched over Otto's lumpy face.

'Like he's scared of it,' Stormy added, as the idea suddenly occurred to him, 'as if he dare not eat it.'

'Listen,' Otto said, 'I know you want to go back up there, but if you stay, Stormy, I'll give you a better job in the kitchen. We could work at it. We could find a way –'

'To do what?'

'To pay Al back. That's what I'd like,' and he rubbed his hands together wildly, a dangerous glint sparking in his eyes.

But Stormy didn't want anything to do with Otto's revenge. It was Otto's sad past, not his. Nothing must get in the way of him going back to the Academy.

'I'm sorry, Otto,' he said. 'I have to go. There are things up there . . . unfinished business I have to attend to. I was meant to be with the spitfyres!'

Otto nodded. 'I see that. I understand, but I'll miss you. I'll be thinking about you, remember that.'

It was hard to believe, almost impossible to take in: Stormy had another chance. And this time he was actually going to be a student, a sky-rider. He wouldn't have to do what Al told him – in fact he'd be able to boss Al about himself!

He went over and over what Mr Topter had said, trying to think who his mysterious benefactor could be. Every time he came up with the same answer: the Director. The way Mr Topter had kept saying 'he' but that it could be 'she' made him wonder if Araminta was involved too.

Being singled out by the Director made him feel enormously proud and special.

He could barely eat or sleep. He thought all the time of the Academy and the spitfyre in the thirteenth cave. Was she still alive? She had managed to survive before with very little care – surely she'd be all right? He would help her properly now. He'd ignore Al. Would *she* remember *him*? Would she forgive him for leaving?

Then there would be his spitfyre. What would *his* winged horse be like? As huge as Sparkit? Blue, or purple or green? Fierce or gentle? There was so much to think about.

He didn't mention his great new opportunity to anyone, and nor it seemed did Otto, because no one asked him about it and no one treated him differently, until the day some books arrived for him.

'Wow! Look at those!' Tex said, lifting the books and weighing them in his hands as if the weight was a measure of what was inside. 'Wow! All about spitfyres! Where did they come from? Who paid? Why have you got them?'

And then Stormy told him.

'Wow! That's amazing! Haven't you any idea who it is?'

'No.' Stormy shook his head.

'Wow! I wish I had a bennyfact-what's it. Not that I'd want to go up there if I had, but still . . .'

'But I do.' Stormy was looking through the books longingly. He would read every one from cover to cover and absorb everything there was to know about spitfyres. He didn't want to be bottom of the class. 'I was a spitfyre skivvy last time; this time I'll be a student. I'll be riding spitfyres. Tex, I'll be a *sky-rider*!'

For a fleeting moment he saw the Director's face, his

expression of disappointment when they last met, and a sharp little pain clutched at his insides. Then he thought of Araminta and her silly ribbons and he smiled again. She had tried to help him before and he felt certain she would be glad to see him again. Everything would be fine.

That week he found himself avoiding his friends, even Tex. He kept imagining himself in his new uniform striding across the Academy courtyard, and how could that person be a friend to a skivvy like Tex who snored and had dirty fingernails? He would probably never see the other skivvies again anyway, so better to begin the separation now.

He passed the time reading his new books. He began to discover things about spitfyres that he'd never dreamed of. He learnt that there was a *'naming of the spitfyre ceremony'*, that normally took place when the spitfyre was between one and three spitfyre years old, by which time it was considered unlikely to die from some terrible disease or accident. The name chosen depended on how the spit-fyre behaved and how the owner felt about it. In other words it could be just about anything, as long as it suited. He spent hours trying to imagine what name Al might have given the spitfyre in cave thirteen.

On his last night he dreamed he was walking up the path to the Academy and that the path was narrow and went on and on, winding round like a snake. The faster he walked, the further away the Academy gate became.

He panicked that he wasn't really called Stormy.

He panicked that perhaps he was the *wrong* Stormy. He was the *wrong* Stormy in the *wrong* kitchen.

The benefactor lost all his money before he could pay for Stormy's place at the school.

Spitfyres bit him.

The littles laughed at him.

Al chased him out of the servery, brandishing a bottle of pink rum.

Finally, at long last, morning came. Stormy slipped out of his bunk and opened up the big box with the Academy crest on it which contained his new uniform. He had refused to open it before so it was only now, this last morning, that he put it on for the first time. What if it was too small or too big? What if they laughed? They might easily laugh.

He had grown massively since that day so long ago when he had been dressed in the Academy work clothes. Mrs Cathcart had measured him very carefully this time and the new suit fitted perfectly. It transformed him; in the mirror he looked just like a real Academy student.

The green jacket was knee length, with a stand-up collar, and made his shoulders look wider and stronger. A red crest showing a leaping spitfyre adorned the breast pocket. Narrow trousers worn inside short boots neatly covered his ankles, and made his legs look longer. The shirts were white, some with stand-up collars, others with a strange soft tie at the neck made of the same material. There was woolly underwear. Several pairs of sheepskin boots, a thick coat to keep out the cold and two different caps.

Of course he couldn't get away without being seen, and as soon as the dormitory was awake, there were cries of, 'Look at his nibs!' and 'We've got a toff in our dorm!' as the boys gathered round him.

'Doesn't he look grand!'

'Sir Stormy, he is now,' someone joked. 'Don't forget your old friends when you're up there, will you, Sir Stormy?'

'Bring your flying horse down here, please!'

'I'll miss you, all over *again*!' Tex said, slapping him on the back.

Stormy hated it. He just wanted to be gone, and so he hurried away to say his goodbyes to Mrs Cathcart and finally to Otto.

'Stormy,' Otto whispered, 'you take care. You don't belong up there and I think you'll find out soon enough. You can always come back to the kitchen, I want you to know that.'

'Thank you, Otto,' Stormy said rather stiffly. 'I shan't be coming back.'

As if! He was going to be a sky-rider! He would have a spitfyre of his own. He was never coming back.

23

Student

Mrs Cathcart arranged for a man from Stollen to help Stormy up to the Academy with all his cases.

'It's very kind of you, Mrs Cathcart, but –'

'But nothing! You're an Academy student now; you can't be expected to carry your things yourself. And you're rich. Careful!' she cried, as the man dropped a bag of books. 'Those are precious!'

Stormy had looked forward to making his triumphant return journey alone. He was even more sorry when he saw the man was using an old lame donkey to carry his stuff.

When the time came to leave, no one was there to say goodbye because Stormy had kept the precise moment secret. He was starting a new life and it meant casting off all parts of the old; the sooner he began the better.

All Stormy could focus on was the awful noise of the scraggy donkey huffing and puffing like an old pair of bellows and its patchy dusty coat as he followed the hobbling man and the donkey up the path. The man from the village whistled constantly and tunelessly. Stormy longed for quiet, to be alone with his thoughts.

They stopped at last at the Academy gates and rang the bell. The littles were quick to open the door. They both bowed low, 'Come in, Stormy, student of the Academy. Beneficiary of the Benefactor. Come in. This way, this way.'

They bowed and gestured and walked backwards on their fat little legs, bumping into each other, giggling noisily and falling down and rolling like skittles. They were making a spectacle of his arrival, he thought, just because he used to be a skivvy. He looked everywhere else rather than at them.

He waved for the villager with the donkey to come along in, wondering if anyone was watching him and believing that he gave people orders all the time.

Students stood around chatting in the courtyard, and it seemed to him that everyone stopped talking when he arrived and turned to look at him.

Stormy's cheeks burnt hotly. He was sure no one else had arrived like this; they'd have had servants and carriages. He turned his back on the man and his donkey as if they were nothing to do with him.

'Here we are, young sir, here we are,' the old man called, hurrying after him and pulling the reluctant noisy donkey with him.

A student started baying and hee-hawing loudly. Everyone laughed.

Ignoring them, Stormy went straight up to the Director's

181

house and knocked on the door. He could feel a million eyes on him and hear their whispered comments.

No one answered the door.

He had never seen such a closed door in his entire life, and no matter how hard he stared at it, it stayed shut.

Why didn't someone open it? Where was Maud? Perhaps she no longer worked here; after all, he'd been gone over a year. They couldn't be friends now, he knew that; she was only a maid.

Eventually he came back down the steps. The donkey man was unbuckling the straps and putting the bags on the floor, whistling softly as he worked. Stormy looked round at the sea of faces; no one smiled back or offered to help.

Then a figure came towards him, wearing the dull suit of grey servery clothes that he'd once worn and carrying an iced cake beneath a dome. For a split second he thought he was seeing himself again, all that time ago . . . but this boy's head was too big . . .

'*Purbeck!*'

Purbeck grinned and came towards him. 'Hey! Stormy!'

'Hey, Purbeck!'

A ripple of laughter and hoots of disdain rippled around the students.

'He's talking to the poo shifter.'

'He's hobnobbing with the staff!'

'Riff raff – I hear that's what he is too . . .'

'. . . From the kitchen.'

They both fell silent.

Stormy's extended arm dropped to his side and he stared at the ground. He bit back what he'd been going to say. Instantly Purbeck did the same, and the smile died on his lips.

'I'm taking a cake to the Director,' Purbeck mumbled to the glass dome. 'Hang on, Ralf will be here in a moment.'

Stormy wanted to say he was sorry. He *was* sorry, but he couldn't say so now, not in front of everyone. Purbeck knocked and the door that had not opened to Stormy opened for him and he disappeared inside.

A few minutes later Ralf appeared. They looked briefly into each other's eyes, then away.

'I can carry my own stuff,' Stormy said, quickly trying to pick up the bags. 'You don't need to do it all. Oh, please . . .'

But Ralf had already hoisted the heavy bags up onto his shoulders.

'Please, Ralf.' He picked up the last three and trotted after him, feeling like a puppy dog. 'I can manage. Please!'

Ralf didn't speak until they were alone inside the vast building.

'Well, well, Stormy, here's a turn up for the books,' he said quietly. 'Fancy *you* coming back. They don't usually let boys back in who have tried to poison the boss's daughter.'

'I never tried to poison anyone, and you know I didn't!'

Ralf chuckled. 'Suppose anyone can come here if they pay,' he added. 'And you've paid a lot, I've heard. Well I never, a rich skivvy.'

'Ralf, don't be unfriendly, please. This is hard . . . And

it's so great to be here, to be inside these walls, a real Academy student.'

Stormy was gazing round at the interior of the Academy castle, where he had never dared set foot before. The walls were panelled with dark wood and hung with portraits of students holding medals and silver cups. Massive chandeliers were suspended from the ceiling. In the hallway sad stuffed animal heads – deer, moose and bear – stared mournfully down at them. The large wooden staircase was covered with a red carpet held down by shining brass runners. There were huge paintings of flying horses on the staircase wall, smoke and fire curling from their nostrils and open mouths.

'Al's in a grim old gloom, knowing you're back,' Ralf said.

Stormy shrugged. 'I suppose he's worried I'll tell the Director how you two set me up,' he said. 'Aren't *you* worried?'

'Naw, couldn't care two pence. Don't care if I get the sack.'

Stormy followed Ralf up the stairs. The wide polished boards creaked loudly underfoot, and Stormy found himself creeping as if he didn't have the right to be there. *But I do, I do,* he told himself. His benefactor thought he had potential. For the first time someone believed in him. He had to believe in himself.

They tramped up to a wide landing that ran right round the hall, like a gallery. 'Staff bedrooms,' Ralf said, 'then up here is students.'

They followed a narrow flight of stone stairs to a second smaller landing.

'Those are the night larders,' Ralf told him, pointing at tall grey cupboards stationed down the corridors. 'Each one stocked up with goodies in case you can't sleep; wine, tea, and cheese and stuff.'

Stormy nodded, hardly listening. He was trying to remember their route – right, left, along the corridor, up the stairs . . . Easy to get lost.

'Here's your room,' Ralf said, throwing open a door. 'Bathroom and books and desk and Lord knows what. All yours.'

'*All* mine?'

The room was as large as Mrs Cathcart's office, bigger than any bedroom he had ever seen. It was high up and the windows looked down over the terrace below and across the valley to the ring of dark mountains. The curtains fell to the ground in thick folds and were patterned with oriental spitfyres and large orchids. Padded hot pipes running along the base of the walls made the room cosy. There was a big desk and books and plenty of empty shelves for his new books, a wardrobe and chest for his clothes. The bathroom had gold taps and a large mirror with silver spitfyres leaping and jumping around its frame. The pink soap had a spitfyre shape embossed into its surface.

But the best thing of all was the vast bed.

The top of the wooden bed was shaped into a spitfyre's neck and head; the wings formed sides that curled round

185

the pillows and down to its end. The four feet had giant hooves. The bed cover was a rich golden yellow trimmed with fur. The sheets were thick and white and freshly ironed.

Stormy stared at it, open-mouthed.

'Posh, isn't it?' Ralf said, grinning. 'This is your timetable, here.' He showed him a chart on the wall by the desk. 'Stop gawping, you'll swallow a fly! You wait – you've got more work than we have.' He laughed. 'Enjoy! Oh, and go see the Director as soon as you're ready,' he added. 'He's in his green room at the bottom of the stairs on the right.'

'Thanks. Thanks, Ralf.'

'No worries. It's not even my job, as you know, but I wanted to say hello, for old time's sake, and you know later . . . well, we won't be able to talk. See you!'

Alone, Stormy went round and round the room, admiring the furniture, feeling how soft the bed was and opening and closing the drawers in the desk, finding pens, pencils and notebooks. The books in the shelves were all about flying and spitfyres. Finally he gazed out at the amazing view. Spring was almost here and although the peaks were still snow-covered, the snow was receding and some of the hills were green and fresh, glistening like salad leaves.

Now for the Director.

As he went down the stairs his pulse was racing; he'd been anticipating this for ages. He had never met anyone as intoxicatingly powerful or as fascinating as the Director. No one else had ever shown an interest in him the way he had. Those blue eyes looking into his and the sense of power and strength had filled Stormy with a feeling of strength too. Every word the Director had ever spoken to him was etched on his brain.

'Come in,' the Director called when he knocked.

Stormy went in. The panelling in the room was so dark it was almost black and underfoot was a thick green carpet. The Director looked up from his large desk.

'Yes?'

'It's me. Stormy, sir. I was told to come and see you.' He went towards the desk eagerly. 'Hello, sir.'

There was a flash of something fierce in the Director's eyes and then it was gone and he was smiling. He got up and closed the door behind the desk, giving Stormy the distinct impression that there was someone or something there that he didn't want him to see. Then he held out his hand. His palm was dry and firm as he pumped Stormy's hand up and down.

'It's you! *Stanley!*'

'*Stormy*, sir . . .'

'Stormy, of course, Stormy, the troublesome boy from the kitchen – mouse in the custard –'

'Gravy.'

'Ha, ha, yes. The boy with the benefactor.' He shook his hand again. 'The boy who got so very, very lucky; so very, very rich. Yes. Now I remember you *exceedingly* well. That was a bad business. All over and done with now.'

'I'm back as a student,' Stormy said, patting the crest on his jacket. 'A sky-rider.'

187

The Director smiled. 'Have a piece of cake. Otto's cake.'

He waved at the chocolate cake on the table; it was the cake Purbeck had been carrying. Stormy almost giggled; the cake was following him.

'So you have a benefactor.' The Director winked. 'A benefactor, eh?'

Stormy smiled back and nodded.

'It's wonderful news and I understand we are not to ask whom.' He sat down again at his desk and gently nudged some papers with the tip of his finger so they slid into a neat pile. 'I'm sure you'll settle in here, clever boy like you. Work hard and perhaps I'll be handing out a medal or a silver cup to you at the next ceremony. I always liked you, Stormy. I thought there was something special about you right from the first time we met. Araminta did too, didn't she?'

'I hope so, sir,' Stormy said.

'And someone must think most highly of you, mustn't they,' he added, 'to pay for all this.' He indicated the Academy. 'It's a mystery.'

He was as good as admitting it, Stormy thought.

But before he could say anything, he was being shown out. He found himself standing in the corridor feeling that somehow he hadn't said what he wanted to say or conducted himself quite the way he'd wanted to. He went slowly back to his room feeling strangely heavy-hearted.

A boy was lurking in the shadowy corridor by his door. Purbeck.

'Hello, old chum!' Purbeck said, flicking a duster at

some imaginary dust. 'Glad you're back. It meant a lot to you, being here, didn't it?'

Stormy looked around anxiously, hoping no one would see them. 'Yes. How's it going?' he whispered.

'Fine. Can't you see I've got fat?' He patted his belly. 'Otto's glorious food goes straight into my big gob! Hey, you didn't tell Otto what we do with his nosh, did you?'

'No.'

'What you don't know can't hurt.'

'Hey, Purbeck, the spitfyre in the last cave, the thirteenth,' Stormy asked. 'Is she still there?'

'As far as I know. I haven't seen it. I didn't know it was a she, but – *she's* there all right.'

Stormy felt a bubble of lightness inside him: he wasn't too late. Every time he'd thought about her waiting for his visit that never came, the pain and guilt had got worsened; it was like having a giant splinter lodged in his heart, the spike digging deeper and harder as the months went by. Now he really would do something about her.

'I heard the big D's given you one of the best rooms,' Purbeck went on. 'And you're in all the good classes with the decent teachers. On the top table for dinner as well! Hey, Stormy, the Director could be your mystery benefactor. Ever thought of that?'

'No, I never thought of that,' Stormy said, not meeting Purbeck's smiling eyes.

24

Test

Stormy sat down on his grand bed and waited.

He heard the dinner gong sound, followed by a rush of feet thundering along the corridor. Now what was he supposed to do? Someone hammered on the door and a boy put his head round.

'Hiya! Grubs up! Come along with me. I'm Tom.'

'Thanks!'

Perhaps they weren't all so bad, Stormy thought, jumping off his bed. Food! The dining room! He was going to be inside that wonderful place he'd glimpsed so many times through the swing doors.

The narrow corridor was crammed with students flooding towards the dining room, stampeding down the stairway. 'Come on!' Tom pulled him in and they were carried along in the current.

Students craned to get a look at this new boy. Stormy wished that he were different, taller, stronger, better-looking, smarter . . . anything other than the weedy orphan skivvy he was. The tangle of bodies rushing along was so rough that twice he nearly fell when someone else's leg got tangled in his.

'Watch it!'

'Clumsy!'

'New boy!'

He just couldn't seem to get out of their way and finally he did trip and come tumbling down the remaining steps of the big staircase, landing up beneath the glass-eyed glare of a brown bear head.

Everyone laughed. He tried to laugh too, but he didn't think it was funny.

When he got up, Tom had vanished.

Nervously he followed the others as they streamed through a doorway and into the great dining room. This time he was part of it, not peering through a crack in the door like a lizard. He belonged in it.

It was just as he'd hoped it would be; just as grand, with long covered tables, gilt chairs, black-suited waiters like statues against the wall. Bright lanterns shone from the walls and candles adorned the tables.

'You're up *there*!' a girl said, pulling at his arm. 'You're on the top table.'

The top table. This was on a stage, set at a right angle to the room, and it boasted elegant silver candlesticks, crystal glass and a white cloth hanging to the floor.

'It's only 'cos he's so rich,' someone whispered. 'He's nothing to write home about as far as I can see.'

'He's taken Tarik's place!'

191

'Can you imagine having to eat with a skivvy?'

So they all knew where he had come from. There was no hiding that. Stormy grew hotter and hotter.

'Hi, I'm Bella,' a dark girl said, pushing him towards the front. 'Ignore them,' she added. 'Some will hate you because of what you once were, others will hate you for having more money than them and some won't know or care, so just brazen it out.'

She pushed him up three steps to the top table and plonked him in a seat. He checked the place card in front of his plate; there was his name in gold letters. On his right, Araminta; on his left, Hector Grant. *Boom bang boom* went his troubled heart.

'Chin up!' Bella called as she slid away into the crush of bodies.

The Director and Araminta came in and a hush fell over the room. The students turned to watch the Director and then studied Stormy too as if he were a rare exhibit in a zoo.

When the Director sat down, the chatter started up again. Hector had taken his seat but was looking in the other direction; Araminta had turned away. He had an uninterrupted view of the blue ribbons wound through her long plait as she chatted to her neighbour. Stormy stared ahead with a fixed grin, practising what he might say as an opening conversation piece – should an opportunity ever arise.

The doors at the far end of the dining room swung open and Stormy strained to see, hoping to catch a glimpse of Ralf or Purbeck – seeing them would make this real – but he saw only a flash of grey uniform before the door closed. He wondered if they'd tried to catch sight of him too.

The waiters served the food to the top table first, golden roast potatoes, succulent chicken with herby sauce, tiny sprouts and rich gravy. Knowing how everyone had slaved away in the kitchen to make this, he was glad to be here, gladder than ever, and yet, thinking of Otto made him feel suddenly sad too.

He pulled himself together, sat up and chanced another look to his left, but Hector still had his back to him. He turned the other way. Had Araminta possibly asked specially for this seating? Then, suddenly she was speaking to him.

'I never expected to find myself sitting next to you,' she said, cracking a chicken bone between her teeth.

'I came into some luck,' he said. 'I'm a student now.'

'Hmm. I hear you're paid up for years and years. Daddy's thrilled. Did someone die?' she asked.

'I don't think so.' He searched her profile for some hint of her knowing more.

'Don't stare at me so,' she said and he instantly reddened and looked away.

'You've grown a lot,' she added. 'Much taller than the servery boy I used to know. Why don't you look at me when I talk to you?'

She was at it again, saying one thing and then the opposite, and he felt confused and anxious – just how she always made him feel.

'I'm not a servery boy now,' he said, making eye contact for a split second.

'He'll be in your classes, Hector,' Araminta said loudly, leaning forward to speak to Hector. 'He's a sky-rider.'

Hector didn't recognise Stormy. He looked blank. 'Say that again?'

'He's a sky-rider, the new boy. Stormy.'

'*Stormy?*' He looked puzzled. 'Weren't you the boy mucking out the stables?'

'Yes, but –'

'And now you're a rider?' He raised his eyebrows. 'How?'

'Don't you ever listen to the gossip, Hect? He's just got loads and loads of money.'

Stormy clenched his hands under the table. 'Yes, I got some luck, I –'

'Now I remember. I heard the Director talking about it to Mr Jacobs. You're an orphan?' Hector's nose crinkled up as if '*orphan*' wasn't a word he really liked to say. 'A *skivvy?*' he said, with even more contempt. 'And now you're in the Academy? What is the Director thinking of?'

'Money, I expect,' Araminta said.

It was true. Stormy knew in his heart of hearts that what she said was true.

'He might join you in the Star Squad,' Araminta said.

Hector smiled. 'That would be interesting. The Star Squad is for the elite of the elite, new boy, and I'm not just talking about family here. You need to be able to fly like a bird and shoot fire like a cannon . . . Can you?'

'Yes,' Stormy lied. Quickly he reached for some butter for his bread – anything to occupy his hands.

'Oh dear, table manners! This is what I was worried

about,' Hector said, tapping Stormy's outstretched arm with his forefinger. 'No training in the niceties of life. We don't use *that* knife for the butter; there's a special one there. And that's my napkin you're rubbing over your grubby mouth.'

'Sorry.' Stormy handed him the napkin back.

'No thank you, you keep it . . .' Hector threw it back. 'Let me give you a bit of advice, Stormy. One thing you require for the Star Squad is straight As and we've tests in aerodynamics and warfare tomorrow, so if I were you, I'd do some revision tonight.'

'Oh, thanks,' Stormy said. He would prepare all night long if he had to. 'Those are my favourite subjects.'

'And on the top table, we do not drink water, we drink wine,' Hector said. 'I know you want to mix in and not look out of place.' He poured Stormy's water back into the jug and replaced it with red wine. 'Drink.'

'I really don't –'

But Hector was smiling and pushing the glass into his hands and up to his mouth and he had to take it. 'There!'

It took a moment for Stormy to get his breath back and wipe the dribbled wine from his chin.

'I just want to make my benefactor proud,' he said quietly, hoping Araminta would understand his meaning. But even at that she didn't move a muscle and he thought she must be the best, strangest actress in the world.

By the end of the evening Stormy had drunk so much wine he could barely make it up to his room. He had almost told Araminta that she was the most beautiful girl he had ever met and that he thought of the Director as his new father and Hector his greatest friend. Thankfully he was incapable of saying anything. He fell into his room with the help of a mighty push from some kind boy, and crashed onto his bed.

He woke early. He always woke early, ready for work in the kitchen, but there was no such work today. He had a bad headache, but after drinking three glasses of water he felt better. He remembered the previous night with a groan. Why had he said those things to Hector that weren't true? Who was he trying to fool?

He peered at his new timetable; several of the sessions were taken by the Director and marked 'Star Squad Only'. He looked at the plan for that day; there were tests in ancient spitfyre myth and legend at ten thirty, but no mention of aerodynamics or warfare. He must have misheard Hector. He'd had so much wine to drink he'd probably got the subjects mixed up. Thank goodness he'd looked at the timetable because now he would revise the correct subjects. He settled down to work, but somehow he was hungry again and sneaked out to the hall larder – it was stocked with goodies – and brought back croissants, sausages, fruit and yogurt to his room. *Brain food.* He set about learning as much as he could from his new books, determined to impress.

It took him a while to find his classroom because none of the students he asked knew where it was; one directed him outside into the courtyard and two sent him back down to the servery. When he did reach it, the teacher, Mrs Lister, welcomed him kindly.

'Good morning, Stormy,' she said. 'I teach ancient winged horse ceremony, history, myth and legend. I'm pleased to have you in our group.' She was thin with pale grey hair and small spectacles that she peered through as if she was very short-sighted. 'It's nice to have a new face in the class.'

'Yeah, specially when it's a rich face!' a girl called out.

'Now, now, Petra,' Mrs Lister said, laughing, 'let him alone, the poor boy. Be kind to him.'

'Come and sit by me,' Petra said. 'I'll be kind and there's lots I want to ask you.'

'You don't know the meaning of the word. Kind, huh. No, come sit next to me!' Bella said.

'He's quite handsome, isn't he?' Petra added in a low voice. She pushed her blonde hair out of her eyes. 'For a skivvy.'

Stormy glared at the floor. The other girls were looking him over too. Was he good-looking? He knew Mrs Cathcart thought so, but she didn't count, she was just squinty-eyed, fat Mrs Cathcart . . .

Hector was the last to arrive and he was in such a hurry he tripped over Stormy's foot as he walked past, landing him a mighty kick on the ankle.

'Sorry, I do apologise,' Hector said. 'Oh, it's *you*, Stormy. Fancy me kicking a new boy. I am *so* clumsy . . . Ready for the tests? Aerodynamics, isn't it?'

197

'Isn't it myths today?' Bella shrieked. 'Please tell me it is! Myths and legend, surely!'

'It is, Bella,' Mrs Lister said. 'Don't worry. As if I'd test you on aerodynamics! I know nothing about them at all.'

'Oh, is it? My mistake,' Hector said with a laugh. 'I hope you didn't waste time revising the wrong things, did you, Stormy?'

'No. I didn't,' said Stormy.

'Is that what he told you?' Bella said, raising her eyebrows. 'The *toad*!'

Hector winked at Stormy. 'My mistake.'

Stormy guessed he'd been tricked. That's what happened to new boys. That was OK. He'd just ignore it.

He looked at the papers: some of the answers seemed to just erupt out of him from a memory bank that he didn't know he even had. It was as if anything about flying horses concerned him. He sailed through the questions.

'Only a few weeks now before the Silver Sword Race,' Mrs Lister reminded them as she gathered up their answer sheets. 'Is anyone in this group – apart from Hector – entering?'

Petra and Tom put up their hands.

Mrs Lister smiled. 'It's a tough one; I'm not surprised only you Star Squad riders are taking part. You see, Stormy,' she explained, 'it's only every ten years. The race is fast and hard. No one knows where the Sword will be until the last minute, so they can't prepare, and sometimes people get hurt. Sometimes they never come back and one wonders whether the race is really worth it, just for the title and the honour . . .'

'And the Director has made it even tougher,' Petra said, 'because the last one back loses their mount – they have to give their spitfyre to the winner. It keeps the race small and very competitive.'

'And the winner –' Tom said.

'Which will be me!' Hector said, banging his fist on his chest.

'– Goes down in history.'

Stormy had been trying not to think too much about meeting his own spitfyre and having his first ride, but by the end of the lesson, he could think of nothing else and was desperate to get to the stables. He'd flown so many times in his dreams and now it was going to be the real thing. Finally he asked Bella when they might go.

'Usually no one goes down to the stables before lunch – at least not if you have a West-side spitfyre,' Bella told him. 'The light, you know.'

Stormy knew this was true. 'But I *could* go now?' he asked.

'You're a bit of a keener, aren't you?' Petra said.

'I suppose you fancy beating Hector? Everyone feels like that when they start here,' Bella said. 'Forget it, new boy, Hector is always the best.'

'I don't want to beat him,' Stormy said, glancing over at the other boy, knowing it wouldn't pay to be on the

199

wrong side of someone like Hector. 'I just want to do well, that's all.'

Hector smiled. 'How charming.'

'Come and have break with us first,' Bella said.

They took him to the Snook, a small room where coffee, hot chocolate and cake was served. Petra and Lizzie squashed alongside him on the bench and Bella sat on the opposite side of the table.

'So exactly how rich are you?' Lizzie asked him, snuggling up.

'And did your benefactor give you loads to spend?' Petra asked. 'There's a good shop here where you can buy extras. I'll take you there later.'

'My father's got three spitfyres, you know. All very rare breeds,' Lizzie said. 'You must come stay in the holidays.'

They wanted to know if he thought his parents were really alive, if he thought his parents were noble or flying horse masters, or perhaps royal? The boys weren't much interested in him, but he didn't care, although he wished Hector found him interesting enough to talk to. He didn't mind what questions the girls asked; he liked being the centre of attention.

'Well, I think I'll go and –' Stormy stopped as suddenly a dull bell sounded.

The girls groaned.

The bell rang in a slow and heavy, thudding way, like the one in Stollen did when someone had died.

'You won't want to go out now,' Tom said.

'Why? What does that bell mean?'

'It means convicts are being moved.'

'Oh, let Stormy go see!' Hector's friend Bentley said. 'He might recognise one! His father, perhaps?' He laughed.

'*Bentley!*' Bella looked embarrassed. 'Ignore him, Stormy, he's such a poser.'

'No, I'm only telling the truth, Bella,' Bentley said, smoothing his hair off of his forehead. 'He's an orphan. He may be rich, but no one knows anything about his family or his breeding.'

'I'm not a prize cow, Bentley,' Stormy said.

'I didn't think orphans were allowed at the Academy,' Petra said.

'I do think one should know who one's parents are,' Tom said. 'Imagine, they could be anyone!'

Stormy straightened his shoulders and marched out through the nearest door.

'Not that way!' Petra called, but Stormy couldn't turn back. He was so angry he thought he might hit someone. He went down a short corridor and opened the door at the end; it gave straight onto the courtyard.

He stopped, dazzled by the bright sun in the clear blue sky. It was cold and the breeze was as sharp as needles. The bell had stopped ringing, and the air seemed to hang emptily around him, waiting.

The littles were swinging like children on the large handles of the open gate; the iron hinges squeaked as if they hurt. They were giggling and all the while darting sidelong glances up at the tall house where the Director

201

stood like a rock, staring at the tower in the far corner of the yard. The usual guards were not there.

Somewhere out of sight, a door creaked open and four guards appeared, slowly rising up from the sunken stone staircase beside the tower, like spirits from the grave, their heads and necks emerging first, then their shoulders and bodies. Behind them came a group of convicts – *grubbin* convicts – and behind them, more guards. At the sight of the convicts, Stormy felt his stomach contract and a coldness came over him; it was an old fear mixed with pity. There were six of them, linked together by chains that were bound to their heavy metal cuffs at legs and wrists. They lifted their heads up briefly, blinking against the blinding sun. Their clothes were nothing but rags; their feet were dirty and bare.

Why were they all grubbins? What terrible crimes could they all have committed?

As they shuffled past Stormy found himself studying each of their grimy faces, looking for *his* grubbin and hoping he wouldn't see him.

Petra appeared beside him. 'They told you not to come this way. See,' she said, linking her arm through his, 'it's prisoners. They're being moved somewhere. The dungeons must be full or something.'

'But they're *all* grubbins,' Stormy said.

'Crime enough,' Petra said.

'Do you think that?' Stormy said, shifting away from her. 'I hate that talk. There's a chef I know, called Brittel, who thinks like that about grubbins, but it isn't true. I can't believe it.'

Petra shrugged. 'They're so dirty,' she said. 'They smell wormy. They're short and stupid and greedy. Why should they have all that gold?'

Stormy gritted his teeth. 'They find it, don't they – on their own land?'

'But what do they want with it? Nothing. I think the world would be a much better place without them,' she added. 'And we could have all the gold.'

The group clanked over the stones and out of the gate. *His* convict was not amongst them; hopefully it meant he was still free.

The littles swung the gate shut with a clang, then went rolling and cart-wheeling merrily back into their gatehouse as if they were in a circus act, and slammed the door shut.

'All gone,' Petra said. 'Wonder where they – '

'So here you are!' It was Lizzie. 'I've come to show Stormy the way to the stables,' she said, linking her arm through his spare one.

'We don't need you,' Petra said, pulling him the other way.

Stormy didn't like to remind them that he had worked here and knew the way.

'West or East?' Lizzie went on. 'Which are you?'

'Oh.' He hadn't given it any thought, but surely, yes, surely it would be West. 'West,' he said confidently.

Lizzie led him down a wide corridor that opened onto a small disc-shaped terrace facing due south. Circular steps led down from here to the terrace. These south steps had been out of bounds for the servery staff.

Stormy paused, looking round at the wide view of mountains, slopes covered with pine trees and craggy rocks. He filled his lungs with the cool, fresh air. Down in the kitchen he could never have believed he'd ever get to breathe this high-altitude air again. Never see this view. He felt full of energy, purposeful and hopeful. He was desperate to get to his spitfyre.

'Are you sky-riders too?' Stormy asked as they walked towards the caves.

'Yes,' Lizzie said. 'My spitfyre is Daygo. I'm going to major in psychiatry – study the mind of a winged horse, you know; though I adore flying too.'

Stormy remembered Lizzie now from her visits to the lovely green spitfyre; he also remembered, unfortunately, how she had wacked the spitfyre with her riding crop when it didn't behave to her liking.

'I want to study every bit of their life,' Stormy told her, 'but more than anything I want to ride.'

At the bottom of the steps they turned right and so came onto the West terrace. In a few paces they had reached cave thirteen. Stormy forced himself not to turn and look at it.

'This is Kyte here in twelve,' Petra said, ignoring the thirteenth cave as if it wasn't even there. 'Mine is further on. Polaris.'

Stormy knew Polaris. He was a member of the Star Squad, a golden-brown colour with greenish tints and very bad-tempered.

'So, which is yours?' Petra said. 'When did it come?'

204

Stormy stopped dead.

When did it come in? He had no idea!

'If you didn't bring it,' Lizzie said, laughing, 'someone else did. You can't *not* have one if you're a sky-rider.'

'I am a sky-rider. I mean, that's what I'm supposed to be.' He stopped breathing. Why had he not thought of this before?

'So where is it?' Lizzie persisted.

'I don't know!' Stormy felt the tightness give way to a great emptiness in his guts. Dread and disappointment mingled, making him weak and sick. 'It must be some-where,' he said, looking around desperately. 'I must have one, mustn't I?'

25

Where?

There was the noise of the dragon-wagon trundling over the stone slabs and Purbeck and Ralf appeared. They were chatting, and their shoulders bumped together as they walked. When Purbeck suddenly burst out laughing, Stormy felt as if he'd been stabbed. For an instant he was jealous of them; he'd loved that job, he'd truly loved it. For a second he wished he were still cleaning out spitfyre stables instead of trying to be something that he wasn't and hobnobbing with the likes of Hector and these girls whom he didn't understand at all.

'Purbeck! Ralf!' he shouted.

The girls winced. 'We don't talk to them,' Lizzie hissed.

Stormy's ears were ringing and his heart was banging painfully against his ribs. 'Ralf! My flying horse? I do have a spitfyre, don't I? Don't I? Do I have one?'

'Not as far as I know,' Ralf said.

He spun round. 'Purbeck?'

Purbeck shrugged. 'I don't think so. I haven't seen one,

Stormy. Sorry, mate. Maybe there's been some sort of mistake . . . '

The girls looked amazed and vaguely amused.

'Is it some sort of joke?' Lizzie asked, but Stormy had already spun on his heel and was running to the servery.

Al was standing outside the servery door, beside the low wall, throwing crumbs into the air. A cloud of tumbling, swooping birds surrounded him, squawking and piping.

'Al!'

The tall man pivoted round slowly.

'Hi, Al! It's me! Stormy!'

Al's face had become more cadaverous than ever. The deep creases in his face were so black they looked like they'd been drawn in charcoal. There was no smile, no sign of recognition. He turned back to the clamouring birds.

'Al, you remember me! You do! It's me, Stormy.' He tugged his Academy jacket off as if that would make Al see who he really was. 'Stormy.'

'*Stormy?*'

'Yes. Hell's bells, Al, don't do this to me!'

'What?'

'Don't be so cold and distant, please. I haven't told anyone what you did – the mouse thing. I won't. Al, please, I need a spitfyre. I'm a sky-rider. You're the spitfyre keeper. Don't I have a winged horse?'

Al smiled, but there wasn't a jot of humour in it. 'You do not have a flying horse.' He sat down on the low wall and faced Stormy. 'I would know if you did. I would have logged it in and it would have a new stable. Not that any are empty . . . Your benefactor doesn't know much about the Academy, does he? What sort of a fool wouldn't know you need a spitfyre? Too much money and no sense, I expect.'

'But, *you* could have said!' Stormy roared. 'When you knew I was coming, why didn't you tell them what was needed? You could have told Mrs Cathcart or that Mr Topter. Why are you against me?'

'I'm not against *you* in particular, Stormy, just the whole world.' Al looked down at the crumbled squares of toast in his hands.

'Well, all right, Al,' Stormy said bitterly. 'So where can I get one? I'm sure I've got enough money. I'm sure my benefactor will pay for one. He must if he wants me to be a sky-rider.'

Al was staring up at the circling birds, crying for more food.

'You can't. Oh, no, Stormy, you can't just buy one, I'm afraid,' he said. 'No. No.'

'What do you mean?'

'Just that; winged horses don't get bought like cakes.'

Stormy smashed his fist on the wall. 'Rot your bones, Al!' he yelled.

He was about to head back into the Academy, when he stopped as an idea struck him. Turning, he flew past Al, past Purbeck and Ralf and past all the spitfyres, down the whole length of the great terrace. He passed thirteen. *There* was a spare spitfyre, he knew, but what use was it? He wanted a proper one.

He went on, right round along the circular steps and on to the East side.

Most of the day the East side was in deep shadow, which made it much colder than the West, but right now it was bathed in morning sunshine. He didn't want a gloomy East-side spitfyre, but who was he to pick and chose? It would do. It would have to. Anyway, he'd make it good, the best.

The tightness in his chest was worse than ever. He stopped, bent double, trying to get his breath.

'Hello!' Troy – or was it Roy; he didn't have the time to look for the earring – came towards him. 'Is that you, Stormy? Heard you were back.'

The other brother popped out from the next cave and grinned at him. 'Look at him, the fine gentleman!'

'Posh, eh?'

'I'm not posh. I –'

'We heard you're so posh you can't even speak to poor old Purbeck.'

'No. Yes. I can. I just – I just had some luck, that's all.' He breathed deeply. 'I was just wondering,' he went on, fighting to keep himself under control, 'if by chance my spitfyre was here? I'm a sky-rider and I must have a spit-fyre to fly, but it isn't on the West side.'

The twins looked at each other, identical faces smiling identical smiles.

'Flying horse?'

'Do you have it here?' Stormy asked.

'Do we have it here?' one said.

'Do we have it here?' said the other one.

'I don't think so,' the other said, without a shred of regret in his voice.

Stormy looked along the row of caves. There were spitfyres here just as there were on the West side, blue and silver and red and green: large and small and fierce and smoking. He needed one. Any one at all would do.

'Is there –'

'Oh, put him out of his misery,' one twin said and Stormy's heart leapt – they were teasing him! An East-side spitfyre wouldn't be so bad . . .

'The truth is, no. Sorry, no.'

'What?' He looked from one to the other desperately. 'Are you sure?'

They shook their identical heads.

'Absolutely sure.'

'You do not have a spitfyre here.'

'No spitfyre.'

Stormy turned away to hide the distress and despair that surely showed in his face. He went slowly back the way he'd come, his feet like lead. Something was broken inside him.

No spitfyre. *No spitfyre!*

Somehow he made it back to his bedroom, shut the door and lay down on his bed.

What was he going to do?

Stormy didn't move for a long time.

His thoughts kept returning to cave thirteen. There was

a spitfyre in that cave; a flying horse no one wanted. He wanted one . . . But it was crazy to think of it – the creature was ill and useless and he wanted a really fantastic one. No, he wasn't even going to consider it.

He had been staring, unseeing, at the wall of books above his desk, and now one particular title stood out: *Owning Your First Flying Horse*, by Professor Georgie Blink. He had not seen it before. He took it down and began to read.

> *. . . there is no particular shop where you can buy a flying horse. It would be foolish to think winged horses can be purchased over the counter like bags of flour; it would be like buying a human child from a market. Plus it would be highly immoral. Flying horses come from dealers who have them from the egg or captured as a hatchling. Unless you have your winged horse from very young and you undergo the naming ceremony with it, you will never bond or receive any loyalty from your beast. There is some evidence of winged horses being captured when around five years old and being trained and named, but few are known to this author personally and hence not recorded in this book.*

Hatchling? Egg? He had no hope: he was doomed.

He stared out of the window at Hector and Bentley flying past, one silvery spitfyre and one dark blue. They swooped and glided and tipped and twirled, using the

211

thermals to rise and fall, almost as if they were performing on purpose, to mock him, to show him how much fun it was. He watched the ease with which they could turn their spitfyres, sail down invisible air currents, and rise, circling higher and higher. How skilfully Hector commanded his spitfyre – to fly, to dive and soar.

There was only one hope left. The Director. If he explained the situation to him, the Director would surely help.

Maud opened the door of the tall house.

'Oh, Maud! Hello!'

She didn't look surprised to see him. She didn't look *anything* for a few moments, or even speak.

'Hi. It's me, Stormy.' And he knew he should have sought her out and spoken to her earlier and went a guilty, embarrassed red. She'd helped him before; she'd been a friend and he'd ignored her. 'You do remember me, don't you?' he said. 'You've grown, Maud. It's nice to see you again.'

That little sparkle that he remembered so well glinted in her eye and he felt suddenly cheered to see her. After a few seconds the dimple appeared in her cheek too. 'You do remember me!' he cried.

'Of course I do,' she said. 'I've been expecting you, but then I realised that now you're so grand and so rich you'd never want to speak to me.'

'Oh, no, that's not it!' But she was a little right and they both knew it.

She glanced behind her at the long corridor. 'Araminta will be furious if we chat!'

'Don't worry, I'm sure she won't . . . I've got a problem.'

She smiled shyly. 'Go on.'

'I don't have a flying horse and I'm supposed to be a sky-rider. I'd buy one, I'm rich enough, apparently, but I can't. I mean, the books say you can't just buy a flying horse.'

She shrugged and smiled again. 'I don't know anything about them.'

'I thought the Director might help.'

'He might not,' said Maud.

'Well, there's no one else. I need to see him.'

'You'd better come in, then.'

Maud led him to the Director's room and Stormy knocked on the door and went in.

'Good to see you, young man. How can I help you?'

'I'm sorry to bother you, Director, but there is something . . . The thing is, I need a flying horse and I haven't got one.'

The Director sat at his desk. He touched his fingertips together, pursed his lips and nodded. 'That is unfortunate. I see. No spitfyre. Who is responsible for this? Is it our fault – the Academy's? Or your benefactor's?'

Stormy wished that just for an instant the Director would crack and let on that *he* was his benefactor, but the Director's stare was cool and gave away nothing.

'Well, I wouldn't like to say exactly, I mean . . .'

'Are you able to get in contact with your benefactor and discuss this?'

'No. I have no idea who he is and Mr Topter, the lawyer, told me not to ask. I don't know what I can do.'

'But everyone knows that the spitfyre rider brings their own spitfyre . . . Well, don't worry, Stormy, of course we will send word to Mr Topter and it will be sorted out and you shall have your flying horse.'

'Oh, thank you!' he said, ready to leap on the Director and hug him. After all, he was only pretending that he needed to speak to Mr Topter – he could provide Stormy with a mount as easy as pie.

'But,' the Director went on, stroking his two white curls of hair up into peaks, like horns, as he thought, 'it will take a very long time. There aren't spare spitfyres just floating around, you know.' He was staring not at Stormy but into a glass dome on his desk. The dome was facing away from Stormy so he couldn't see what was inside it.

'*How* long?' Stormy managed to gasp.

'Perhaps two years?' The Director smiled at him. 'But during that time you can study hard and I'm sure you'll do very well. There are other aspects of study apart from sky-riding, you know. Psychiatry, behaviour, customs, history – the list is endless.' The Director's eyes glazed over slightly and he glanced meaningfully towards the door, stifling a yawn.

'I must go,' Stormy said, taking the hint. 'Thank you, sir.'

'Not at all. I look forward to seeing you around the place. Goodbye.'

Stormy shut the door carefully with numb fingers.

Araminta had been lying in wait. She leapt on him as he came out, and grabbed his arm. 'What did you say to him? Why did you want to see him?'

Stormy sighed. He felt as if a bottomless pit was opening up at his feet and he was sliding into it.

'Nothing.'

'Go on. Go on!' she urged. 'Were you telling tales again?'

'No,' he was suddenly angry. 'And I never told anyone you rode Bluey that time, either.'

'Shush!' She tapped her finger to her lips. 'Shush, that's our little secret, isn't it?'

'Is it? What about *my* secret? The yellow powder Ralf gave the spitfyres?

'Which yellow powder would that be?' Araminta said. 'I've never heard of such a thing . . . Now, tell me what you were talking to my father about!'

He sighed, knowing she wasn't going to let him go unless he explained. Briefly, he told her.

'Poor little boy,' Araminta said sweetly. 'I wish I could help, but I don't know anything about spitfyres at all.'

'Well, but . . .'

'And if I did, I wouldn't help *you*!'

26

Thirteen

'Al. Al, can you hear me?'

Al was draped over the servery table like a crumpled dishcloth. Stormy shook his shoulder. 'Al, please.'

'What is't? What yerwant?'

'I want your flying horse, Al.'

Al shrugged him off. 'Want what? Do what?' He peered at Stormy from under half-closed lids.

'Please open your eyes. Sit up. Listen to me!' He pulled Al upright. 'I want your permission to see number thirteen. To try and get her fit again.'

Al moaned and Stormy let him fall back over the table again.

'Oh, what's the point,' Stormy said. 'The poor thing won't be able to fly anyway.' He stared at Al's limp body. 'How could you neglect her like that?'

Al's face was flat against the wood of the table. 'Years of training,' he said coldly, 'years of it.' He sat up sharply. 'Years!'

Picking up his knife he went on cutting up a bit of pie into small chunks.

'Well, so, I can try, can I?' Stormy said.

'I told you she is wild and crazy. I told you what she did to me. She'll kill *you*.'

Stormy stared at him. 'Otto told me it was your fault she did what she did.'

Al winced.

'She was all right before you made her do that thing!' Stormy went on. 'That Spin, when she wasn't ready and you were drunk!'

Al heaved out a big sighing moan. 'Leave me alone.'

'Why? Why? I don't understand!'

'I told you. That spitfyre is deranged, mad!' Al looked at him from the corner of his eye. 'And even if she weren't, you'd never ride her. You can't.'

'Why?'

'Because a spitfyre needs a name, Stormy, you know that, and she hasn't one.'

'She must have one and you must know it. Please tell me.'

'I've forgotten it,' Al said. 'It's the truth. It's gone. When she did this –' he stamped his wooden leg on the floor, '– when she did that . . . the shock, I don't know. I forgot it. I've never spoken it. Never thought it.' He gathered up the tiny fragments of food and limped out onto the terrace with Stormy hopping along at his heels.

'*Al!*'

When Al reached the wall he threw the food scraps up

217

into the air and, as if by magic, scores of small birds swooped down and snapped them up before they fell.

'Al, please! Please help me!'

'Otto's lovely, lovely food,' Al said sadly. 'We must feed the birds when it's cold, Stormy.'

'You're impossible!' Stormy cried. 'Why d'you waste the food like that? Why do you waste a spitfyre like that? Why are you wasting your life like this? Please, didn't you write her name down somewhere? Can't someone else tell me what her name is. Please!'

'Oh, Stormy. I haven't spoken it since that day. I've wiped it from my mind and cast it out so as never to hear it again. I swear that's the truth. I should have killed her,' Al went on. 'But I thought this was a better punishment, and who's it hurt, eh? Me. Me more than anyone.'

'Maybe . . .' Stormy was thinking aloud. 'I bet I can get her flying again without it. I'm sure I can. Oh, I hate you for doing this, Al!'

'Me too,' Al said wearily. 'Me too.'

Stormy raced down to the stables. There was no one else about; the eerie sound of the birds crying was the only sound in the still, misty air.

He grabbed a lantern.

The smell was terrible in thirteen's cave, wafting out of it so richly and thickly that he imagined he could see it, a solid rope, coiling through the clean air, as it had been with the poor, stinking convicts.

Guilt washed over him in hot, shameful waves. Ever

since he'd arrived at the Academy all he'd done was think of himself. He should have come here first.

But what was he going to do, anyway? He knew the spitfyre was weak and couldn't fly. He had no plan.

I'll just look at her, he told himself, easing around the rock that blocked the cave entrance. *Just look. Make sure she's OK.*

It was worse than he'd feared.

It was like returning to the first time he'd seen her. The spitfyre was lying on her side with her head on the hard cold floor. Her ribs hardly moved. The only sign of life was the thin wisps of smoke drifting from her nose and a small rumble coming from her belly. Her wings lay flat like damp fabric on the ground. Her last food bucket looked untouched.

His pathetic dreams evaporated. This spitfyre would never fly again.

'I'm sorry,' he whispered. 'I'm *so* sorry. I promised I'd help you last time I came, do you remember? Do you remember me? Oh, why didn't I come straight away? Why didn't I rescue you before?'

She stirred and her small ear flicked towards him.

'Did you hear me?'

He felt a twinge of hope. His skin prickled with anticipation. He crept closer and squatted down.

'Might you remember me? I'm your friend, a bad friend. I didn't mean to be so useless . . . I'm Stormy.' The spitfyre lifted her head an inch off the floor and opened her sore eyes a fraction. 'Listen, poor thing – I'm sorry! I'm so sorry, but I'll make it up to you. I promise.'

He was appalled at the blankness in her eyes, the complete and utter lack of hope.

He knew he'd let her down but he wouldn't ever do that again. He would help her all he could.

She was very weak. She closed her eyes again.

He swore to himself that nothing, nothing, would stop him from trying to get her better.

Stormy was learning so much in his classes, things the books never told you, that he didn't want to miss any of them. There might be something that would help the spitfyre. He would go and see her straight afterwards. He had stayed up late reading up on animal welfare and medicine in his new books, taking notes, thinking of potions and creams he might use. He remembered the shelves of glass bottles in the storeroom where the overalls were. Might there be something there? He would try everything.

On the way to breakfast he spotted Maud, dusting the tall silver candlesticks in the hall. He tried to sneak past her, but she wouldn't let him, and flicked her duster right in front of him.

'Stormy,' she whispered, avoiding looking at him directly.

'Yes?' He put his bag down and tossed a book onto the floor near her, then kneeled to pick it up. He didn't look at her either.

'I know where they keep all the names of all the flying horses that come in here.'

'What?'

Her eyes were shining. She made a cheeky face at him. 'Meet me tonight in the courtyard, at that bench near the gate. Ten o'clock.'

Then she was gone, twirling her feather duster merrily along the windowsills as she went.

Stormy stood up, clutching his fallen book. He couldn't stop a grin spreading across his face.

'We don't talk to the staff here,' a voice said loudly in his ear. It was Bentley.

'Not unless it's to tell them what to do,' Hector added, striding up. 'We realise that it is hard for an orphan and ex-skivvy to learn the ropes, but really, Stormy, you're not even trying.'

'Leave me alone,' Stormy said. 'I'll talk to whoever I want to.'

His cheeks blazed hotly, but it wasn't the boys that embarrassed him; it was that he'd tried to avoid Maud, his only friend. And she knew where the spitfyres' names were!

He went to pick up his bag, only to find that someone had tipped all his things in a heap on the floor.

Because Stormy loved spitfyres, all the books he'd read about them and all the snippets of information he'd ever heard had sunk into his brain and taken root there. He found the lessons easy.

Mr Jacobs taught psychology and said he was a natural, that he might be one of the very few who could become

221

a spitfyre whisperer. The teacher explained how spitfyres were motivated to work with humans and how they interacted in a squad and as individuals. 'No tame spitfyre should ever be out of control,' Mr Jacobs told them, 'but just in case I carry my NSD with me. That's the Numb Spitfyre Dart.' He brought out a small dart gun. 'Don't worry; it only brings instant sleep to the disobedient spitfyre. Later in the term we will make the drug that goes into the dart. You'll need to carry one with you. At all times.'

Stormy came top in the myth and legend test and beat Hector by five marks. Mrs Lister said his work was exceptional.

'So, Stormy,' Hector said. 'I'm going to have to keep my eye on you, aren't I? I don't believe anyone has ever beaten me at anything before.'

'Oh, it was just luck,' Stormy said, truly believing it had been.

'So it won't happen again?' Hector said. 'Will it?'

'Maybe, maybe not,' Stormy said, refusing to cringe beneath Hector's awful glare.

'Any luck with getting a spitfyre?' Bella asked him.

Before he could answer, Tom butted in, 'Course not. Where would he find one?'

'Stormy's made history,' Bentley said. 'He's the first sky-rider without a spitfyre to ride.'

'I *have* got one, actually,' Stormy said suddenly.

'How?' Hector asked. 'That's not possible. How could you?'

The others were listening with interest. Stormy wished he'd never opened his big mouth. He coughed. 'It's Al's spitfyre, number thirteen,' he said.

Everyone burst out laughing.

'I thought you were being serious,' Hector said, with a hard little laugh that couldn't hide his relief. 'Al's old castoff doesn't count. It's a dud.'

'Thirteen!' Tom said. 'Rubbish. It's an old bag of bones.'

'It's crazy, that one!'

'You are an idiot, new boy.'

'Or I'm an optimist,' Stormy said. But he knew probably better than any of them just how sick and weak the spitfyre was and he did not feel very optimistic at all. After seeing her yesterday he had almost completely given up any idea of ever riding her.

'Still, I happen to know that Al's wiped her name from his memory,' Hector said. 'Or the rum has wiped it for him. You'll never find it out. You are totally doomed.' And they all laughed. 'No name, no game!'

'I know it already,' Stormy suddenly said loudly. Oh why, why did he speak? Why must he lie? He felt on the brink; if he spoke he'd fall in, over, down. He could stop now, but he couldn't.

Hector had gone still and was staring at him hard.

'How?'

'I found it.' He was shaking. It was such a lie. 'In the records.'

'What is it?'

'Starlight.' It was the first thing that came into his head.

'Starlight,' he said again, as if saying it twice might make it true. 'And she's a good spitfyre. She's fine.'

Stormy got away and ran down to the terrace. Why had he been so stupid? If only they hadn't laughed at him and made him feel so small.

He went to the storeroom and put on some overalls, boots and gloves. Just because Hector niggled him, he'd lied. If anyone ever looked in cave thirteen they'd see that she couldn't fly. They'd see she didn't respond to the name Starlight.

In the storeroom, as he'd remembered, the cabinet contained small glass bottles: lotions, powders, pills and ointments. He could not see the one with the yellow powder in. He guessed that Ralf carried it with him. He found something called *Solomon's Spitfyre Tonic*, suitable for all spitfyres, and pocketed it. Also, *Biogenic Vitamin Supplement for All Weary Winged Animals*. He stuck a hose, a bucket and a spade in a wheelbarrow and tramped down to stable thirteen with everything.

He carried in three lit, half-shuttered lanterns and arranged them around the dark cave so he could see the spitfyre clearly. Right, this was it.

'Hello,' he said softly. 'It's me.' He went slowly up to her, talking quietly all the time, and lowered himself down until he was sitting beside her head.

Her sticky eyes blinked open, then closed. A shiver rippled over her skin when he touched her.

'First I'm going to clean this muck up, then I'm going

224

to make sure you eat something,' he said. 'You haven't eaten properly for days, have you? You must eat; you're too thin. I'm going to help you. I promise.'

He got up and set to work on the straw and dung that had been there for so long it had formed a thick carpet all around and under her. It was hard work chiselling at it with the spade and Stormy was soon hot and his arms were aching. He shovelled up the stinking stuff and threw it into the wheelbarrow; when that was full he tipped it over the side of the terrace and let it tumble down onto the rocks below.

There was nothing he could do about the dirt under her, but after an hour the place was a lot better. Now she was watching him, her eyes following him as he moved around the cave.

'You're clever,' he told her. 'When Al talked about you he said you were his best, the cleverest of them all. We'll be a great team, we'll be the –'

'Stormy! What are you doing?'

Stormy jumped and spun round.

Purbeck and Ralf were standing at the mouth of the cave, peering round the rock at him. 'You can't go in there, mate,' Purbeck said. 'Come out! Come on! She's dangerous.'

'No she isn't. Look at her! She's not dangerous!'

'Isn't she? I've never even set eyes on her,' Purbeck said, crouching down and staring at the spitfyre. 'Small, isn't she? And sickly-looking. Is she all right?'

Stormy pushed past them with the empty wheelbarrow. 'No, she's not all right,' he said.

225

They followed him out.

'What are you doing, then?' Purbeck said.

'What should have been done before – cleaning her stable. It was disgusting. Do you know her name, Ralf?' Stormy asked, looking him in the eye. 'Did Al ever tell you it?'

'No.' Ralf shook his head.

Stormy didn't think he was lying. 'Al says he's forgotten it.' He saw no reason to tell them his stupid lie. 'I'm going to call her Starlight for now,' he told them.

'You can try, but they only respond to their real name –' began Ralf.

'I know that.'

'Shame no one knows her real name,' Purbeck said.

'Yeah, 'cos even if you got her fit, you'll never train her without it,' Ralf said. 'Hey, maybe it really is Starlight?'

'Is that her food there?' Stormy asked.

'Yeah, but she hasn't been eating. I've been pulling out her buckets half full.'

'And you didn't do anything about it?' Stormy snapped. 'Here, give the food to me, and none of that yellow stuff!'

Ralf reddened. 'You idiot! That's not for her!'

Stormy gave him a long, hard look. 'He gives the Star Squad a yellow powder, Purbeck. Makes them overexcited and wild.'

Purbeck made a face. 'So? They're meant to be sparky. They're fighters, aren't they?'

Stormy shrugged. 'I don't think it's good for them.'

'And you know everything, of course!' Ralf snapped.

226

Stormy frowned; Ralf was right. He was only going on his instincts. He didn't know anything. He took the food into the cave.

'It's your dinner, thirteen, ' he whispered. 'It'll make you better. You have to eat to get strong.'

The food consisted of long orange worms wiggling through the leaves and seeds, not something he fancied eating himself. He remembered how Mrs Cathcart had tempted sick little Karl with Otto's famous chicken broth. Wincing, Stormy took up a morsel of the food between his fingers. 'You need food. We all need food. Come on, thirteen, open your mouth.'

Her nostrils quivered as she sniffed it and her tongue came out and licked weakly round her dry mouth. Water. She needed water more than anything else. Karl had too. Mrs Cathcart had held a wet flannel against his cracked lips . . . Quickly he went out to get fresh water.

Purbeck and Ralf were standing outside the cave, whispering together.

'Phew! You're not dead, then?' Purbeck said.

'Course not. She's not going to hurt anyone. Though I might – I feel like throttling the pair of you for letting her get like this . . .' It made him feel better to say that, but he knew he was just as much to blame. He looked round for his things. 'Hey! Where's my hose and barrow gone? Where's my mop?'

Purbeck pointed. 'Him,' he said, nodding at Al.

Al was trudging back up towards the storeroom with Stormy's things.

Stormy rushed after him. 'Oh, thanks, Al, thanks very much for your help!' he said sarcastically. 'But it'll take more than that to stop me.' He pushed past Al and grabbed the water bucket back. Water sloshed over Al's feet. 'You're cruel, Al, you know that?'

Al looked down at his wet shoes, up at the high cliff face of the Academy, then back to the ground. He looked everywhere except at Stormy. He was smiling.

'Don't try and stop me again!' Stormy shouted.

He took everything back to the cave. Inside, he soaked some water up from the bucket with his hankie and squeezed it over the spitfyre's closed mouth, hoping some would dribble in. She licked and this time he saw her swallow. He repeated it again and again, adding a few drops of the vitamins and other medicine, until finally she shook her head slightly and her mouth stayed closed. Enough. Now he began to tempt her with the food. He was sure she wanted it but hadn't the strength to take it. Gently he prised her mouth and teeth apart and slipped a tiny morsel inside. At the first mouthful she choked and coughed and he scrambled up in a panic thinking she was going to burn him or die. But she didn't. She coughed and coughed and then managed to chew and swallow and after a little wait he did it again and she swallowed again. She took seven small mouthfuls and then stopped, tired and panting.

'Enough. Well done. Good girl. I shan't hose you down, poor dear spitfyre; it will be too much. Just as well Al took it away,' he told her. 'How does this soft sponge feel?

Is it good?' He began to wipe the grime from her shoulder but she was too tired and her neck went limp, her eyes were closing.

'I'll be back,' he told her. 'I promise I'll be back soon. Don't you worry about Al. He's not going to stop me. No one will stop me this time – Starlight. And maybe tonight I'll find out your real name.'

She was sleeping.

'Goodnight.'

He crept outside. By the cave entrance someone had placed a bottle of pills: SPITFYRE STRENGTHENING SUPPLMENT: ONE TO BE TAKEN DAILY.

It might have been Ralf or Purbeck. It could even have been Al. Stormy took them gratefully.

27

Names

Ten o'clock. The night air was icy. Stars hung in swathes, like lace scarves across the black sky. Stormy turned up the collar of his jacket against the bitter wind that nipped at his cheeks and ears as he went across the courtyard.

It was deserted.

The guards were in their tower behind closed shutters; a thin strip of yellow light was all there was to show they existed.

Laughter and shouting came from the students' common room. Someone was thumping a piano. He could hear Hector's voice above the rest, leading the singing.

Stormy kept close to the walls. The bench, in deep shadow, was on the left of the gates and he made his way to it almost blindly. Maud was already there.

'Hello,' he whispered. 'It's me.'

'Shh!' She pulled him towards the littles' house. 'Shh. Come.'

'In there?'

'Yes. They have to record everything that comes into this place,' she said. 'They'll know all the spitfyre names.' She tapped on the door and it opened enough for one little to peep out.

'It's me, Mr Small,' Maud whispered. 'I've got Stormy. And I've got the cake. It's coconut with buttercream icing –'

She had hardly finished saying 'buttercream icing' when the door was yanked open.

'In!' squeaked a voice and they slipped inside.

The room had a low ceiling and was furnished with very small furniture. There was a fire burning in the hearth and an old-fashioned kettle hanging above it.

'Must be quick,' Mr Small said. 'Might be seen. Mustn't be seen. We'll be in trouble.'

'I know. Here.' Maud set the cake on the table. 'Otto's cake. There's always too much. And I've got biscuits too.'

'Love a bisky,' the other little said. 'Love cakey.'

'Good. Glad to make you happy, Mrs Small.'

Mrs Small? He stared at the plump, smiling little. She was dressed just like the other little in trousers and jerkin but her long hair was tied back in a bun and she had softer, more feminine features.

The room was crammed to bursting. The shelves bulged with official-looking leather-bound volumes with gold numbers on their spines. Portraits of littles, both old and young, covered the walls; some were circus performers and wore diamond-patterned tights and funny hats with bells on. One hung suspended in a trapeze. A large painting of a lady with dark hair intertwined with ribbons and bows hung above the fire. She wasn't a little, and he wondered who she was to have such an important place in their room. Two wooden armchairs were either side of the fire and there were two chairs at the table. There were tiny cups and saucers, minuscule glasses and teaspoons. It was very snug and very small.

'Do take a seat if you can fit your bum on it,' Mr Small said, sitting at the table. 'Try the stool.'

Stormy sat down on the stool. It was uncomfortable, like sitting on a post.

'Thank you,' he said. 'I don't mean to be rude, but I've heard the Director doesn't like grubbins very much and –'

Mr Small jumped up indignantly. 'We're not grubbins! We're tiny, weeny things, yes. We're *littles*! He hates *grubbins*! He loathes the blighters, but we're not *grubbins*.'

'He likes all small people – except grubbins – because being around them makes him feel tall,' Mrs Small said with a laugh.

'I was only wondering . . .' Stormy said, wishing he hadn't spoken at all.

'He hates grubbins because grubbins are rich,' Mr Small said. 'That's all it is. Grubbins make money; they can make money out of anything. They dig a bit of soil and up comes buried treasure. They hit a rock with a pickaxe and oh, look, there's a streak of silver! He thinks that's dirty luck. He thinks grubbins are dirty lucky blighters, and he doesn't like that.'

'Aren't *you* lucky, then?' asked Stormy.

232

'Not a bit of it. We're miserable shorties and so he doesn't mind us one bit.' Mr Small laughed and picked up three tiny cups and began juggling them. 'He likes our tricks, you see.'

'Oh, do take care, Mr Small!' Mrs Small shrieked, getting out of his way. 'He won't let off with his clowning. We hardly have a matching cup and saucer in the house.'

Mr Small put down the cups and grinned at them. 'Old habits,' he said, shrugging as if juggling were out of his control. 'How can we help?' he added, taking another piece of cake.

'The Entry Books,' Maud said, nodding towards the leather-bound volumes. 'We want to find out the name of Al's flying horse. It must have come in when he did, and so its name has to be in one of the books.'

'Everything's in the books,' Mrs Small said. 'You're in there, Stormy. Twice. And that's unusual.'

'Is it?'

'Oh yes, got a habit of being a one-way place, this. Peoples come in but somehow peoples don't go out and come back. Leastways I haven't seen it much. Have you, Mr Small?'

Mr Small shook his head. 'No.'

'Al had me sent back,' said Stormy. 'He made up a story about me; it wasn't true.'

'Well, be glad he did,' Mrs Small said. 'Other boys weren't so lucky and just vanished off the face of the mountain when they weren't wanted.'

'I see.' Stormy was remembering Ollie.

233

'So, can we check the books?' Maud said.

'Yes, yes. What year was it?'

Maud and Stormy looked at each other and shrugged. Stormy dug in his pocket and fished out the handbill for the circus, hoping it might have a date on it. As soon as Mrs Small saw the paper she grabbed it.

'Skippety slip! Look at that!' she said. 'Cosmo's Circus! *We* were in that circus!'

It seemed everyone in the Academy had been in the circus.

Mrs Small smoothed out the creases in the flyer and spread it out on the table. 'Haven't seen that picture for a long time. Wasn't Al handsome those days?'

'We were the comic act, got up to all sorts of high jinks and silly pranks,' Mr Small said. 'We used to roll in the sawdust for the punters. Fall in the buckets of water for them; trip over our feet for them. We still do it now, to keep *him* happy.'

'But Al had a bad time,' Mrs Small said. 'We don't talk about it. Do we, Mr Small?'

'We don't, Mrs Small.'

'But this is wonderful!' said Stormy. 'If you were there, surely you remember the spitfyre's name? The name of Al's winged horse that went crazy and attacked him.'

The littles shook their heads. 'Bad times. Bad times get blotted out,' Mrs Small said. 'We never did know it.'

'Dates. Dates,' Mr Small muttered. 'We were the first to come here. Al came soon after. Let me think, that would be volume seventeen, I think.'

Mr Small went over to the shelf and reached up for one of the leather-bound books. 'Here we go.' He brought it over to the table and just as he opened it, there was a loud rapping on the door.

Stormy jumped up, banging his knees against the little table so the milk jug spilled. He glanced at Maud. The blood had drained from her face instantly; she looked terrified.

'I'll be in such trouble if I'm found here!'

Stormy took her hand. 'It's OK.'

Mr Small pointed to a staircase in the corner of the room and held his finger to his lips. 'Shh!'

Stormy and Maud scuttled over to the stairs and quickly went up, ducking under the low ceiling as they went.

Mrs Small snatched up the cake and whisked it out of sight into a cupboard. Mr Small chucked the book under the little table and pulled the tablecloth down to hide it.

The hammering on the door sounded again, louder.

'Coming. Coming!' Mrs Small checked the room showed no signs of her other visitors and went slowly to draw back the lock.

Upstairs, crouching in the tiny bedroom, Maud and Stormy strained to hear what was going on.

It was Hector.

Immediately Stormy wished he'd stayed downstairs to confront him but he couldn't go down now – he'd look a fool, and anyway Maud's fingers were locked around his arm. She needed his support.

He heard Hector stride boldly into the room below. 'My God, you are *so* titchy!' Hector cried, then there was a horrible crunching thud.

Stormy unpeeled Maud's fingers from his arm and crept to the top of the stairs to peek down.

'Ouch!' Hector had smashed his head against a low beam. 'Ouch, ouch!' he yelled, clutching his head. 'What a totally stupid place to put the ceiling!'

'Oh, Hector, sir, I'm so sorry,' Mr Small said. 'I can't think what made me put that beam there. How foolish of me. If you'd perhaps ducked a little sooner? Or were just four, five inches smaller . . . '

'I'll get him some ice,' Mrs Small said. 'Won't you take some ice for that, Hector? It helps with the swelling.'

Petra and Bentley followed Hector in. 'You all right, Hector?'

'Isn't this so cute!' Petra said.

'It's like a flipping doll's house!' Bentley said.

'Oh, Hector, you've got a massive bump!' Petra said.

'You have. I'm thinking duck eggs,' Mrs Small said kindly, staring at Hector's forehead. 'Even aubergines, that bump is so big.'

'Will you all just shut up and leave me alone,' Hector said. 'Shut up!'

The room fell silent.

'That's better,' Hector said. 'Now listen, midgets, you've got something I need –'

'Excuse me, but technically we're not midgets,' Mr Small butted in. 'We're –'

'Be quiet, will you?' Hector shouted. 'Something you've got! I *need* something you've got!'

'Of course, of course,' Mrs Small said. 'Don't interrupt him, Mr Small. It doesn't matter that we're not midgets. Or pixies or –'

'I'm warning you!'

'Let me get it for you,' Mr Small said. 'What is it? What can it be?'

'Ice?' Mrs Small suggested.

'Not ice, you idiot! Volume seventeen. Spring, the time when Al came. Quick!'

At the top of the stairs in his hiding place, Stormy felt a jolt like lightning shoot through him. Hector knew!

'Yes, yes, Hector, sir,' Mr Small said.

Mrs Small went to the shelves. 'It doesn't seem to be there,' Mrs Small said. 'I don't understand it. Mr Small, do you understand? Where could volume seventeen be?'

The littles began taking down volume after volume and piling them up on the floor.

'I am sorry, it seems to be –'

'I really can't imagine where it might have got to.'

'Fancy it going missing,' Mrs Small said, 'how could that happen?'

'Yeah, how?' Hector said, kicking a chair over. 'Don't worry, we'll find it.'

'We will!' Petra started throwing the cushions out of the armchairs and tipping the wood out of the wood bucket. 'Must be here somewhere.'

'Ever seen me do this trick?' Bentley asked and yanked

the tablecloth as if he could take it off without moving the crockery.

The cups, saucers and plates went flying and smashed on the stone flags.

Stormy jumped up, ready to go and fight, but Maud held him back. 'Better you don't,' she whispered. 'Better for me –'

'Ah ha!' someone cried.

They had found the book.

'Well done, Bent!' Hector said, as Bentley handed it to him. 'Weren't trying to hide it, were you, Mrs Small?'

Hector laid the large book on the table and flicked through it. 'Just need . . . *this*!' And he ripped a page out.

'No!' Mrs Small cried.

'You can't do that!' Mr Small shouted. 'That's stealing. That's destruction of Academy property!'

'But I have and I did,' Hector said. 'And now, let's see what it says.' He looked up and down the page. Suddenly he roared with laughter. 'Oh, that little rat! Stormy lied! He dared to lie to me.'

'What does it say, Hector?' Petra said.

'Never mind, never mind what it says, what it *doesn't* say is Starlight. It's best no one else knows this. This can be my little secret.'

'Watch out!' cried Mrs Small. 'The fire!'

'Oh, mercy me, I'm so clumsy . . .' Hector was holding the torn page over the flames. 'The page has gone and fallen in the fire!'

'No!' The two littles rushed to the fireplace, but Bentley and Hector held them back.

'Let me go!' Mr Small cried.

No, please, no, thought Stormy, seeing the burning paper. *That's my last chance.* He turned and looked at Maud; there were tears in her eyes. She knew how much hope he'd pinned on that book.

'Hector, you are *so* naughty!' Petra squeaked.

They watched the page burn.

'If that skivvy comes along searching for it, he won't find it. Will he?' Hector said.

'No, sir.'

'And you won't know where it went, will you?'

Mr Small shook his head.

'Here, something for your trouble.'

Hector threw a coin onto the floor; Stormy and Maud heard it roll over the flagstones, followed by the clomp, clomp of three pairs of feet as they went out, slamming the door shut behind them with a crash.

Stormy and Maud hurried downstairs. The littles were scrabbling around in the fireplace. Mr Small was trying to lift out an ashy bit of paper with the fire tongs. Mrs Small was fishing through the coals with a long toasting fork.

'What bad luck!' Mr Small cried. 'Why would Hector come tonight of all nights?'

'It's my own stupid fault,' Stormy said. 'I told him I knew where it was – I mentioned records.'

'Oh, Stormy,' Maud said in a hushed voice.

'I know; I'm an idiot. I even told him I knew the spit-fyre's name and now of course he knows I was lying.'

'The rotten thing,' Maud said, kneeling down by the fire and grabbing at bits of burnt paper. 'Oh dear, all black and scorched.'

'Quick, here.' Mrs Small held up some charred paper. 'Look, it's high quality; the very best parchment. We might save a bit . . .'

But there was almost nothing left of the page. Mr Small held up another fragment; Stormy peered at the faint lines on the grey paper. It was scorched right through, but because the paper was so thick it hadn't disintegrated and some words showed like ghostly writing, but nothing that could be read clearly.

'Was this the only time Al came into the Academy?' Stormy asked.

'Yes, like I said,' Mrs Small said. 'Only in, no one goes out. Specially Al.'

'Al's scared of Otto,' Stormy said.

Mr Small nodded. 'He says Otto's waiting for him,' Mr Small said, 'that Otto stands guard on the path with a meat cleaver ready to chop off his head.'

It wasn't true, but they weren't that far wrong.

'And the big D wants him here,' Mrs Small said, 'just as he wants us here. We don't cause a fuss, you see. We let things be.'

Al let things be too. He let Ralf feed the spitfyres the powder and let the Star Squad behave badly, let the other spitfyres get poor care, let his own animal suffer . . . He had a lot to answer for.

'I'm sorry for the trouble and the mess, Mrs Small,' Maud said as she and Stormy left. 'You were so kind to help.'

'Don't worry, my dear Maud,' Mrs Small said. 'Goodnight.'

The door closed behind them and Stormy walked Maud back to the house. 'I hope no one missed you,' he said.

'Me too . . . I've heard the other students talking, Stormy,' Maud said quietly, giving him a sidelong glance. 'I've heard you've got a real way with flying horses – they say you could be a spitfyre whisperer. Even when you were just clearing them out, a skivvy, you got a reputation for being brilliant with them. They're jealous, that's why Hector did this. He doesn't want you to have a chance.'

Stormy shrugged. His heart was heavy.

It was flattering to believe what she said, but flattery was no good right now. All he needed was the spitfyre's name, and it looked as if his only chance of ever finding it had gone for good.

28

Nightmare

Stormy was woken by an awful scream. He went to the window and pulled back the curtains. Everything was bathed in a spooky silvery blue; the moon was high in the sky in front of him, shining right over his body so he glowed white.

There was another scream and a shout.

Stormy felt his pulse quicken.

He opened the window and leaned out as far as he could, staring into the night sky.

All of a sudden he heard the whoosh of wings nearby, like giant umbrellas violently opening and closing. Three winged horses came into view. Instinctively he ducked down and crouched there, watching.

The spitfyres were Bluey, Sparkit and Polaris – Star Squad.

There was another scream. Stormy peered up at them trying to see who – or what – it was.

For a moment the light shone on Bluey; he seemed to be

carrying something in his mouth, something alive and wriggling, but before Stormy could work out what it was, the spitfyre flew over the courtyard and disappeared from view. The other two circled, criss-crossed and swooped lazily over the castle, and within seconds they'd disappeared too.

Stormy got back to bed and snuggled under the covers. He was shivering violently. He didn't know what he'd seen, but his instincts told him it was bad. He pushed it to the back of his mind, refusing to dwell on it; it wasn't his business. It was the Star Squad going about their secret work, their work to make a New World. Alone in his room he felt excluded, a little jealous, even. Perhaps one day, he thought, he might be part of the Director's plans – even though he wasn't sure what they were, wasn't sure that they were even good, he needed to belong.

In the morning when he woke, he was able to tell himself that it had been a dream. That was all. He didn't even call it a nightmare, though the truth was, it had felt like one.

Araminta searched him out after breakfast.

'I hear you've adopted Al's old spitfyre,' she said.

'You hear a lot of things, I expect,' Stormy said. Had she perhaps seen Maud go to the Smalls' house and sent Hector along? He wouldn't put it past her.

'Hector told me. He knows everything. Anyway, here's something totally different. There's a charity I support,' she went on, 'for old and injured spitfyres, and I was hoping you might contribute to it. It's called the Happy Home for Spent Spitfyres. You could support it, couldn't you, now you're rich?'

'I suppose I could. I'd have to ask Mr Topter.'

'These poor worn-out spitfyres are kept on farms in the lowlands,' she went on. 'They can't fly or make fire so they're no use to anyone, but this refuge looks after them until they die a natural death. But of course it costs a lot.'

Stormy didn't want to talk to her but found it impossible to get away. He was impressed she was involved in charity work.

'Please, Stormy.'

'Of course I'll sign, and I'll write and ask Mr Topter to give them some money.'

'Oh, thank you, Stormy,' she said, handing him the board. 'That's very generous of you. Just there, your full name and your signature, and over there the name of your spitfyre. Well, that doesn't matter, just leave it blank. Or put thirteen, if you want.'

Stormy spent as much time with the neglected spitfyre as he could while trying to keep the visits secret. He told everyone that she was dangerous and that she'd tried to attack him. He didn't want anyone going in and seeing the progress she was making.

These days the terrace was busier than usual as the Silver Sword Race was coming up and the sky-riders were training for it. A form had been pinned up in the hall and those wishing to enter the race had to put their names on the list. Hector had been the first to do so. Only a few other brave riders did the same.

244

One day Stormy went in to cave thirteen and the spitfyre was standing on her feet for the first time, wobbly, but standing.

He stood and gazed at her in delight and she looked back at him with a spark in her dark eyes that was quite new. He wanted to reach out and hug her but stopped, not wanting to frighten her. 'Dear thing,' he whispered instead. 'It's so good to see you like this. So good.'

Mrs Cathcart had once shown him a tiny dried seahorse sent from far away by her sailor brother. This thin spitfyre was delicate and beautiful like that, with an air of mystery, as if, like the seahorse, she had come from a long way off, seen a great many things and was very wise.

She puffed out two small clouds of green smoke and pawed the ground with her front hoof.

Stormy took the bucket across to her and she immediately started to eat, stopping every now and again to lift her head and look at him.

'You look so much better,' he told her. 'I can hardly believe you're the same creature! I've just got to get all that dirt off you. Your tail is solid with muck and your hooves . . .'

She tossed her mane and flicked her long tail. He couldn't be sure whether it was a yes or a no.

'If only I had a name for you,' he added. '*Your* name.'

Stormy racked his brains to try and think of any other way of finding it now the paper record had been burned. Who else might know it? The littles didn't. Ralf didn't.

What about Otto? They'd worked at the circus together, so he just might remember it.

Later, when he was back in the servery, Stormy composed a note:

Dear Otto,
Please help me if you can. Remember you told me about the circus? And Renaldo? Do you remember the name of the flying horse that caused all the trouble? Al keeps that spitfyre here and won't tell me her name. Please, please, if you can remember it, let me know. It's a matter of life or death.
Love to Sponge.
Best wishes,
Stormy

Stormy put the sealed note into the food lift, tucking it behind the dirty dishes. He had no way of knowing if it would reach Otto; he just had to hope that it would.

A magnificent black and gold carriage, drawn by six ordinary white horses, was standing in the centre of the courtyard when later Stormy went that way to his lessons. The name GRANT was written in gold letters on the side. Hector's parents had come for a visit. There was a small crowd of students and staff beside the carriage, chatting.

Stormy sidled by, wanting to keep out of the way, but Araminta, who was talking to Hector, called him over.

'Hey, Stormy, come here!'

Stormy did not think to disobey her.

'Think you're grand enough for this sort of company, do you?' she whispered when he joined her.

He shook his head, ready to go; she was so confusing.

'This is Stormy,' Araminta said to Hector's father.

Mr Grant looked just like his son, with the same crinkly hair pulled back from his forehead, only his hair was grey. He leaned back and looked down his nose at Stormy as if he was a very long distance away.

'Sky-rider?' he asked.

'Well, not quite, you see –' Stormy began, but was interrupted by the Director.

'This is one of our most promising students, Mr Grant,' he said, patting Stormy on the shoulder. 'He's new. He has a secret benefactor. Very wealthy,' the Director told Hector's father with a wink. 'We are very delighted to have him join us.'

Stormy felt his face freeze into a stupid grin and tried to think of something to say.

'I don't know how good a rider you can become,' Mr Grant said, 'with the skills not being in the blood. Hector has the history, you see: generations of sky-riders.' He turned back to the Director. 'It's not long to the race now, is it?' he said. 'Is Hector still favourite to win it, eh? Want his name in the gallery, don't we?'

The Director nodded. 'Of course he will win. Of course he will.'

'Like father like son,' said Hector's father. 'I've got money on him bringing back that sword, a lot of money. There is no such thing as failure in the Grant family.'

'You won't be disappointed,' the Director said. 'I'm coaching Hector. Got money on him myself too.'

'And of course I hope to have a new spitfyre in our stables,' went on Mr Grant. 'Hector will take the loser's spitfyre for himself, won't he?'

The Director nodded. 'No doubt,' he said. 'That's the rules.'

The gathering began to head towards the house and nervously Stormy began to move with them. *I have every right*, he told himself. *I'm a student, Araminta invited me.*

'Look, there's Tom! Come and join us, Tom!' Hector called, walking straight across Stormy's path. 'And Bentley. Come over here, Bent!'

'I think I'll go,' Stormy muttered. He didn't belong. No one wanted him.

As he walked away, he heard the Director introducing Tom to Hector's father, 'This is one of our most promising students,' he said.

He might just as well have stabbed Stormy with a knife.

Stormy had 'borrowed' a freshly made lavender wing-lotion from his care and hygiene class. Lizzie had concocted it and it had proved to be the most effective of all the lotions the class had made. He was eager to get the spitfyre's wings clean and try it on her.

Ralf and Purbeck were sitting in the sunshine outside the servery. Ralf was playing his harmonica and Purbeck was balancing a plate of chocolate éclairs on his knees and slowly munching his way through them.

'Hey, what are you doing, Stormy?' Purbeck called as he went past them.

'I'm going to my spitfyre.'

'Ha! Joke!'

They watched him warily as he struggled with a big bucket of warm water.

'Heavy, is it?' Ralf said.

'You could help,' Stormy suggested.

'We could, but we won't, thanks all the same. Not on our list of duties, getting hot water for spitfyres and namby pambying them.'

'Hey, don't forget your thork!' Purbeck shouted as Stormy made his way down the terrace.

'Don't need one,' Stormy called back.

The stable was spotless and even smelling sweet now, with the fresh straw on the stone floor. There was just the spitfyre to clean; she was still caked all over with grime.

'I'll get all that dirt off you and then you'll feel so much better. And you must go on eating to get strong,' Stormy told her. 'We're going to fly, you and I; we're going to fly together and be *so* good!

He went on talking to her all the time he cleaned, rubbing gently at her with a soapy cloth and warm water. She stood very still, letting him work the lather over her body as if he had done it a hundred times for her before. The dirt dissolved and underneath the grime her true colours gleamed.

'Look at this! And look here!' Stormy whispered, as more and more of her coat was exposed. 'Who'd have thought it, hey? Who'd have thought you'd be the most beautiful spitfyre ever in the whole world?'

He used a shorthaired brush to massage her neck and shoulders and each delicate leg. She was a rainbow of purple and blue and pink, and as she shifted her feet and the lantern light caught her coat, she glimmered and shone like the pearly scales of a trout. Her wings were softest silver but they were torn and lacking in strength. They should have felt tightly drawn between the ridges of sinew and tendon; instead they were flabby and soft from lack of use. He spread the lavender lotion over her clean wings and worked it in circles into the dry, broken skin.

He scrubbed each hoof, which she lifted docilely for him, letting him pick out pebbles and straw that had lodged there. Her hooves were ragged, cracked and overgrown and he filed them down neatly for her. He shampooed her tail and beneath the dirt her tail was purple and fuchsia coloured, interlaced with silver threads. 'You're the best spitfyre in the world. The finest, most beautiful.'

Her mane had already begun to grow back and no longer stuck up in a tattered ridge. He brushed it and washed it and then combed out the silken violet-coloured strands against her neck.

The sunlight angled through the mouth of the cave and lit up two or three metres of black rock. 'The sun would do you so much good!' he told her. 'And you could stretch your tattered wings! Oh, Al, how could you let this happen?

Poor thing . . . I do believe he's scared of you, Starlight, really, that's the truth.'

Around her back leg where the shackle held her tight the skin was sore. Stormy needed the key to take off the cuff so he could bathe and clean it properly and put on a healing ointment. He had seen a key around Al's neck when he first came and guessed it was for this leg iron, but how would he ever get it?

He stretched up to reach her ears and try and clean them. 'You're too tall, thirteen. I can't, I need –' He was about to say he needed a ladder, when he felt a blast of hot air down his back as she bent her head down for him.

'Thank you.'

He rubbed and brushed around her delicate chin and mouth; the small leathery scales here were pale pink like the inside of seashells. He whispered into her ears that he loved her and she was his own dear spitfyre and he would never leave her. She lowered her head onto his shoulder, resting her chin so he could clean her forehead, between her eyes where the hair grew short and whirled around in a beautiful pattern. Finally, he wiped her crusty eyes clean, clearing her long eyelashes and bathing them with clear water.

When he finally stopped, she blinked several times, then opened her eyes wide. He was startled to find himself so close to such large dark blue eyes staring intently back at him. Intelligent eyes. Then she nudged him with her nose and lifted her head up high, proud of herself again and wanting him to know it.

A great bubble of hope rose up inside him. Maybe he *was* a spitfyre whisperer, like they said. And maybe he'd surprise everyone with what he could do, even if he had been just a skivvy from the kitchen. And maybe he could train her and ride her. Maybe not having her name wouldn't matter. She trusted him; that counted for so much.

She unfurled her wings and shook them out. The holes in the delicate membranes would tear if she flew; she wasn't ready yet for that, but one day . . .

Suddenly she trembled violently, as if fearfully cold, and stamped her hooves sharply towards the entrance. Alarmed, Stormy jumped out of the way.

'*Stormy!*'

The spitfyre quivered and shifted back against the wall, puffing loudly, blowing sparks around the cave.

It was Al. He didn't come into the stable; his long narrow shadow lay on the wall as he stood at the entrance.

'What is it?' Stormy yelled.

'What are you doing?' Al called back. 'That's my spitfyre!'

'You don't deserve her!' Stormy marched out and almost collided with Al, who was standing there as stiff as a dead tree. 'You don't deserve her!' he yelled again.

He was horrified when Al sank down onto his knees and started to moan.

'I'm sorry, I –'

He stopped. The chain around Al's neck swung free from his shirt and Stormy's eyes fastened on the key as it slipped along its length. He needed that key.

252

'I know,' Al whimpered, 'I don't deserve her.' He covered his eyes with his hands. 'How is she?' he whispered. 'How is she now?'

'Come and see for yourself.'

'I can't. I can't ever look at her again,' Al said with a groan.

'She's recovering,' said Stormy, 'eating well. She could fly again, Al, if only . . .'

Al shook his head. 'If she sees me – if I see her – her eyes will show it. She will fix me with those eyes and I will never bear the guilt! I've done everything wrong. Everything!'

'But Al –'

'I shouldn't have done the Spin . . . I went after my own selfish desires . . . Then I blamed her and I've punished her all these years . . . But it was *my* fault.'

'Oh, Al . . . Listen, you can help her now. Give me the key to her chain,' Stormy said. 'I'm not afraid of her. She trusts me.'

'How can she ever trust again?'

'She does. I'm sure she does.'

Al wiped his eyes and looked up at Stormy doubtfully. 'She would be a fool to trust anyone ever again.' He tore off the key and threw it at Stormy's feet. 'Take it. I'm done with all this!' He staggered to his feet and limped away.

29

Night Visitor

Stormy lay awake for hours thinking about Al and the spitfyre. He fingered the key to the leg iron that was now safe on a chain around *his* neck, longing to use it and to set the spitfyre free.

It was wet outside and the wind whistled in the chimney like a frightened animal.

What was that?

He sat up. The room was in total darkness, the curtains drawn tight over the windows. Once or twice he had thought he'd heard slates shifting overhead and put it down to the wind; now he wasn't so sure. There was a new, strange noise outside his window that made no sense, because he was miles from the ground. There it was again; something was scratching and scrabbling at his window!

Stormy slipped out of bed and flung back the curtains. The rain beat against the windowpane. He couldn't resist opening the window and checking . . . The wind rushed in, bringing with it a voice.

'*Norphan!*' And a body threw itself through the window and dropped onto the floor with a damp thud.

Stormy recognised him immediately. The grubbin convict! The moleman rolled over and knelt up, grabbing Stormy round the knees.

'My little norphan!' he said, a big smile showing all his broken and yellowing teeth. 'At last!' He flung his arms round him.

Stormy was appalled. The grubbin was filthy, his long hair a tangle of mud and twigs and leaves. He smelled of the underground, of caves and dankness, and wet herbs . . . What was he doing in here, in his room, in the Academy?

He tried to move but the grubbin's arms were locked round him.

'Oh, you're wonderin' what I'm doing here, aren't you?' the grubbin said, grinning up at him. 'You're wonderin' how I found you out, eh?'

Stormy nodded. 'Shh! Please, quiet. Could you, would you, let go?'

He was straining to hear if there were any creaks on the boards outside his door. How would he explain this? A grubbin here?

The grubbin released him and sat back on his heels. 'It's a long story, lad, but I'll tell it. Got a drink or a bite of food? I'm hungry as a wolf.'

Stormy nodded. Motioning him to stay back, he quickly unlocked his bedroom door. The corridor outside was empty. He tiptoed to the night larder and came back with some food.

'Cheese, grapes and a flask of hot tea,' Stormy told him, putting it out on the desk.

'*Cheese, grapes and hot tea!* Remember me, eh, Stormy?' the grubbin said as he crammed the food into his mouth. 'By the blazes, but I was hungry *then*! Years in prison's made me like that.'

Stormy glanced towards the corridor. Was that the click of a door opening somewhere? His heartbeat quickened.

'Don't worry,' the grubbin said, 'no one saw me come. I'm a good climber, I am.'

'Why did you come back?' Stormy asked. 'It's so dangerous here! *How* did you get in?'

'Oh, a grubbin can climb, you know; like monkeys over ground we are; over the rooftops, no problem; down the rough wall, no problem. And like moles underground, ha ha! And why have I come? Why, I've come to see that you'd got what you wanted,' the grubbin said. 'To see how you'd become a fine student at the Academy and got all them things you wished to have.'

Stormy went on staring at him with amazement and horror; what did his welfare matter in the slightest to the grubbin?

'You've sure as sure have got a nice place here,' the grubbin said, looking around and licking his lips. 'Very nice.'

'I had some good fortune,' Stormy told him. He didn't want to explain to him about his mysterious benefactor; all he could think of was getting the grubbin out before anyone saw him.

'Got lucky, did you? How was that, then?' The grubbin was looking at him with his head on one side expectantly, his eyes glittering, a dimple forming in his cheek as he smiled.

'I . . . I have a benefactor and he or she – I know nothing about them – they paid for me to come here.'

'Did they, then?' His look suggested he knew something that Stormy didn't. Stormy didn't like it. It made him feel uneasy. 'Well, well.' The grubbin paused to stuff more grapes into his mouth and drink some more tea. 'Sorry, manners not needed in a dungeon,' he said, wiping the dribble and crumbs off his chin.

Stormy reddened and tried to smile as if he wasn't repulsed.

The grubbin shuffled closer to the heating pipes with a shiver. 'Cold outside. Very cold.'

'So, how can I help you?' Stormy asked, folding his arms.

'Oh, it's not *you* going to help me,' the grubbin said. 'It's *me* that's helping you – this time.'

'How is that?'

'Why, remember how you helped me? Remember how you stole me food and got me the pincers to cut my chains?'

Stormy nodded.

'Well, I never forgot that. I never forgot it even when they put me back in prison and locked me back down in the dungeons. Thought about that kindness a lot. When I broke out again I left my leg iron for you, a sort of memento, like. I wasn't planning on wearing *them* again!

I wanted you to see them, Stormy. I hoped you'd see them, know I was out.'

'I did,' Stormy muttered. He didn't like the way this conversation was going. There was unease growing like some awful fungus creeping through his insides and it was making him weak and giddy.

'Well, you see, Stormy, I never forgot and I wanted to reward you. I went and dug out buckets of gold dust. Rubies the size of my fist! So then I could do it; reward you, and I did. So it's me! There!' He hit Stormy on the knee. 'I'm your benefactor!'

Stormy shook his head furiously. 'You can't be!'

'Why not?' The grubbin looked disappointed. 'Why not? We can make money out of the dirt, we can.'

'But I thought . . .' Stormy's voice trailed off.

'I shall tell you everything,' the grubbin said, settling down comfortably on the floor with his arms around one of the big heating pipes. 'I'm not a thief, Stormy. I'm not a bad man. And you reminded me of how I wished my own child might have been, in your kind ways, you did.'

'This is too much! It's all too much!' Stormy said. 'I can't take it all in.'

'I know, I know,' the grubbin agreed, laying his cheek against the warm pipe and yawning. 'Listen, young man, why don't we just settle down for the night and I'll go on with my story in the morning?'

The thought of spending the night with the grubbin in his room was horrible and Stormy couldn't disguise a shiver of disgust at the thought, but he had no choice.

'OK. It's late. That's a good idea. You could have a bath if you like,' Stormy suggested, and to his delight the grubbin agreed. 'But do it quietly, won't you?' he begged as the moleman turned on the taps and the water rumbled out. What would his fellow students think to him having a bath at this time of night?

While the grubbin scrubbed himself and splashed around merrily, Stormy sat resting his head in his hands, staring sightlessly at the wall. He would have to give the grubbin his bed. He would have to hide the grubbin in his room. He would have to be kind to the grubbin. But worst of all he knew what the grubbin had told him was true. It had to be. Why would he make it up? And who else but a grubbin who'd been locked away for years *wouldn't* know you needed a spitfyre to be a sky-rider?

The Director had no secret plans for Stormy.

Araminta did not admire him.

The simple truth was that he was an idiot.

30

Secrets

In the morning Stormy pinned a DO NOT DISTURB sign on the bedroom door.

He left the grubbin asleep and a note not to open the door to anyone, while he went to see to his spitfyre.

She greeted him with a blast of soft, warm smoky air and rested her head gently on top of his. 'I can't stay,' he told her, rubbing her neck. 'You'll never believe what's happened. Who's come . . . Oh, my . . . It's dreadful!' He could hardly think straight, the grubbin might wake up and go out or . . . He worked the key in the rusty lock, but it wouldn't turn. 'It hasn't been opened for ages,' he said. 'I need oil.' He bathed her sore leg as best he could. 'I can't stay too long. Oh, why did that grubbin have to come and spoil everything?'

He gave her some of her medicine, finished his duties quickly and said goodbye to her. All along the terrace he kicked an empty food bucket noisily. Everything was ruined!

By the time he returned to the main building, the other students were awake and several were in his corridor.

The grubbin was awake too.

In the light of the morning, and after a bath and a shave, he looked much better. The bald centre of his head shone like a boiled egg and his hair was now pale grey not black, but no amount of scrubbing would remove the grey *moley* sheen to his skin. Stormy winced, remembering what a poor reception he'd given him last night, and determined to be kinder. He had brought some breakfast up for him and after the little man had eaten it, savouring every mouthful and praising the pastry and the fruit and the newly baked bread, he began his story.

'My name is Mungo Muddiman. I have a brother called Sylvester and once I had a wife and a daughter . . .' He paused and wiped a tear from his eye. 'Dead,' he added, nodding at Stormy. 'Long time ago. As you see, I'm a grubbin; but not *pure* grubbin, not both parents. My pa was a human bean. It was my ma, bless her heart, that had the grubbin blood and she passed it on to me and to Sylvester; only I got the most of it. *Very* pointed ears, *very* short height. Big brains, though!' he chuckled. 'My brother, Sylvester, he was so ashamed of his grubbin blood, he went and cut off his points!' He felt his own ears tenderly. 'Right off! He wanted to scratch out his grubbin heritage entirely, have not a jot of it left, so he left home and went adventuring. He changed his name as well as his looks and we lost track of him. Didn't see him for a long time, didn't know where he was, even. Then Ma and Pa died and I

261

searched him out. Was I surprised to find he was now passing himself off as a human bean and not a grubbin? I was astounded, I can tell you! I had a lot of money then, earned honest, too. I'd been deep in the hills mining and got lucky. Lucky? I should say so, diamonds as big as an albatross egg. Nuggets of gold like loaves of bread, hee hee. All safely stashed away. When Sylvester found out I was so rich he set me up, set me up to steal it off me. My own brother!' He shook his head and banged his fist down. 'Hard to believe, eh?'

'What did he do?' Stormy urged him on. 'How did he set you up?'

'Got a filthy lawyer to say I'd stolen the money off my dead folk and had me locked away in the dungeons. He didn't get it all, though; I'd more hidden in my secret, secret places. We grubbins always have. I never saw my wife and babe again. He told me they was dead. I was alone. I didn't care about being locked up when they was dead; they was all I lived for anyways.'

Stormy smiled encouragingly.

'But when I realised what he was doing . . .'

'What was he doing?'

Mungo took a deep breath.

'The dungeons are here beneath the castle, are they not, young lad? And I was prisoner there for many years, was I not? And you, no doubt, have seen the convicts here, and did you not wonder, young lad, why they was all grubbins?'

'I did, yes.'

262

'Is it only grubbins that are thieves and liars and cheats in this world?'

Stormy shook his head.

'No, it is not. And why do they get moved on out? Because there's no space for them down there! Why? Why? Because they brings in more grubbins and fills it up again. The dungeons are full to bursting of grubbins! Bursting at the seams with us blighters! Packed to the brim! Overflowing!'

Stormy took a big breath. 'You are saying they are locked up in the dungeons *just* because they're grubbins?' He hesitated, remembering Lizzie had said something similar. He realised too that he had put a certain memory to the back of his head so that he hadn't had to deal with it. He said, 'One night, I heard a scream. I saw three spitfyres flying . . . one had something . . . ' He let his voice trail off.

Mungo nodded. 'The Director has trained them bat things to find and capture grubbins.' He lifted his shirt and showed Stormy some terrible white scars, running across his chest. The skin had been stitched untidily; it was puckered and pulled tight. 'Got snatched myself. They bring them here and lock them up. If my brother has his way there won't be a grubbin left this side of the moon . . . '

'But hang on!' Stormy stopped him. 'You were talking about your brother Sylvester first, then the Academy, the Director . . . I don't . . . '

'Yes.' The grubbin nodded furiously. He stared him

263

squarely in the eye. 'His name is Sylvester Muddiman. The Director is my brother.'

Stormy reeled backwards and fell heavily on the bed. He lay sprawling there for a moment staring sightlessly at the ceiling; so this was what being hit by a cannonball felt like.

The Director a grubbin!

Mungo's brother.

'The Director steals the grubbins' money then locks them up and lets them fester down in the dungeons. He treats them worse than animals. And I was the one he wanted most to keep hidden,' Mungo said, 'because I was the awful reminder, the one that could expose his lie. Least he didn't bump me off; he could have . . .'

Stormy groaned. 'I wanted to be here so badly, so . . .' His voice trailed off. 'I wanted to be a sky-rider and I ignored all the clues, ignored every hint that something bad was going on. Now I can't stay here! How can I stay and be part of such an evil plan . . . And does that mean the Director knows what's going on with the spitfyres? Surely he doesn't? Surely he must!' Stormy clutched at his hair. 'I'm going crazy! It's probably all the Director's orders.'

'Don't get het up, lad,' the grubbin said. 'I understand, I really do. You are a norphan an' all and you want better things. What's wrong with that?'

'But this isn't better things!' Stormy cried. 'What'll we do?' he added. 'How can I stay here with such horrible people?'

'Course you can stay, lad. You int bad! What we'll do is wait for night-time and then I'll be off again. I can get

264

out of most places, you know, and this castle is a doddle compared to them dungeons. Now you know my story; why I wanted you to have a chance in life as I have never had. And I knew you'd not be after hunting grubbins, you weren't the sort. I had the idea maybe, that you'd help stop it . . . And perhaps I hoped you might find out what happened to my wife and daughter, how they died. Poor dears, poor dears.'

Stormy's jaw dropped open. 'Me? Stop the Star Squad? It's like saying I could stop an avalanche. A rock slide. A typhoon.'

'It was just an idea . . .'

'But I'll try and find out about your family. I will do that, I promise. Oh, Mungo, you're in danger here. We need to get you somewhere safe.'

'I can go the way I came, norphan. It only took a day of crawling and creeping; up the wall, over the roof . . .'

'Too risky.' Stormy shivered. It suddenly dawned on him just how dangerous Mungo's trip to see him had been. Never mind someone seeing him and knowing Stormy's benefactor was a grubbin, Mungo was risking his life coming back here. If he were caught he'd be tossed straight back in the dungeons. 'You really shouldn't have risked coming,' he said.

'Ah, it was stupid, Stormy, I know, but I had to see you, I had to.' He grinned and shook his head at his own folly. 'Now, do you have any friends here that might help?'

Stormy immediately thought of Maud but it wouldn't be fair to involve her in this. And the littles would be too scared of losing their jobs. He shook his head. 'No.'

'Your flying watsit!' the grubbin cried. 'That's our answer! It will take us to safety. If you drop me in the village – well not literally *drop* . . .' He chuckled. 'I'll be safe. I've got friends there.'

Of course Mungo Muddiman didn't know that he didn't have a spitfyre. He didn't want to explain; he never wanted the generous little man to know the mistake he'd made.

What if thirteen were a grubbin catcher too? What if it was in her blood and she couldn't help it?

Mungo must have read his mind.

'*Your* spitfyre wouldn't be one of them, would it? You don't think that, d'you?' His expression was so hopeful and expectant.

'Well, no, I don't think so,' he answered truthfully. 'She couldn't hate grubbins; she just isn't that sort of animal.'

And she isn't a member of the Star Squad, he reminded himself. *And she's never been given any yellow powder.*

'Well, there we are, then, lad.'

'Yes, yes, there we are,' said Stormy.

Just supposing he could get thirteen to fly, how would he direct her to Stollen? He knew almost nothing about flying.

'Let's do it!' Mungo said.

'When?'

'Dawn.'

His heart missed a beat.

He nodded. 'Dawn,' he repeated. He sighed. He had a whole day and night to get through first. 'Dawn it is.'

Stormy made the grubbin promise to stay in his room while he went off to his classes. 'Don't open the door to anyone!' he warned him.

'Not on your life, I won't,' the grubbin said. 'I'm going to read up all your books here. Which ones has the nicest pictures in it?'

When the sky was just beginning to lighten, Stormy and the grubbin crept silently from his room.

'You all right, Stormy?' Mungo Muddiman was dressed in Stormy's dressing gown and had covered his bald patch with a towel, turban style, so if anyone caught a glimpse of him they'd think he was a student who'd just been taking a very early shower. 'You seems a bit shaky.'

'Sorry, sorry,' Stormy muttered.

The school buildings were still and silent but every board creaked beneath their feet and even the carpets and curtains seemed to swish loudly at them as they went by. Stormy's insides were churning and his heart beating horribly fast and hard. He was so busy looking round to check they hadn't been seen that he twice bumped into a wall.

'Don't fret so,' Mungo said. 'We'll be fine.'

At last they reached the terrace. The sky was colourless and the air was damp and cold. The mountain peaks were hidden by low, grey cloud. Nothing moved. Everything was still and quiet, and Stormy was just beginning to think they were safe when, nearing Sparkit's den, he realised his mistake.

The enormous silver flying horse had jolted awake as

they came near and was now noisily sniffing the air. He swung his head from side to side, stretching his neck out of the cave, snorting and blowing. He turned towards them and breathed in deeply.

They both froze.

'I think Sparkit's caught your scent, Mungo!' Stormy spluttered. 'He's one of the chasers! Back, back!'

Sparkit was wide-awake now. A low whinny erupted from deep inside his belly and bubbled out of his open mouth, along with tiny sparks which flared and fell sparkling to the ground. He began to paw the ground with his right hoof and to strain against his clanking chain.

'He'll start roaring any minute! Hurry!' Stormy hissed.

They backed off until they were behind the curve of the wall and out of view.

'Phew,' Mungo said, wiping his brow. 'That is one scary beast!'

They stood there for a few moments waiting for Sparkit to quieten down.

'Is your flying thing as huge as that?' Mungo asked him, wide-eyed. 'I never saw such an enormous monster!'

'Er, not quite so big or so fierce,' Stormy said. 'Come on, this way.'

They scurried back into the main building, along numerous corridors, until they at last reached the south staircase.

'But Stormy, where are we going?' Mungo whispered loudly. 'It'll be light soon.'

'Trust me,' Stormy said. 'We've got to avoid those Star Squad spitfyres. This way we'll come out at the South point and the first cave on the West is mine. Thirteen.'

The sun's rays were beginning to burn off the mist and low cloud and now light appeared over the mountaintops on the east. Everything was starting to come to life. Birds wheeled above their heads and cried forlornly.

'Is she very fine, your flying horse?' the grubbin asked as they bustled down the stairs. 'I so hope you have a fine one.'

Stormy wasn't sure which was worse, trying not to lie to Mungo while still keeping him believing in his flying abilities and sky-rider skills, or trying to fool himself that he knew what he was doing.

'She's the best,' he said quietly. And he meant it.

As they approached cave thirteen they heard the jangle of the spitfyre's chain rattling.

Mungo covered his ears. 'I 'ate that sound. I 'ate it!' he said huskily and grabbed at his leg where for so many years he had worn a metal cuff. 'Oh, it 'urts me, it does.'

'She's usually really quiet,' Stormy said. 'Hold on, I need to go and get a lantern.' He ran to the stores and came back quickly with a light.

They went in cautiously; still thirteen was rattling her chain.

'What's the matter? What's the matter?' Stormy whispered soothingly. *Don't let it be the grubbin*, he begged her silently. *Not that.*

She was straining at her chain, all fidgety as if she had

been stung by a bee or bitten by a rat. Her neck was arched tensely. She peered at him with a worried expression, as if he wasn't who she thought he was going to be. Stormy didn't dare go any closer.

'She's small – but then I appreciate small!' Mungo said peering round Stormy. 'She's a beauty! Real pretty!'

'Er, yes, er, just hold on there, Mungo.' Stormy forced himself back to the present. 'Stay back – she's very excited and I don't know why.'

Surely, surely she wasn't a grubbin chaser?

'It's only me, thirteen, your friend. Only me,' he said. 'It's Stormy. What's the matter?'

She settled a little, stopped dancing about and puffed out a little cloud of acrid smoke.

'There, there, it's all right. It's fine. We're going out, we're going out flying!'

Her ears twitched backwards and forwards as she listened to him, her head cocked on one side, and she fixed her eyes on his, watching him closely. But every now and then, she would dart a look towards the entrance, past Mungo, as if she thought someone else was there.

Keeping a wary eye on her, Stormy reached up for the bridle, reins and goggles that hung on the wall.

'Oh!'

'What's the matter, young man?'

'Nothing, nothing,' Stormy said, staring at the spotless riding gear in his hands. He had been meaning to clean the tackle, but hadn't . . . Someone else had, though; it was smooth, supple and shining. He stared at the spitfyre and back at the bridle and reins. Who? His fingers were trembling as he untangled the leather straps.

'Is everything all right, Stormy?' the grubbin whispered. 'Can't we hurry?'

'Fine. It's fine.' Stormy said.

Someone had been in here.

Someone had frightened thirteen.

She nuzzled his ear with her soft mouth. 'Clever thing!' He stroked her neck. 'It's all right now. We're going out. We're going to take Mungo back home. Hold the reins, would you, Mungo?'

As if it were the most natural thing in the world, Stormy lifted the reins over her head and somehow a strap fell over her forehead and another slipped neatly over her nose. While Mungo held her, he buckled the straps below her chin.

'Phew!' Stormy said.

'What's the matter?'

'Oh, nothing, nothing. Hot in here.' Stormy wiped the sweat from his brow. 'See, she likes you,' he added. 'She's not a grubbin chaser. I'll unlock her and we can go.'

He pushed gently alongside the spitfyre, knelt down and slid the key into the leg iron.

'Nasty thing, that is!' Mungo said and spat.

The spitfyre was standing very, very still now, as if she knew – and he was sure she did – that she was going to be set loose. The key turned smoothly, the lock had been well oiled – another surprise – and the cuff fell to the rock floor with a clatter.

Immediately she lifted her unshackled leg and shook it

like a cat shaking a wet paw. She snorted and tossed her head and pushed towards the cave entrance.

'Hey, hang on!' the grubbin cried. 'Hold on!'

The spitfyre was pulling the grubbin with her.

For an awful instant Stormy saw her flying off and the grubbin being carried away, dangling from the reins, but she stopped suddenly outside, breathing fast, thrashing her tail against her haunches like an angry lion.

Steam and smoke billowed from her nostrils. Sparks flew.

'Stormy, she seems really furious . . .' Mungo said.

And then they saw why.

It was Al.

31

Remorse

Or it was the ghost of Al? He was so thin and gaunt and his skin so pale that he might easily have been a spirit. The spitfyre spat a shower of golden sparks on his hair, setting it sizzling and smoking.

'Going somewhere?' he asked, brushing absent-mindedly at his hair. He barked out a dry laugh.

'Al, please don't try and stop us,' Stormy said. 'Please don't –'

Before he could utter another word the spitfyre made a dive at Al and sent him staggering backwards, limping and tottering towards the edge of the terrace.

'Thirteen, stop!' Stormy cried.

Thirteen's eyes were blazing. Narrow streams of dense black smoke curled from her nostrils like ribbon.

When Al had got his balance again he turned to them and laughed. 'Look! Look at her!' he cried. 'She hasn't forgiven me! She wants me dead. She hates me . . . I cleaned her gear, did you see? While she slept, I crept in and oiled the lock. She'd have killed me if she'd seen me, she could have!'

Stormy waited for Al to go on.

'She was angry, she wanted to bite me. Wanted my other leg, didn't you!' He pointed to a large burn, the size of a saucer, in his jacket. 'That's what she did when she woke and saw me. Bad girl!' He laughed and then quite suddenly burst out weeping, as if a cork had burst from his throat and his tears could now overflow. 'It is all my fault, Stormy . . . My life is torture. Everything. Otto sending up delicious stuff and knowing I won't eat it. I can't eat it! It would kill me; I know it would. Mayra was *his* sister! His dear little sister, and it was my fault she died. I was too proud and vain. I wanted the Spin. I wanted to show them how brilliant I was. Since then . . . everything has slipped, slipped away.'

Suddenly thirteen lunged at him. Al hopped and hobbled out of the way as a ball of flame spun towards him, rolling along the ground like an orange Catherine wheel.

'See what you've done, Stormy!' Al roared. 'You've made her fit and strong. I tried to stop you before and then I saw I couldn't. But she'll kill me!'

'Why didn't you just look after her properly?' Stormy cried. 'Why didn't you? If you'd treated her better she wouldn't have –'

Al was teetering near the edge of the cliff.

'She'll kill me. I –'

But his words were lost as the spitfyre puffed out her chest, spread her wings and went for Al again. There was

274

nothing anyone could do to stop her. She was poised like a snake about to strike, and dashed at him. With a scream Al turned and ran – not towards the safety of the buildings, but towards the edge of the terrace. He hesitated briefly, looked over his shoulder at the spitfyre as she came towards him, and then flung his arms out wide and jumped into the emptiness.

Stormy was struck dumb.

Thirteen screeched to a halt, wings held out as brakes, hooves grinding horribly against the stones. A dreadful tremor rippled over her; she shook and shuddered, then rocked on her four legs, settling her balance.

Silence.

Stormy and the grubbin raced to the edge, crouched and stared down.

'By the blazes!' Mungo cried. 'He's *there*!'

Al had landed on a ledge about four metres below. He was absolutely still, lying flat on his back. His eyes were open.

'Al? Al? Can you hear me? Are you all right?' Stormy yelled. 'I'm coming down!'

Al groaned.

'He's moving!' Mungo said. 'He's alive!'

But before Stormy could start the descent, Al started to roll; over and over he went, slowly, as if an invisible force was driving him down the hill.

'What are you doing, Al?' cried Stormy. 'Mind the edge!'

But Al didn't stop. He fell right over the rim of the rocky

ledge and thumped onto the grassy hillock below. Then he went tumbling and spinning down that and rolled away into the nothingness and disappeared.

'Al! Oh dear, oh my, oh goodness,' Mungo muttered.

'Is he all right?' Stormy said. 'We could try and –'

'No, don't worry, lad,' Mungo said. 'You've got other things to do. You've other things on your mind.'

The spitfyre was still trembling; her wings quivering like giant leaves shivering on a stem; her breathing was fast and hard. She stood with her head low as dark, tarry smoke streamed from her nostrils and curled over the rim of the cliff. Stormy stroked her. 'There, there,' he murmured. 'It's all right.'

'Don't you worry about Al,' Mungo said, brightly, 'he'll mend. This is his spitfyre, is it? Don't you have your own one, then?'

'Oh, Mungo, it's a long story.'

'And we haven't time, have we? Are you still up for our ride, lad? Only the morning's on its way and I think I hear peoples . . .'

'I like Al, you know, despite everything; I know he's good underneath,' Stormy said forlornly.

The grubbin patted his shoulder. 'Yes, yes, I knew you was a good lad the first time I sets eyes on you,' he said. 'You was how I wanted my little girl to be, kind and honest and helpful. Now, dear boy, are you going to take me off here or what?'

'Sorry. I keep getting distracted. The thing is . . .' Stormy said, gently guiding the shivering spitfyre over to a

276

mounting block. 'The thing is, Mungo, I've never actually flown her before, and I need her name to fly her.'

'Why didn't you say?'

'Al oiled her lock and gave me the key and . . . I think he really wants me to be her rider, but with him gone, I'll never find out what her name is. I hoped he'd remember it.'

'Well, my bet is you can make anything fly, even a mole, name or no name. Born sky-rider you are. I saw the marks you've been getting for your school work.' Mungo went round and flapped his arms in the spitfyre's face. 'Come on, you, we're going *flying*!'

The spitfyre gawped at him in amazement.

'She knows what I mean. Come on, let's get on.'

'I really don't think . . .' But Stormy climbed gingerly onto her back, settling with his knees tucked in behind where her wings emerged, hoping against hope that something magical would happen and he'd instantly become a master sky-rider.

Sitting on her back was extraordinary; to have so much of his body touching hers, and to feel the heat radiate from her, as if he were astride a stove. He felt he should have asked permission to get on to her – it seemed almost rude just to sit on her as if she were a chair – but she didn't object, and what else were you supposed to do?

The grubbin scrambled up behind him and clasped his arms around his middle. 'Off we go!'

The spitfyre smelt strongly of earthy herbs, and just-struck matches. Stormy could feel her muscles and tendons

277

and sinews writhing beneath her skin as she flexed her wings and tested her legs. Her expanding ribcage rose and fell; her beating heart throbbed like a drum.

'Isn't she gorgeous!' Stormy whispered. 'I think I might pop with joy.'

Mungo chuckled. 'She is beautiful,' he said cheerfully. 'Even more beautiful if she'd get a move on . . . Make her go, can't you?'

How? Stormy whispered in her ear, 'Come on, thirteen, please. *Starlight?* Please, let's go. We must fly. We must!'

She swished her tail and her wings twitched, and Stormy's hopes soared, and then fell as she stayed rock still.

'Try kicking her.'

'I can't kick her! She isn't an ordinary horse! I don't want to hurt her. Come on, thirteen, please. Up, up, UP!'

Her ears flicked backwards and forwards and she tensed the muscles in her back and limbs so her body tightened and prepared, like a spring, beneath them. She was like a runner in a race, on her marks, but she wouldn't go without the whistle blowing. And Stormy had no whistle.

'Up!' Stormy urged again. 'Fly!'

She unfurled her wings, and her body stretched and shifted again, but didn't move.

'What's in a blooming name?' Mungo said. 'Never knew they were that important. Ah, never mind, young Stormy. It doesn't matter.' He slipped off the spitfyre's back and patted her side. 'She's brilliant. Beautiful. She really is.'

'I'm sorry,' Stormy said. He got off and stared at the ground. 'I've let you down . . .'

'Not at all, not in the slightest,' Mungo said, patting his shoulder. 'Flying would have scared me anyway; molemen prefer the ground, something solid beneath them. Even a roof is more solider than the air, isn't it? It's that Al's fault,' he added thoughtfully. 'Well, I said I'd go after him, and I will.' His round face glowed with the idea. 'I'll go after him and make him tell me her name. I'll drag it out of him. There.'

'But *Mungo*, it's so dangerous. If anyone sees you!'

'I'll be all right. No one will see me. I'll sneak down through the weeds and the rocks. It was fine meeting you, Stormy. Fine. I'll make him remember that name for you, and *you* find out about my little child and her mother, will you?'

'I will. I promise I will do my best.'

They hugged and Mungo patted him hard on the back; then he was gone, leaping over the side and rolling and tumbling down the steep side of the mountain as if he were a hedgehog.

32

History

Stormy felt as wrung out as an old dishrag as he led the spitfyre wearily back into her cave. She folded herself neatly onto the clean straw again with a sigh. Stormy stroked her neck thoughtfully and stared into her trusting, bright eyes. The way she looked back into his really made him feel she understood every word he said.

'I'll fight anyone and everyone to keep you,' he said. 'And when Mungo finds Al, maybe Al will do something to remember your name. Then, nothing will stop us!'

Thirteen snorted gently, letting tendrils of sea-green smoke trickle in wayward curls from her nostrils. Settling her head trustingly on his lap, as if having no name didn't really matter, she drifted off to sleep.

Stormy felt like running away with her – not that he could, or had anywhere to go – and anyway he'd promised Mungo to find out what happened to his wife and baby. And there was the Star Squad to deal with. And the Director. What a fool he'd been to think the Director cared about him! How conceited he was! 'I'm not going anywhere,' he told the sleeping animal. 'I have a lot to do.'

The two guards outside the tower in the corner of the courtyard stood so still they might have been dead, and they were the only living things Stormy saw as he went back to his room. Everyone was having breakfast now.

On his way to wash and change before classes began he realised he needed to explain what had happened to Al to the Director. The door to the Director's green room was open, and he knocked, but got no answer. He pushed the door gently open and looked in.

The room was empty.

Stormy's heart was suddenly beating very fast, and he almost backed out; but then something through the second doorway behind the desk caught his eye. He crossed the room quickly and pushed the door wide.

The next room housed a collection of glass domes and jars arranged on the shelves. He went a little closer. One large dome in the centre was facing him directly. He looked at it.

He blinked and stared again.

What on earth was it? He leaned towards it and looked closer, squinting. What – it couldn't – *what*? Were those actually eyes? Was that shaggy fur really hair? Pointed ears . . .

It was a *grubbin's head*.

Stormy staggered backwards, his mind reeling. The other domes contained other heads; heads of birds, cats, rabbits,

281

even a horse. He felt hot bile rise up and flood his mouth. He swallowed hard.

He stumbled out of the room, retching and moaning. Somehow he got out into the fresh air and stood by the door, breathing in deeply. If he'd ever had any doubts, any *whispers* of doubt about wrongly condemning the Director, he had them no longer.

He couldn't eat breakfast; he couldn't think about food at all. What he needed was a friendly face and someone he could trust to talk to.

He went to the little gatehouse and knocked loudly. Mrs Small opened the door a crack. Her round wrinkled face split into a grin when she saw him. 'Cakey?' she whispered.

'This is no time for cake.' He didn't meant to sound so grim, but he felt miserable. He wished he could wipe out the image of the grubbin's head, but he guessed it was going to stay with him forever. 'Can I come in?'

With a sigh, Mrs Small ushered him in quickly. 'In my opinion,' she said, 'all times are cake times.' She closed the door behind him. 'I told you, my dear, we've nothing here that can help you.'

'I know,' Stormy said. 'But . . .' Mrs Small must have guessed at his low feelings because she patted his hand and began to toast a small crumpet for him.

'Sit down. Stay a while,' she said.

'Hello, Stormy!' Mr Small leapt into the room. 'How are you?' He did a somersault, walked on his hands to the table and backflipped into his chair. 'How's things?'

'Really, Mr Small!' Mrs Small snapped. 'There's a time and a place for that sort of thing.'

'Exactly,' Mr Small laughed, 'and that was the perfect moment for a backflip.'

'Mr Small!'

'Sorry, dear. Old habits die hard, you see, Stormy. Mrs Small and I,' he went on, 'we depend on the Director for our livelihoods. We cavort and trip over and juggle to make him smile. Anyway,' he rubbed his round middle, 'it keeps me fit.'

'Fit? *Fat,* more like,' Mrs Small added. 'I dream about leaving the Academy, Stormy, but where would we go? We've no papers. No references. Nothing.'

'See, after the business in the circus – well, anyone involved with that night and the death of Mayra was doomed.'

'That's why Al is here too, isn't it?' asked Stormy.

'Yes. He was lame, remember, and since his skill is with flying horses, this was the only place he could get work, and of course it's nicely out of the way up here.'

Where was Al now? Was he all right? Stormy wondered. Had he made it past Otto's window or had Otto leapt out and grabbed him and was he now boiling him alive in the stockpot?

'Otto's sister, Mayra, was a lovely young thing. Only seventeen,' Mrs Small said, 'and Al adored her. Otto wanted to take her home.'

'I know. Otto told me.'

'Mayra didn't care about Al; she was planning to run away with Cosmo. Isn't it always the way?' Mr Small said.

283

'When Al found out he went wild, as you know, and tried the Spin.'

'The Director has picked his staff carefully,' Mrs Small said. 'Al with his broken, guilt-laden heart is perfect to keep his dark secrets.'

Mrs Small passed Stormy a cup of tea and a crumpet. They were both extremely tiny and he demolished them in one swallow.

'It was the same for us,' Mrs Small said.

'Because I was one of the littles who put up the cage,' Mr Small said sadly. 'After the accident Cosmo said we hadn't put it up properly and that was why the spitfyres escaped. It wasn't true. They would have got out from anything. No one believed me. So it was the Academy or nothing . . .'

'And to begin with this seemed like a lovely place,' Mrs Small said sadly.

'But recently it's got bad. We've seen the Star Squad at work,' Mr Small said. 'They've got careless and we've seen them – bringing in grubbins and locking them up.'

'I saw it too, one night,' Stormy admitted sadly.

'Terrible, terrible. The poor grubbins,' Mrs Small said.

'They steal their money,' Mr Small said. 'Grubbins can't resist carrying their precious knick-knacks around with them. They store the stuff underground too.'

'We take extra food in to the prisoners, it's the very least we can do to help,' Mrs Small said. 'There's little passages and ways under here that only a small person can get to and we take down treats and things. Otto's leftovers . . .'

The missing food from the servery was explained at last. Stormy smiled. He was glad it went to a good home.

Mrs Small started sobbing. 'We would have gone away – we *wanted* to go – but there's Maud to think of too. I love her like my own, and she won't go . . . She knows she's an orphan, she knows it in her heart of hearts, but at the same time she has this feeling . . . Just suppose her father were still alive, if there were the smallest hope – well then, he'd come here to look for her, wouldn't he, and so she must stay put. Well, how could we leave the poor little mite alone with Miss Araminta and *him*?'

Mrs Small wiped her eyes and pointed at the portrait of the woman with the dark hair and the ribbons. 'Can you see the likeness in the eyes? She was Maud's mother. She died when Maud was a child.'

The woman in the picture did have the same eyes as Maud; bright, dark and about to smile. At least Maud knew what her mother looked like; Stormy had no idea about his own parents.

Mr Small waddled over to the bookcase and brought a small book over and opened it on the table in front of Stormy.

'Now Maud was asking us about yellow powder, Stormy – for you. I've checked the books. Here we are,' he said. 'It's called *Star Vitamin Plus*.'

Stormy pursed his lips. 'It's not a vitamin at all. Next time it comes up, could you get rid of it? Hide it or throw it in the bin or something?'

Mr Small raised his eyebrows questioningly.

'It's a drug. The spitfyres shouldn't take it,' Stormy explained. 'It makes them wild; it makes them grubbin chasers. I'm sure of it.'

'But we can't just throw it away,' Mr Small said. 'We'd be in trouble.'

'You could lose it, somehow, surely?'

'Course we can,' Mrs Small said. 'Really, Mr Small, where's your spirit? We must help Stormy.'

'Who sends it to you?' Stormy asked.

Mr Small pointed at the writing in the book:

Otto's kitchen.

33

Ceremony

Otto's kitchen? How could the hateful stuff come from there? He could hardly believe it, yet the book showed *Star Vitamin Plus* came up every month straight from there. Did Otto know about it? Surely it wasn't anything to do with him; Otto had never said a bad word about grubbins . . . On the other hand, Brittel hated grubbins and had not been ashamed of speaking his mind. It *must* be Brittel.

Stormy left the gatehouse and hurried to his classes, but midway across the courtyard Maud stopped him. She looked worried.

'Have you seen Al?' she said. 'He's vanished. He's never gone out of the Academy before, not as long as I've known him.' She looked about to cry. 'Have the Smalls seen him at all?' Maud looked at Stormy intently. 'You *do* know something.'

'Yes. It's all right, don't worry.' He led her over to the bench, ignoring the whistles and catcalls from the other students. They sat down and turned their backs on them. 'This morning I went to see my spitfyre – Al's spitfyre – and Al, he jumped off the terrace.'

Maud gasped. 'Is he all right?'

'I think so. I was with his spitfyre,' Stormy explained, 'and the spitfyre went for him, and Al jumped.'

'Oh!' She reached her own hands round her neck as if it might be broken. 'Poor Al. Will he come back? I can't imagine this place without him.'

'I don't know.' They both stared at the ground.

'What were you doing at the gatehouse?' Maud asked him.

'Oh, Maud . . .' Suddenly the awful vision of the grubbin's head in the dome came to him again. That dear Mr and Mrs Small had made him forget it for a while. 'The yellow powder! It comes from Otto's kitchen. The only person I can think of who might want the grubbins caught is Brittel.'

Maud was obviously struggling with some idea, twisting her hands together she stared at him worriedly. 'They're all against you . . . If you had the spitfyre's name, do you think you could make her fly?'

Stormy nodded. 'I do.'

'Can I come and see you and your spitfyre tonight?' she said.

Stormy turned on her in surprise. 'Well, yes, if you want, but –'

'I'll be there at eleven. OK? It's number thirteen, isn't it?'

'Yes, but –'

'I've got something – I think. I think it'll help.'

What could Maud have that would help him? he wondered.

After his classes Stormy went to the servery. Purbeck and Ralf were lounging at the table, surrounded by that morning's breakfast remains.

'Look who's here. It's His Lordship Sir Stormy,' Ralf said.

'What are you doing here, hobnobbing with the workers?' Purbeck interrupted. 'You might dirty your Academy uniform.'

'Oh, Purbeck, don't . . .' Stormy frowned.

'Al's gone,' Ralf said. 'Vanished.'

Already the servery seemed less dreary and sad without Al's melancholy shadow cast over it.

'He kept saying he was sorry all the time yesterday,' Ralf said. 'And he remembered something for you.'

'He left you a note,' Purbeck added, pointing to an envelope on the table.

'A note for me?' Stormy grabbed the envelope. 'It must be her name!' He paused, looking at the envelope. 'You've opened it!'

'Not us. It was Hector.'

Stormy felt his chest tighten. 'If he's taken it, if he's stolen the name, I'll kill him!' Stormy reached inside the envelope and found a folded, hand-written note.

289

THE SPITFYRE IN CAVE 13 IS YOURS.
ABSOLUTELY.
FOREVER.

Al, alias, the Great Renaldo
P.S. I can't remember her name, I really can't.

Stormy had his own spitfyre at last! He felt enormously proud and glad, and then just as enormously disappointed. He dropped into a chair. 'He's given me his spitfyre,' he told them . . . which meant he must have planned to leave, Stormy thought. He had meant to jump. 'Al's given me thirteen, but not her name. He can't remember her name.'

'Good luck to you, mate!' Purbeck said. 'You wanted a spitfyre and you got one, sort of . . .'

'Talking of cheating . . .' Stormy said.

'Were we?'

'Al put that mouse in the gravy, didn't he?'

'Yes.' Ralf grinned. 'He wanted you out, mate. He liked it as it was here, sad and decaying and sinking, like him. And Araminta wanted you out too . . .'

'*Araminta* did?' Stormy was surprised to hear that. 'Are you sure?'

'Yes, that's what Al said. So he came up with the mouse plan. But Al didn't want you to have an accident and disappear. Not like Ollie. He thought too much of you. Said you had skills.'

'Did he? I'm glad,' Stormy said. 'Listen, Ralf, now he's

gone, you can stop putting that yellow powder in the Star Squad food, can't you?'

Ralf made a rude face. 'Who are you to give orders all of a sudden?'

'Just the same old Stormy. But if you so much as put a grain of it near any of those spitfyres,' Stormy said, 'I'll . . . I'll make you eat it!'

Ralf laughed. 'Try!'

Stormy lunged at him and quick as a flash had the little bottle out of Ralf's pocket. *Star Vitamin Plus.* The writing on the label wasn't Otto's, but he recognised it.

'Brittel!' Stormy said. 'It's Brittel's writing. I thought as much!'

'What, him? I never liked Brittel,' Purbeck said. 'He's a mean sort. Even Otto said he was mean.'

'Do you know what this nasty stuff does to them, Ralf?' Stormy asked, shaking the bottle at him.

Ralf shrugged. 'All I know is, it's the Director's orders and he's boss. So you'd better shut up.'

Stormy did shut up. Not Al's orders? *Director's orders!* Of course it was. Why did he never listen to his innermost voice, his deep suspicions? He had been so naïve, wanting to believe the Director was a good man despite all the evidence to the contrary.

And Stormy had thought he'd been so clever telling the Director what was going on. How the Director must have laughed at him!

He felt like running away, but he knew he had to stop the Director. He had to save the grubbins. He had to help

Mungo. He was not going to give up his spitfyre now. Nothing anyone ever did or said would make him do that.

It was nearly eleven; the air was sharp and the sky was clear with thousands of stars twinkling in the blackness.

Stormy had taken four lanterns from the store cupboard and lit them. He kept their shutters almost closed, so only a chink of light escaped as he carried them across the terrace past the sleeping spitfyres. Now he was outside stable thirteen, waiting for Maud.

'Stormy!' A whisper came from the dark.

'Here.'

Maud appeared out of the blackness. She was wearing a large cloak that covered her from head to toe and hid most of her face. Only her eyes glinted above the folds of fabric.

'You're not scared?'

She shook her head.

'Take two of these.' He handed her the lanterns and slid back the shutters so light flooded out across the terrace and into the black of cave thirteen. Maud didn't hesitate but followed him inside.

The spitfyre was half awake and lifted up her head, blinking as they came in. She snorted gently in welcome and Stormy went and patted her head and smoothed her mane. Quickly he unfettered her leg – he had padded her leg iron so that it didn't hurt her but he felt he must keep her chained in case she decided to go after Al if he came back – or in case Hector tried to steal her.

'Wow,' Maud breathed. 'She's lovely. I love her. Look at her blue eyes, she looks so clever and wise . . . and everyone's always made out that she is so horrid.'

'She *was* sick, but never horrid. Al spread rumours about her being crazy . . . She's much better. I think she's fantastic . . .' He hesitated. 'But, sometimes, when I watch her face when she doesn't know I'm looking, it's like there's a darkness inside her, an emptiness, as if she might collapse inwards . . . It's hard to explain. She's been alone for so long. It's a sort of blankness – I think she's been badly hurt.'

Neither of them said what they both were feeling, that the spitfyre and Maud and Stormy had all been abandoned, were all orphans of one kind or another.

'You can make her better, Stormy, I'm sure you can. You have to!'

They set the lanterns down on the rocky ledges round the cave and then crouched in front of the spitfyre.

'I love her wings!' Maud whispered. 'They are so beautiful, like pearly fabric, and I love the colour of her coat. She looks magical, almost as if she were a fairy horse . . . I wish I could ride winged horses.'

'Is that why you wanted to come tonight?' Stormy asked.

'Yes. No.' Maud took a fragment of paper from her pocket and laid it out on her palm. It was charred and burnt at the edges. 'It's from the ledger. I rescued it from the fire.' Stormy met her gaze. 'It's got writing on it. I bleached out the burnt bit and re-stained the paper and the writing came up and . . .'

A buzzing started in Stormy's ears; he felt light-headed. 'Oh. I can't look,' he murmured. 'Tell me, does it say something on it, really does it?'

'There's a name on it. It must be this spitfyre's name. I'm sure it is.'

Stormy was so thrilled and surprised and amazed he could hardly speak. 'Thank you, thank you,' he said. 'I don't know what to say.'

'It's nothing.'

'It's everything.' He paused. 'When a spitfyre is passed on to their new owner, they have a little ceremony . . .'

'Yes. I know. I got these to help.' Maud dug into her pockets. 'Cotton wool represents a cloud, the pebble here is land and the bottle of water, er, is water. It's air, land and sea, places the spitfyre will go.'

Stormy nodded. Maud was racing ahead of him.

'And we ask permission from the Spirits to let her move through the elements and be kept safe, don't we?' he said. 'I've read about the naming ceremony too . . .'

They turned and faced the spitfyre and looked deep into her eyes.

'This is your naming ceremony,' Stormy said. The spitfyre scrambled to her feet and tossed her head, snorting warm sparkly air. 'Are you ready?' Stormy asked her. 'Right . . . Sun, Moon, Stars, all you that move in the heavens, hear me!'

The quiet in the cave was enormous. The spitfyre was concentrating on Stormy; her eyes never left his face and her ears twitched upright.

'Make the path of the winged horse smooth so that it may journey well,' Maud said and put down the pebble.

Stormy glanced at her. Maud's eyes were shining, and her cheek was dimpled. She grinned back at him and gave him the thumbs up.

'Winds, Clouds, Rain, Mist, and all you that move in the air . . .' he laid down the cotton wool, '. . . make the path of the winged horse smooth so that she may journey well.'

'Hills, Valleys, Rivers, Lakes, Trees, Grasses, all you of the earth . . .' Maud put the bottle of water and a leaf onto the floor. 'Make the path smooth for this spitfyre so that she may journey well.'

'All you of the heavens, all you of the air, all you of the earth, hear me! Make her path smooth so she shall travel beyond the four hills. We name this spitfyre . . .'

Stormy read from the burnt fragment of paper.

'*Seraphina*,' he said.

The spitfyre suddenly sighed loudly, as if a valve had burst or a door opened, as if something had been set free. Tossing her head so her mane flicked left and right, she blew out a cloud of tiny silvery sparks. The sparks spun and twisted and spiralled, flying upwards until they fizzled out against the roof of the cave. Turquoise smoke billowed in long trails from her nostrils and curled round her head. She shook herself as if shaking off an invisible heavy coat; or, like a reptile, casting off an old and unwanted skin.

'*Seraphina?*' Stormy said, enjoying the sound. He laid his hand on the horse's head. 'Seraphina. Dear Seraphina.'

'Seraphina. Beautiful Seraphina, angel of the air!' Maud said. 'Now she'll fly for you, Stormy. I know she will.' Maud turned towards the cave entrance. 'I must go back,' she added. 'I'm cold and I still have chores to do. Goodnight!' The light from the lantern fell across her smiling face; for a split second she looked quite different, like someone else he knew. 'Maud?' He wanted to look at her again. 'Wait!'

But she had gone.

Who? He was suddenly confused. He felt as if he'd known her before in a different life or time.

He turned back to study Seraphina, *his* spitfyre, and she stared back, her eyes bright and full of intelligence. Stormy quickly got down the bridle and put it on her and led her outside onto the terrace.

'Now, my dearest Seraphina, this is the moment,' he whispered to her. 'This is the moment we *fly*.' He remembered his vain attempt to fly with Mungo. He blushed hotly, thinking about it. What a disaster! He knew this would be different.

Seraphina knew it was different too. She understood, he could tell that she did – the way she was looking up into the sky, imagining it, just like he was. She wanted it in the same way he did.

Gently he got up onto her back. She was warm and shivering, gently expectant. He leaned down and whispered in her beautiful ear.

'*Seraphina!* Let's fly.'

A tremor ripped through her body as if she'd been struck

by gentle lightning. She flung back her head and made a strange sound, half whinny and half croaking dragon's roar. Every inch of her body twanged and vibrated with energy. She lurched forward, as if a brake had been released, and Stormy nearly fell, just grabbing at the reins in time. Her hooves rang loudly on the stone flags but he had no time to worry about the noise. As she sprang towards the edge of the terrace, picking up speed, he felt as if he were sinking into her back, as if his legs and body were melding into hers and they were one being. He wasn't bouncing at all, despite the speed, but was snug on her back as if glued there.

Then she was at the edge and springing forward and upwards. And at that moment he felt something extraordinary, not just that they had left the ground, but rather that they had pushed the earth away and were suddenly free.

Seraphina was a bird. A kite. An angel.

As she leapt up, a great weight in his heart dissolved and something, some inner spark of great happiness filled its place. The sensation passed from her to him – or from him to her, it was hard to tell – all he knew was a great joyousness speeding through his veins. Tears filled his eyes. It was the first time he'd ever felt so close to another living thing in his life.

They moved smoothly, almost silently as her large leaf-like wings flapped and they swooped effortlessly up and down in the dark sky.

Stormy laughed out loud. There was nothing below them, nothing surrounding them; they were flying. *He* was flying. At last! At last! 'I've waited all my life for this,' he told her. 'Seraphina! Thank you!'

The air was startlingly cold against his cheeks and hands, but Seraphina was warm beneath him.

They flew away from Dragon Mountain and the castle, into the depths of the dark sky. He felt he was actually flying amongst the speckling of tiny brilliant stars that surrounded them. Far away, the lights of Stollenback were twinkling and he could make out one or two lights in the village below. He didn't want to be seen. How could he make her turn round? He felt a moment of panic, then squeezed his left foot and leg into her side and she obligingly moved in that direction. The smallest pull on the reins encouraged her to turn and fly that way. He sent her round in a figure of eight, pressing and urging gently, sharing with her the thrill of working together and understanding. He asked her to fly upwards just by wanting it, by thinking it, and she did exactly what he desired.

'Fire,' he whispered and she blew out a rush of yellow and gold flames. 'Sparks!' She lit up the sky with a cascading shower of white and silver sparkling dots.

He didn't know, but it would have taken any other sky-rider years and years to reach such an understanding with his spitfyre.

He was born for it and they were meant for each other. When at last his ears were numb and his hands were locked painfully round her reins from the cold, he turned her gently back towards the castle. 'Home,' he whispered. It wasn't much of a home, he knew, and she probably didn't want to return to her dark cave, but he had no choice.

Seraphina flew back quickly. He had a moment's panic as the terrace seemed to rush up to meet them, but Seraphina was a flying creature who knew how to land without his help.

Stormy slipped off her back and led her past the sleeping spitfyres in eleven and twelve and back into her own dingy cave. He rubbed her down and gave her fresh water and wrapped his arms around her neck and kissed her nose.

'You are wonderful,' he told her. 'Thank you, thank you.'

He did not want to leave her and stayed with her until she had fallen asleep; then he crept back to his room and his bed, the happiest boy in the world.

34

Race

Stormy loved Seraphina. For hours he brushed her coat and mane and, as he did so, he talked to her, telling her about his life in the kitchen, about Otto and about Tex and his skivvy friends. He talked about Al, too, and hoped that one day she would be able to forgive him; that Al would forgive her.

Seraphina flourished.

She was fatter, rounder and glistening like a ripe fruit. Her eyes were bright. Her wings had mended; her rainbow coat gleamed. Her hooves were polished, trimmed and oiled.

Now, as soon as Stormy came into her stable, Seraphina blew smoke rings and spark showers of all different colours that lingered in patterns in the air. She pawed the ground with her delicate hooves and tossed her mane that was now silky and luxurious. Stormy hoped he'd never again see the closed, blank look on her face that made him so sad.

On the rare occasions when Ralf and Purbeck were off somewhere and there were no other students around, he took Seraphina out onto the terrace and let her run up and down, flapping her wings to exercise them. He took her out at night and they practised diving, soaring, circling. Each outing was a joy, and he learnt more and more about flying.

One morning, on his way to his classes, he saw a rush of students making their way to the noticeboard in the hall.

'What is it?' he asked Lizzie.

'The Silver Sword! The competitors' names have been put up!'

Stormy experienced a little pain of exclusion. *We might have stood a chance*, he thought, making his way to the paper pinned on the board, *in a month or two. Next year! Next year Seraphina and I would have won it!*

'You are some crazy guy!' Bentley said to him, pushing past him rudely as he made his way back through the throng around the board.

'What?'

'Did you read the small print?' Bentley added.

'What are you talking about?' said Stormy, confused.

'Well done, mate!' Tom said, slapping him on the back. 'Loser!'

Before he could get any closer to the list, Stormy saw Bella and grabbed her to ask her what was going on.

'Don't pretend you don't know,' she said.

'But I don't!'

Bella shrugged. 'You don't have to lie to me, Stormy . . . I just wish you'd told me you were thinking of it, I'd have warned you off.'

'Thinking of what? I honestly don't know what you're talking about.'

'Come here.' She pulled him along with her, pushing through the students to the noticeboard, where a large sheet of paper headed THE SILVER SWORD RACE had been pinned. 'Look,' she said, pointing to the competitor's names below.

Hector on *Sparkit*
Petra on *Polaris*
Lizzie on *Daygo*
Tom on *Condor*
Cindy on *Easterly*
Bentley on *Bluey*

and right at the bottom,

Stormy on *unnamed: thirteen*

Stormy felt his blood run cold and his head burn hotly all at the same time. Words wouldn't come.

'You can't deny it now,' Bella said, putting her finger against his name. Then she saw his expression. 'You really didn't know, did you?'

He shook his head. 'I didn't put my name on that list.'

'That's your handwriting, your signature. I recognise it.'

'It is,' he agreed. With a shiver, he remembered Araminta's smiling encouragement to give generously to sick old spit-fyres. She'd tricked him – how could he ever have imagined

302

that she liked him? It was those ribbons that had made him believe she cared. She and Hector must have planned this together; they were both cheats.

'What will you do?' Bella asked.

'Well, obviously I'll go and see the Director,' Stormy said, 'and get out of it.' But even as he spoke, he was thinking fast. Now his name was down, why not take part? *Because you're not good enough*, he told himself. *You'll make a fool of yourself. The others have been sky-riders for years.* 'I'll explain to the Director that I can't – it would be mad . . .'

'Yes, do,' said Hector, coming up behind them. 'It would be mad. I can't think why you put your name down.' He grinned maliciously.

'I –'

'Mad. Must be the lack of breeding.' He chuckled. '*Starlight!* Not likely!'

Stormy watched Hector swagger away. He had never hated anyone so much in all his life.

'Go and see the Director, Stormy,' Bella urged him. 'Hector will win the race and you'll get hurt, even if you can fly that old creature of Al's.'

Stormy nodded. 'I'll go now.'

He had to see the Director, he had to get out of the race, but the thought of coming face to face with a man who hunted down grubbins and kept a head as a trophy was enough to make him feel sick. Still, he went again to the green office and this time when he knocked on the door, the Director called him in.

'Yes?'

'I'm Stormy, sir.'

'Yes?'

'I've come about the race.'

'Yes?' The Director looked up at him for the first time. 'The Silver Sword Race?' He tapped a pen against a pile of papers. 'And?'

'There was a mistake and I've come to say I don't want to compete, I never wanted to take part; someone else put my name there.' He twisted his hands together. 'I mean,' he went on as the Director continued to stare him down, 'I mean, I can't race, because I don't have a spitfyre. That is, not a real one . . .'

The Director leaned back in his chair. 'I'm a busy man, Storky, very busy.'

'*Stormy.*'

'And I dislike cowards. I understand that Al gave you *his* spitfyre.'

'Oh. Yes, but – I'm so new and –'

The Director handed Stormy a copy of the list of competitors and pointed to some lines of minuscule writing at the bottom. 'Read that.'

No time wasters.
No sky-rider may scratch from the race for
any reason other than
the loss of a wing, a leg or death of
either rider or spitfyre.
Forfeit: the sky-rider's spitfyre.

'So, either you race, or you give up your spitfyre,' the Director said. 'Which is it to be?'

'I've never raced in my life!'

'Which is it to be?'

'I'll come last and I can't really fly,' Stormy protested. 'I'm just learning. I –'

The Director looked weary and bored. 'My patience is running out. Which is it to be?'

'I'll race,' Stormy said. 'But –'

'Good day.'

Stormy stood outside the Director's office and pounded his fist into his palm. *All right, all right*, he thought. *I'm glad. I'll race for the Silver Sword. Let the battle begin!*

Stormy read everything he could about the race. Soon he had narrowed down the possible places where the Silver Sword might be hidden: Moleman Mount, Slender Point, the Strand and Dark Rock. He laid out a map on the ground in front of Seraphina and showed her the rivers, cliffs and mountains. 'If it's here,' he said, pointing to Dark Rock, 'we'll have problems with height. It's the tallest spot and there might still be snow. If there's snow we might think about putting hoof-chains on, but they're so heavy that will slow us down dreadfully. And we may not need them. We'd have to come in from this angle and land there.' Seraphina stared at the map as he showed her what he meant. 'That's the worst of all the options.'

Seraphina blew out softly and shook her head.

'Of course Slender Point will have its problems too,' he

went on. 'Being so narrow, if two spitfyres land there's no room for the next and there could be a squabble. It was Slender Point last time, so I doubt it, but then the Director could be crafty and chose it just to be difficult.'

He ran his fingers over the map, tracing the river along the valley.

'I just don't think it will be the Strand,' he went on. 'I don't know why, but it's so far and it's almost too easy, isn't it? You know, I'm betting it will be Moleman Mount. Moleman Mount will be more difficult. See, there's that peak and then this area around it, so hardly any room for a spitfyre to land. There are horrible updraughts and we'd have to fly in from here.'

Seraphina puffed out pale sweet-smelling smoke and nudged his shoulder with her nose.

'I know,' Stormy said, 'I know. I have faith in you. We'll do fine. We'll practise for Moleman Mount, then, shall we? In honour of our dear friend, Mungo. I wonder how he is? I must go and see the Smalls. They might know something about his wife and child; they know such a lot. But when? When can I go?'

His lessons, combined with his night-time training, was exhausting and Stormy had to put Mungo's request on one side. After the race, Stormy told himself, then he'd address that problem.

The day of the race arrived.

Staff and students gathered to watch, standing along the terrace or leaning from the windows and balconies above.

The air was bursting with excitement and tension, as if something invisible was pulled tight between them all and might suddenly snap and send everyone hurtling off into space.

Stormy took his riding suit out of its tissue paper wrapping for the first time. He laid it out reverently on the bed. There were tight trousers, soft boots and thin leather gloves – this would be better than his old overalls. He also had new goggles to keep the wind out of his eyes. His trembling fingers could barely do up the buttons and tighten the belt. At last it was all on. Finally he would be a real sky-rider.

He stared at his reflection and hardly recognised himself. Stormy, sky-rider! He looked the part, but on the inside, he was jelly. *Stormy, you are an imposter!* he told the mirror. *You've only been flying for a few weeks. You are going to fall off. You'll make an idiot of yourself. You know nothing . . . Just as well you have the best flying horse in the world! So don't let her down! We mustn't come last, that's all. Not last!*

He made his way down to the terrace.

'Hey, nice gear!' Bella said. 'Suits you!'

'We thought you weren't coming,' Lizzie said, looking disappointed.

'Who does he think he is?' someone else called.

'Look, it's skivvy boy!' Tom shouted.

All around he heard mutters of,

'How dare he?'

'Never thought he'd show,' and 'Loser!'

As Stormy made his way through the crowd he had the

307

strange feeling that Seraphina was expecting him; as if a secret thread bound them together and, as he drew near, he could feel it reeling him in. Nerves began to give way to excitement. Dear Seraphina. Wonderful spitfyre.

Ralf and Purbeck came running past.

'Sparkit's had *extra, extra* vitamins this morning!' Ralf said under his breath. 'Watch him, Stormy!'

Purbeck was carrying spare goggles and reins, buckets and thorks. He made a funny face at Stormy as he jogged by, and grinned. 'Good luck!' he whispered, as if he really meant it.

Stormy stood a little taller and straighter. He swung his goggles round nonchalantly. *Sky-rider!*

The crowd was noisy, jeering and laughing, and someone was taking bets, but no one was putting their money on Stormy. *Hah!* he thought. *You haven't seen Seraphina in action. You just wait until you see her!*

The Director and Araminta were seated on two chairs near the first cave. How different the Director appeared now to Stormy; no longer benevolent and wise now that Stormy knew him to be a tyrant. The Director wanted a world without molemen, a world that suited him and over which he could rule. When the race was over Stormy would come back and confront him with what he knew . . . somehow.

Maud was there too, as always, a thin, almost hidden figure shifting around in their wake. Dear Maud, what a good friend she was.

The West-side spitfyres, Sparkit, Bluey, Polaris and

Daygo were outside their stables already. The two East-side spitfyres, Condor and Easterly, were bunched together near to cave thirteen, nervous at being on the wrong side of Dragon Mountain.

The winged horses seemed much bigger and more alive out of their caves. They had expanded, inflating like newly hatched butterflies from their pupae. They pranced on the tips of their hooves, as if the ground was too hot to stand on, jostling each other and snorting out multicoloured sparks. Several students were nervously holding up thorks as if that could protect them. Stormy watched Bentley prodding a thork at a bad-tempered Bluey and couldn't help thinking that spitfyres, like people, might not like thorks waved in their faces.

It was a clear day with a hint of warmth in the sunshine. The spitfyres' coats, all different shades, shone iridescent blues or greens shimmering into gold and silver. As they flexed their muscles and tensed their necks, rippling their skin, the sun glinted on them, a huge kaleidoscope of shifting colours. Smoke spiralled and coiled, hanging in the still air like pale ghostly snakes.

Sparkit stood more than twice the height of Hector and his wingspan was thirty-five paces. His head was square and solid and tapered to his ears, which Stormy had always thought might mean a small brain, like Hector. His eyes were dark and malicious and this morning he was livelier than ever, tossing his mane and pawing the ground – it was the yellow powder at work!

'Here's the kitchen boy!' Hector cried, barring Stormy's

way. There was no pretence now at being even slightly friendly. 'Stormy the boy wonder! I've been expecting your withdrawal from the race every day. What went wrong?'

Stormy stopped and stared at Hector coldly. Hector stared back.

'Well, better get a move on and bring out your spitfyre, skivvy. We've heard so much about her!' He thrust his big chin at him and grinned. 'Need a trolley in case she can't walk?'

Stormy walked past him, smiling. He was amused that Hector was so confident his spitfyre was a wreck that he hadn't even looked in cave thirteen for himself. He was in for a surprise.

'I don't know why you bother,' Hector went on. 'If you take part you might get hurt. You could still scratch from the race, you know.'

Stormy went past him without speaking.

He felt as if he were going home – not that he'd ever gone 'home', but it was a sensation he'd often dreamed about. Home was somewhere safe, where you were wanted and loved. Cave thirteen had become that for him.

He ran into the stable.

'*Seraphina!*'

He threw his arms around her neck. She huffed and sighed, tossing and bobbing her head in greeting, blowing out a shower of ash and silvery sparks. Her eyes were shining, smiling.

'Seraphina. We're going to race! We're going to fly!' He leaned against her and stroked her neck. 'You're the best,

310

the very best spitfyre in the whole Academy, and you'll fly like a bird, speed like a comet, shoot like a star.' She'd been in the circus. She'd done the *Spin*. She was brilliant. He *loved* this spitfyre. A tingle ran up his spine and shot right down to his fingertips. He took down the reins and bridle. He shivered happily. 'We're going to be magnificent!'

She nudged her nose into his chest. A noise, a sort of rolling, clicking sound, gurgled up from inside her like a mechanical cat purring, then burst out into a happy whinny. She could hardly keep still while he fitted her bridle. She jiggled till her hooves clicked against the rock, making sparks, and so many sparks flew from her nostrils too that the dingy cave was quite lit up.

Outside the crowd was cheering and hallooing.

Stormy wished he had something to mark the occasion, something special . . . He'd noticed a small store of dingy jewels at the back of the cave before. Seraphina was the only one with dragon's treasure and he wondered if Al had left it there for a reason. Quickly he searched through it.

'There!' He fitted an enormous armlet with red stones set in it around her foreleg. 'I bet this is worth a few pence.' He stood back and admired her. 'Beautiful thing!'

Purbeck was calling for him; someone was asking if all the entrants were there, and he started to move outside. Whatever happened, he could never give up Seraphina now. If he lost he'd run away with her. No one was going to take Seraphina away from him, ever.

Then somehow they were outside and the sunlight was blinding; the sound of roaring and shouting filled his ears.

'Here he is!' Purbeck cried.

'What a fool Stormy is, I mean, really . . .' Petra began.

There was a hush as they all turned to stare. Their surprise silenced all of them except Hector.

'Look at that! You little orphan nobody! You cheat, Stormy!' Hector marched towards him, pushing past the other students roughly. 'That's not Al's spitfyre!'

'Yes it is. She's mine,' Stormy said, holding Seraphina's reins tightly. 'My spitfyre.'

Hector turned to Ralf. 'Wipe that grin off your face!' he spat at him. 'This is not what you told me!'

Ralf rolled his eyes. 'Why, Hector, it's amazing!' he said, in mock surprise. 'She didn't look like that before!'

'Liar. You'll pay. You'll both pay for this,' he said to Ralf and Purbeck, who was also grinning like a mad thing. So they had deceived Hector! Stormy was thrilled.

Hector turned back to Stormy. 'Well, servery boy? This is it. The last one back is given as a prize to the winner. That'll be me. Right? That'll be me, getting *your* flying horse. Don't say I didn't warn you.'

'And if I win I'll turn her into cat meat,' Bentley said, fixing his dark eyes on Stormy. 'Whatever, Stormy, she's a goner.'

'Don't be so mean!' Petra called. 'What's her name, Stormy?'

'Secret,' Stormy said quickly.

'He means he doesn't know,' Hector said, 'and never will, now.' He laughed. 'You can't win,' he added. 'No chance. I know you still think you might win, just like you

312

think the big D likes you, just like you imagine Araminta likes you. They don't. No one likes you. It's all part of their little game.' He chuckled silently, pushing his face up close to Stormy's face. 'Give up now, before you get hurt. You'll still lose your spitfyre, but –'

Stormy shook his head. 'No,' he said. 'I'm in the race.'

He turned away and bumped straight into Purbeck, who had sidled up to him. 'They'll cheat,' Purbeck said quietly. 'They'll do anything to stop you from winning. Take care.'

'Thanks. I know,' Stormy said, stroking Seraphina's neck. '*We* know. Thanks for everything!'

Mr Jacobs was shouting orders. The sky-riders and spitfyres got themselves into a line along the terrace.

'I'd forgotten all about that spitfyre of Al's,' Mr Jacobs said to Stormy. 'I'm surprised to see her so fit. Can you really fly her?' he added quietly.

Stormy nodded.

'Well, all right . . .' He tapped his pocket where he always kept his NSD tranquiliser, as if reminding himself and Stormy that it was there. 'The others might get rough . . .'

'We're fine.'

'But really, Stormy, if I were you I'd retire now. I don't want to see you hurt.'

Stormy smiled his thanks. He shook his head. 'No.'

Mr Jacobs patted his back and went off, calling to the riders to mount and get ready.

The spitfyres were springy and nervy now to the point of bursting into flames. The tension was awful. Sparkit

313

was making deep, anxious calls in his throat and tossing his head, dragging the reins through Hector's hands, fretful and eager to go. The others were jostling and flapping their wings, neighing, snorting.

Stormy settled as calmly as he could onto Seraphina's back. She was simmering like the copper kettle on the fire, an animal engine, raring to go. He took up the reins and smoothed her neck. Beneath his fingers he felt her respond and begin to gather herself in readiness. She lifted up her head and sniffed the air; her eyes darted all over, watching. Stormy felt his heartbeat quicken.

Mr Jacobs blew a whistle sharply.

'Ready wings!'

Seven pairs of spitfyre wings unfurled with loud snapping sounds, like giant wet sheets on a washing line. A mini tornado whooshed around the terrace as their wings billowed backwards and thrust forwards. The girls shrieked and grabbed hold of their gusting hair and skirts.

Stormy looked along the row of riders, each one dressed in dark clothes, their eyes hidden behind helmet and goggles, crouched forward, and ready to go. They didn't look like students now but warriors and fighters. The power and force that emanated from them was energising.

He felt Maud watching him and was glad. She had done her hair up with white ribbons. Even from this distance he could see she was smiling, and each cheek was dimpled . . .

Suddenly he knew who she reminded him of! It hit him like a blow to the chest. Of course! How stupid he was!

But then there was no time to think about it; another whistle pierced the air. The Director was putting them on their marks . . .

'. . . Get ready, set . . .'

Stormy's thoughts were in a whirl. Maud. *Maud was . . .*

The Director's voice cut through his thoughts: 'The Silver Sword is at . . . *Moleman Mount* and . . . *Go!*'

He had to concentrate, not think about her.

But if he was right . . .

He had to focus. He mustn't let anyone down; so much relied on him. Moleman Mount. He'd been right about that!

Seraphina was off.

The air was filled with the clatter and thunder of galloping hooves and the rush and sigh of the spitfyres' wings.

They raced to the edge of the terrace. In the light of day, the air beyond looked emptier and more like nothing than it ever had in the night. Fear was a sudden cold fist squeezing his stomach, but then the magic of flying took him over and all he felt was a great happiness as they soared off the terrace and into the cold, still air.

The first few seconds were crucial. Stormy had to remember exactly where Moleman Mount was. He visualised the map; he'd thought it out so carefully, and he mustn't spoil it now. Swiftly he urged Seraphina to fly north.

Seraphina was already going that way; stretching out her neck she was heading purposefully down the valley, beating her beautiful wings steadily and powerfully.

He whispered to her that she was the best creature in

the world, and that they were going to win the race. He could feel her silent reply in the slight flicker of her ears and thrust of her wings. She understood.

Imagine Hector taking away his dear Seraphina . . . Never. He would never let anyone –

'Get out of the way!' a voice roared.

Suddenly there were orange wings right beside him as another spitfyre flew by, almost on top of him. The air seemed to be full of floundering hooves, wings, the massive hot body of a spitfyre.

He ducked and spun round.

'Watch out!' the voice behind him shouted again. 'Out of the way, you idiot!'

35

Cheat

The gleaming emerald body of Daygo was right above him. Easterly, the orange spitfyre, was on his left. They were too close; they were crowding him.

Stormy yelped and ducked and Seraphina veered out of the way, dropping like a stone, falling so suddenly that Stormy felt his stomach still hanging above him as he fell.

Daygo and Easterly crashed above him with a terrible smacking sound. There was a horrible squeal and tangle of orange wings with green ones and legs, hooves, a flash of open mouths, teeth and fire. They'd planned to squeeze Seraphina and make her fall, but instead, they collided with each other.

The two spitfyres tore apart, spun, and began to drop. Cindy, Easterly's rider, let out a piercing scream as her spitfyre spun out of control, its wings broken. The spitfyres' wings were like broken umbrellas, spokes pointing this way and that, and all a mess. It was awful. Cindy was crying, desperately pulling on the reins as the spitfyre twirled down.

Stormy quickly glanced back and saw them land awkwardly back on the terrace. Cindy was safe but out of the race.

'Idiot!' Lizzie cried.

Stormy spun round, surprised at her sharp tone, but he could see she was trying to rein back a stunned Daygo. She was desperate. 'That was your fault!' she shouted.

'It wasn't!' Stormy yelled back.

'You shouldn't be here! You know nothing!' she cried. 'Go back! Get out of the way!'

Stormy stared ahead fixedly and ignored her. Purbeck had warned they'd cheat. The stakes were high and they'd stop at nothing to make sure he didn't win. He'd avoided that crash and now they were six.

He patted Seraphina's neck. *Well done, well done.*

Sparkit was way out in front with Bluey, Polaris and Condor. Stormy and Lizzie began to chase after them. Stormy tried to recall and visualise the pattern of strong air currents that charged through the valley and urged Seraphina to fly with them.

On they went, faster and faster.

He knew Seraphina understood everything he was thinking; as if his thoughts echoed inside her, as if as he breathed, so did she. The heat from her body crept into his, they were merged into one being; his hands, holding lightly on the reins, were sensitive to each tiny movement she made.

If I die right now it won't matter, he thought, closing his eyes for a moment to relish the feeling. *This is the best. It can't get better than this.*

Soon they were level with the others and it was Daygo at the back of the pack.

'Watch your wings!' Bentley shouted at him, and Stormy was shaken from his dreams.

'He's a blooming amateur!' Tom shouted. He was riding Condor, a big creamy white. 'He's hired help, remember? Kitchen boy!'

'Stay right back!' Lizzie cried, fighting for space. 'Don't get in Daygo's way again, Stormy!'

They flew on.

Stormy stared ahead and gritted his teeth in a frozen smile. He *was* in the race, he *was* a sky-rider and they couldn't get rid of him.

Beyond the sigh and flap of the wings, another noise was beginning to materialise. Stormy strained his ears to hear it. A strange low, keening whistle was floating through the air. It didn't come from one direction but seemed to be all around them. The sound rose and fell and every time Stormy thought it was fading away, it came back from another direction, stronger and more enticing. He couldn't focus on anything else. It was a fascinating sound and he yearned to get closer to it. The others gave no sign that they could hear it, and he began to feel that it must be directed at him. He strained to hear more of it, wanting to go to it.

The sound reminded him of something promising – a game, or a whistled tune he'd heard when he was very young. Was it Ralf's tune on his mouth organ? Or was it something to do with Al? Was Al trying to call to him?

319

Yes, that was it. He was sure that was it. Poor Al. Where was Al?

'Stop, Seraphina! I must help Al!' He tried to rein her in, but she flew on, ignoring him. He twisted round on her back, searching the empty skies for a clue to the whistling sound. 'Al! Al!' he shouted. 'Where are you?' He scanned the cliffs, but there was no one there.

The noise got louder and stronger. His happiness began to dissolve; he was all anxiety as the whistling filled his head and drummed inside his skull.

'Stop, Seraphina!'

He looked for somewhere to land. 'I hate flying, Seraphina. Let me down. I want to land!'

Suddenly he caught sight of Petra staring at him. Lizzie too. They both looked away quickly, but not before he'd seen how thrilled they both looked. And smug.

Tom was looking back over his shoulder and grinning wickedly. He pointed to his ears. All the other sky-riders were wearing earmuffs and couldn't hear a thing.

Hector was too far out in front for him to see him clearly, but Stormy guessed somehow that the whistling sound came from him. He knew his ears would be well covered too.

Stormy let go of the reins and clamped his hands over his ears. The whistling sound grew faint. 'Stop, stop, stop,' Stormy begged the noise to go. Sweat trickled down between his shoulder blades as he forced himself to block out the noise. The whistling was evil. He'd never been so drained of happiness in all his life or felt so hopeless.

He pressed harder and harder until the sound faded completely.

Gradually, his spirits began to right themselves.

It was just Hector, nothing more sinister than Hector.

Stormy collected himself and calmed his booming heart. He was in a race. He had to get on with the race. Thank goodness Seraphina hadn't listened to him. On she flew, strong and keen and wonderful.

When at last Stormy dared to uncover his ears, the whistling had gone. Now there was an eerie silence with only the wind sighing past, and the beat, beat of the spitfyres' wings.

'We're still in the race,' he whispered to Seraphina.

'Something's wrong!' Lizzie called suddenly. She leaned forward and rubbed Daygo's neck. Stormy thought it might be another trick and was on guard, but then saw that Daygo's right wing, as green and beautiful as a giant leaf, wasn't working properly. 'Daygo's hurt,' she cried. 'It was that crash with Easterly. Your fault . . . Oh, poor Daygo. We've got to go back.'

She wheeled him round and slowly headed back towards the Academy.

Now they were only five.

The sky-riders followed the path of the river that trailed like a dark blue ribbon miles below, speeding between the smooth grey rock walls of the valley. Here and there spindly trees sprouted from crevasses and cracks;

Seraphina swerved by them expertly, ducking and diving like a fish.

A blue ribbon river . . . White ribbon . . . Now Stormy's thoughts flew back to Maud.

White ribbons! Maud had been wearing *white* ribbons in her hair.

It made him felt stupid, very stupid. And glad. *She* had given him the ribbons, not Araminta. He was the luckiest, happiest person in the world. The wind on his cheeks, lifting his hair, whistling past his ears, was the best feeling in the world. Once he'd been a kitchen boy, skivvy, compost-maker, and washer-upper. Now he was a real sky-rider. And he had new friends. Nothing could be better. Somewhere also, in the back of his mind, was that moment of realisation, of seeing something in Maud's expression as he flew off the terrace. Yes, he was sure he was right. He knew who she was!

A bird hurtled by, flying in the opposite direction, and he came suddenly back to the present.

Ahead, the valley split into two like a snake's tongue, and rising up at the V was a tall white cliff with a flat top that was Moleman Mount. Stormy steadied himself. *Concentrate! Don't think about Maud.* It was important to fly round to the west side, then rise up and come in that way to avoid a strong air flow that rose up on the east side. He began to get into position.

Suddenly an amazingly bright and blindingly reflective light burst out from its summit.

It was the sun striking the Silver Sword.

Hector and the other sky-riders were prepared and all pulled dark visors over their eyes. Grimly Stormy squeezed his eyes up against the blinding light.

The light was nothing to Seraphina. She began to pick up speed. She began to creep up on Polaris.

Petra shook her fist at them. 'Go back! Get away!'

Stormy ignored her.

'I'll take action!' she shouted at him. He couldn't see her eyes, but her voice was as cold as stone. 'Go back!'

'It's a race!' Stormy shouted back.

Petra took a stone from her shoulder bag, held it up so Stormy could see it, and then threw it at him with all her force. He ducked instinctively. The stone hit them. Stormy heard a dull metallic clunk. Panicking, he leaned forward and ran his hand down Seraphina's throat and chest, dreading he would feel blood. But there was nothing; the stone had hit her armlet and bounced off.

'Stay back!' Petra yelled. She waved her fist at him. 'Back! Go away! You're not wanted!'

Another stone winged across, but he dodged it and it sailed over his shoulder.

Tom screamed.

It had hit him. He grabbed at his forehead, dropped the reins, overbalanced and began to slither off his spitfyre. Grabbing for the mane, for the reins, for anything, he screamed again. 'Help!' He had caught Condor's mane and was hanging onto it, but Condor didn't like it; he was lopsided, distraught. He bucked and swivelled and Tom finally lost his grasp and slipped into the void.

'Nooooooo!'

He fell, tumbling over and over like a doll, until he hit the trees and disappeared amongst the rocks and greenery on the cliff side.

Petra's shocked face was white with horror.

'That was your fault!' she shouted at Stormy. 'Poor Tom! Tom!'

Condor was confused. He tossed his white mane and circled round, then headed down into the valley after his fallen rider.

Now they were four.

36

Moleman Mount

Seraphina flew on, ignoring everything. She was flying so well that now only Polaris and Sparkit were in front, both going to the west side of Moleman Mount. Tom, Lizzie and Cindy were out of the race; surely *he* was safe. Stormy couldn't be the loser; *they* were the losers. He had nothing to fear now; he might as well battle it out and really go for it.

Hector looked back over his shoulder; behind his goggles his eyes were full of malice. His big chin was thrust out angrily and Stormy recognised that face; it was the face of the sky-rider who'd wrecked his compost heap all that time ago. It was Hector. Of course.

'It's my race! I *have* to win!' Hector shouted. He began to kick Sparkit and slash him with the ends of the reins, urging him to go even faster.

Stormy and Seraphina swerved round to the left of the Mount to let the warm currents help them rise up towards the flat summit where the light from the Silver Sword still blazed.

'Let's not be last to land,' Stormy told her. 'Come on, we can do it. Up, up!'

They shot up over the summit, high into the air, and almost instantly Stormy asked Seraphina to land and she quickly slowed down. She tilted, wings outspread, and began swirling down towards the earth like a kite.

Sparkit was there too. His enormous silver wings hung out in the air like giant sheets as he spun and sailed down. First to touch the soil was Sparkit, then Polaris. Stormy was third.

Stormy felt the solid earth; Seraphina was tucking in her wings. He jumped off her back and ran towards the sword.

The great Silver Sword was set into the top of a heap of richly coloured stones. The sun had shifted and now the sword gleamed rather than shone blindingly. It was misshapen and crooked, but there was something beautiful about the sword's vast size and rough, silver surface.

Stormy and Hector both sprinted towards it.

The ground was covered in short grass and broken stones and Stormy tripped and almost fell. Hector stopped to fling a stone at him; Stormy twisted out of the way.

Suddenly there was a flash of brilliant azure, as Bluey zoomed into sight on the east side of the Mount where the fierce currents were. Both Stormy and Hector stopped. The strong winds lifted Bluey up rapidly, and it looked as if he would shoot past, but he did an incredible turn and flip and swooped down to the landing area.

'Go on, Bluey!' Bentley cried and he yanked hard on Bluey's reins. The spitfyre hit the earth, somersaulted and rolled along like a wheel, throwing Bentley off so that he crashed into Stormy and Stormy toppled over like a skittle.

'Well done, Bentley!' Hector shouted. 'Excellent. Don't move, Stormy!' he roared as Stormy scrambled to his feet. Hector was running the last few paces towards the Silver Sword. 'That sword is mine.'

'It's a race!' Stormy said, scrambling up and leaping towards him. 'It's just as much *my* sword!'

'Don't talk rubbish! Sparkit! *Fire!*' Hector yelled.

Stormy jumped as the grass where he had been standing went up in smoke.

'Fire isn't allowed!'

'Shut up, kitchen boy,' Hector said.

Under cover of another stream of flaming balls from Sparkit, which rolled out one after the other, scorching and burning, Hector got to the Silver Sword. Stormy dodged the flames but a shower of sparks set his clothes smoking. He stopped to pat out the glowing fabric.

'Cheat!'

'When will you learn, skivvy?' Petra said, leaning forward, resting her elbows on Polaris's brown neck. 'Hector always wins.'

Hector took hold of the great sword and, rocking it backwards and forwards, released it from its place. 'So,' Hector said, waving the Silver Sword in the air. 'I win!'

'Congratulations, Hector,' Petra said without enthusiasm.

'We knew you would,' Bentley said glumly. He picked himself up and slowly began taking some rope from his backpack.

'Who did we lose on the way?' Hector asked as he admired the great sword, turning it over and over in his hands. 'My father will be pleased with this.'

'We lost Tom, Cindy and Lizzie.'

'Three?' Hector shrugged. 'Tom? Well, they were careless and it was their fault. Who was last to land?'

'*Stormy!*' Petra and Bentley said quickly and firmly.

'No. It was Bentley on Bluey!' Stormy cried, spinning round to face the other two. 'I wasn't last! You know I wasn't last!'

'I saw you come down after me,' Petra said, looking blankly towards the mountain peaks.

'So did I,' Bentley said. 'I was third, you were fourth.'

'I agree. That's what I saw,' Hector added.

'That's so . . . How could you?' Stormy cried. 'Petra, come on, please, tell the truth! Please!'

Petra flushed red, but still she said, 'No. You were last, Stormy. You were the slowest.'

'Oh, dear, poor little skivvy,' Hector said. 'You lose. That pathetic little creature you're sitting on is now *my* spitfyre!' Hector chuckled. 'I will so enjoy chaining her back up in a dungeon at my castle.'

'You can't. You're all lying!' Stormy looked round at them wildly. 'You're all cheats. I won't let you do this!' He ran back to Seraphina, but Hector was one step ahead of him. He had caught hold of the thin rope Bentley threw to him. He had it round Seraphina's neck in an instant.

Seraphina reared up, and the rope tightened around her neck, throttling her. She dropped to her knees, thrashing her head from side to side in distress.

'Stop! You're hurting her! Stop!' Stormy shouted. He ran to her and tried to get his fingers under the rope but it was already too tight, and squeezing into her skin. Seraphina jumped and kicked, rolling her head to escape the rope. She squealed and spat out dark smoke and sparks.

'I don't think you've got much choice,' Hector said, pulling the rope tighter again.

'Fire! Seraphina! Fire him! Bite him!' Stormy shouted desperately. 'Do something!'

Seraphina snapped at the rope, trying to reach it with her teeth. Her eyes rolled in fear.

'You see, Stormy, you really don't belong,' Hector said, walking away with the end of the rope in his hand. 'You shouldn't have tried to play sky-riders when you're not one of us.'

'Back to the kitchens for you, Stormy,' Bentley said.

'Or the dungeons,' Petra said, 'when the Director hears what you did to poor Daygo and Easterly.'

Hector got back onto his spitfyre's back as calmly as if it were a normal day. 'Come on, Sparkit!' he waved the sword. 'Up we go! Home!'

'Wait! Stop!' Stormy scrambled up onto Seraphina's

back. He dug his fingers under the rope again and managed to loosen it a little. 'Seraphina, dear, don't fight it,' he told her. 'You'll hurt yourself. Don't, don't.' Then he turned and shouted at Hector. 'Curse you, Hector! I hate you!'

He felt a tug as Sparkit moved and pulled the rope taut. They were like a dog on a lead. They were Hector's prisoners. His heart was heavy and full of hatred. Now they had to fly where Hector flew; at the speed that Hector wanted. They were Hector's property.

Sparkit rose up into the sky and everyone followed him. Hector laughed out loud, waving the Silver Sword round his head and making whooping noises. He turned round to gloat at Stormy and make throat-cutting motions with his free hand and laugh.

They flew all the way back like that.

Soon the towers of the Academy castle and their familiar pointed rooftops came into view. Stormy felt like something with no mind of its own or will of its own. He hung his head. He didn't want Maud – or anyone – to see him like this. But what could he do?

Suddenly the rope between the two spitfyres jerked so sharply that Stormy was almost thrown off. He grabbed at Seraphina's mane.

'Stop! Stop, Hector!' he cried.

Seraphina made a choking sound and coughed hoarsely, shaking her head as the rope tightened. She had to go faster. And faster.

'It's all right! Don't fight it,' he called to her. 'Don't pull.'

Sparkit had suddenly changed direction and was speeding straight towards the steep mountainside. He was flying headfirst into the rock!

Seraphina, strung behind, could only follow.

'Stop!' Stormy cried. 'What are you doing, Hector?'

But Hector did not turn round.

Sparkit twisted, changed direction and began to drag them into a narrow gulley. They were so close to the green and grey of the cliffs that Seraphina's wings almost scraped the rock.

'Let go! Let go of her!' Stormy shouted. 'You'll kill us!'

But Hector had his head down low and didn't answer. He seemed uncomfortable. He seemed almost as desperate to cling on as Stormy was, as if, unbelievably, Hector *wasn't* in control.

Seraphina and Stormy could only follow, pulled this way and that, dragged along like a fish on a line.

Then the blue and the brown of Bluey and Polaris were with them too, and the four of them were flying at breakneck speed in the narrow gap. The air was loud with the rush of their wings and throaty cries.

'There's no space! Get back!' Hector roared. 'Back!'

But Bluey and Polaris didn't hear or couldn't understand. Their wings were almost touching. The air was full of tumbling stones, grit and flying leaves.

Polaris came in closer and closer until suddenly his wings tangled with Bluey's and both pulled up, lost balance and began to fall. Bluey spun off and bounced into the rocks. He crashed into loose boulders and they toppled down on him and knocked him to the ground. Bentley was thrown off. The two lay broken and still on a wide ledge.

Polaris tipped head over heels and hurtled into a thicket of bushes. Petra was tossed onto a flat rock with a terrible smacking sound. Polaris tumbled down and down into the valley, screaming wildly.

That was as much as Stormy could see because Hector was forcing him onwards, faster and faster. It was as if Sparkit had caught the scent of something on the wind and was drawn towards it like an arrow speeding to the target, and Seraphina and Stormy were forced to follow.

Then Stormy saw what Sparkit was chasing and his blood ran ice cold.

37

Mungo

It was Mungo.

The moleman had come onto the hillside to see the race. He had no idea how dangerous it was. And Sparkit had got scent of him. Nothing could stop the grubbin-hating spitfyre now.

Mungo was trying to hide, ducking down amongst the bushes and boulders on the side of the mountain. But there was nowhere to go.

Hector hammered the flat of the Silver Sword on Sparkit's rump – not urging him on, but trying to make him turn back!

But Sparkit wouldn't turn.

Stormy and Seraphina swung along behind them, powerless to do anything. Sparkit circled in over the grubbin's head, closer and closer, until his massive wings brushed the overhanging rock, ripping out leaves and twigs. He almost crashed against the cliff, then turned and circled off again, throwing Hector to one side so he nearly slipped off Sparkit's back.

'Stop! Stop, you fool! Sparkit!' His fingers slipped from the reins – and the rope.

The rope went slack. They were free.

Seraphina immediately extended her wings as brakes. She swung away and hovered above the other spitfyre.

Mungo was crouched beneath a rowan tree.

Sparkit had been forced to circle off to avoid crashing into the cliff, but now came straight back at the grubbin, eyes blazing madly, sparks and black smoke billowing from his nostrils. The sun shone off his flanks as if they were made of dull metal. He looked unimaginably fierce and alien, not like a living being at all.

'Help! Help!' Mungo called.

Sparkit snapped at the little rowan tree and yanked it from the ground, roots and all. He tossed it aside; a shower of soil rained down over the grubbin and rattled down on the hillside. Mungo yelped and dived behind a boulder. He began to crawl towards the path, like an animal seeking its burrow, but Sparkit was back. Now he was hanging above Mungo's head, his wings held aloft, poised to strike.

'No!' Stormy cried.

Sparkit's eyes gleamed with malice as he swept down, open-mouthed, and plucked the grubbin from his perch in his teeth.

Mungo screamed. He kicked and thrashed his arms but he was powerless in the great spitfyre's grip.

Stormy watched in horror. What could he do?

Seraphina was gliding round gently, circling, watching.

Now she steadied herself, her shoulders tensed, her wings tipped and curved and she pitched down.

Amazed, Stormy simply held on.

Seraphina swooped silently towards Sparkit. She was a rainbow arrow, diving below him, going down, and then further down, so when Stormy looked up, he could see Sparkit's underside, his vulnerable pale grey belly. And poor Mungo, legs bicycling hopelessly in thin air.

Sparkit, heedless of Hector's shouts and anger, was flying up towards the Academy with his prize, but it was an almost vertical climb, and within a few moments his great wings were beating more slowly with the effort.

Below him, unseen, little Seraphina began to circle. Round and round she flew without any effort or sound as if she'd found an invisible air current that she was riding. Faster and faster she went, then, with no warning, she flew straight at the mountain wall. Stormy toppled to one side, righted himself, threw his arms round her neck, nearly fell, hung on.

'Seraphina!' he cried, seeing the wall rushing up. 'Seraphina! No!'

But at the last moment, just as he thought they'd hit the rock, she twisted and, using her strong legs, ricocheted off the wall with a harsh metallic sound as hooves hit stone. Stormy shuddered at the impact. He was almost knocked off her back, but clung on. Seraphina darted across to the chasm to the next wall and sprang off that in the same way. Then she bounced off another wall, turned and vaulted off the next. Each leap gave her more power and more speed. Now she accelerated until she was going so fast she didn't touch the sides at all, but began to spiral upwards, like a corkscrew rising up on a whirlpool of air.

The Spin! She was doing the Spin!

Stormy laughed out loud. 'Seraphina! You star!'

Round and round they whizzed, as if they were in a vortex.

Hector's goggled face peering down at them was full of horror and amazement.

Seraphina came whirling up with her wings tucked in close to her side. She was a rocket. A torpedo. A bullet. She shot straight into Sparkit's underbelly –

Whoosh!

There was a tremendous collision of body against body and Sparkit somersaulted backwards. Hector yelped and dived forward, locking his arms round Sparkit's neck. The Silver Sword fell from his grasp.

And Sparkit dropped Mungo.

The grubbin plummeted like a stone, tumbling over and over into the valley below, screaming as he went, a whirl of legs and arms, like a broken wheel.

Seraphina shot after him.

Sparkit was winded and flew this way and that in confusion. He was giddy and dazed by the impact. All Hector could think about was his trophy and he jabbed his finger at the fallen Silver Sword. It was lodged in a crevice a few hundred metres below them, shining, tantalising, a dream.

'That way!' he screamed. 'The Sword!'

336

But Sparkit only had eyes for the grubbin. He went for Mungo again.

Now the two spitfyres were racing to reach Mungo, who was still plummeting through the air.

Sparkit jetted out plumes of fire and smoke but Seraphina was nimble as a flea and zigzagged out of his way. She shot down through the gulley like a meteor, faster than Sparkit and more nimble.

Go, Seraphina, go, Stormy urged her.

Mungo was caught on the branches of a small tree jutting out of the hillside. He was flapping like a bit of washing, yelping and shouting.

Seraphina glided in beneath him, hovering with her wings beating gently. Sparkit was coming.

'Jump!' Stormy yelled.

The dangling grubbin squealed, let go of his branch and dropped down behind Stormy. He fastened his arms round him like a crab. Sparkit was seconds behind them. He belched out balls of fire that came rolling through the air at them, but too late, and only the little tree went up in a blaze of orange flames.

Seraphina was away, flying fast. She zigzagged upwards, quickly avoiding the fireballs that Sparkit spat towards her. Stormy was dizzy; he hardly knew which was the sky and which was the ground. His ears hummed and his throat was dry.

'Well done, my sky-rider!' the grubbin wheezed in his ear. 'That's my boy!' He wrapped his arms more tightly round him.

337

Seraphina flew over the courtyard walls and into the square, where the students were peering up into the sky. They cheered as they saw the first flying horse appear. Stormy could hear surprise that it was *his* spitfyre in their shouts and cries of amazement.

Seraphina slowed and landed gently, tucking in her wings as she touched down. She was breathing heavily and her legs almost gave way beneath her as she righted herself. Her chest heaved and throbbed. She was burning hot. Stormy peeled off his helmet and goggles and wiped the sweat from his face.

Sparkit came next, roaring, billowing fire and smoke so he was almost invisible inside the cloud of grey. The students scattered, taking shelter as he skidded into the square.

Sparkit galloped across the yard towards Seraphina, his hooves ringing out loud and hard on the stones. The whites of his eyes showed; dense, dark smoke curled from his nostrils. He snapped his jaws and spat out fire.

Seraphina backed into the corner near the tower. The grubbin clutched tighter at Stormy, whimpering.

'Stop him, Hector! Stop your spitfyre!' Stormy cried.

'I can't. It's the grubbin he wants. Just hand over the grubbin,' Hector shouted. 'It's the only thing that'll stop him. It's his life's blood now. He needs them. He must have them.'

'He can't have this one!' Stormy yelled.

'What's going on?' It was the Director. He flung back the door and marched down the steps.

338

'Control your spitfyre, Hector!' Mr Jacobs shouted, running along behind the Director. 'Keep him back!'

'I can't!' Hector was pulling on the reins and digging in his heels but Sparkit was incensed, like something possessed. Steam rose from his glistening coat. He tossed his head and let out a shrill whinny that set Stormy's teeth on edge. Sparkit was edging closer, snapping again and again at Seraphina, at the wall and now at Mr Jacobs as he tried to get near.

'If you can't –' Mr Jacobs took a dart from his pocket. 'I shall have to quieten him, Hector,' he warned. 'Do something, or I shall have to.'

'No, don't do that!' Hector roared. 'Sparkit, Sparkit, down. Down. Relax!'

Mr Jacobs was already fitting a dart to his gun and aiming it. 'This is your last warning . . .'

'Sparkit, relax!' But Sparkit did not. Could not.

Hector jumped off his back, just as the dart hit Sparkit's neck. Almost instantly the spitfyre's front legs buckled. The rest of his great body slowly began to crumple, his neck flopped, his head hit the stone with a *thonk* and he toppled to the ground in a dead sleep.

Hector strode towards the Director. 'So much for your *vitamins*,' he muttered sarcastically. 'Thanks for nothing,' he sneered. 'Nothing!'

'What *vitamins*?' Mr Jacob asked.

'I've no idea at all,' the Director said quickly. 'Where's the sword? What have you done with the Silver Sword?' He looked round at the gathering of students.

'The Director does know about the vitamins, Mr Jacobs,' Stormy interrupted. 'He knows everything.' The grubbin shivered behind him as he went on. 'The vitamins are a drug. A yellow powder, and they give it to the Star Squad spitfyres. It makes them catch grubbins. That's what the Star Squad do. They bring the molemen here, take their money and –'

'Be quiet, boy. Where are the others?' the Director interrupted. 'And where, Hector, is my Silver Sword?'

'Just a moment –' Mr Jacobs tried, but couldn't get a word in.

'Hector cheated,' Stormy started to say, pointing at Hector. 'He –'

But Hector was just as quick. 'The others had to retire. Injured. Stormy lost – they'll all back me up. Stormy was last to land on Moleman Mount and he's trying to deny it. He doesn't want me to have his stupid spitfyre. Sparkit and I were just trying to –'

Mr Jacobs rubbed his bald head nervously. 'I don't understand. Could you –'

'Where is the sword?' the Director said very precisely and now his voice was icy cold. 'Where is the Silver Sword, Hector?'

'The sword fell. I got it, but it fell and . . .'

The Director's expression was ghastly, all colour drained from his face. 'You *have* to bring it here. That's the condition.' He wiped his hands slowly over his face and shook his head. 'Hector, Hector, have you any idea what you've done? I put a fortune on you winning. So did your father. We're ruined. You've ruined us.'

340

'But why was Sparkit attacking you, Stormy?' asked Mr Jacobs. 'That's what I don't understand.'

'What does it matter?' the Director snapped.

Mungo abruptly slipped out from his hiding place. 'Because of me.' He dropped down to the ground and waved his arms to get their attention. 'Hey there! Hey! Listen to me!' he cried. 'Listen to what I have to say!'

'My God, it's Mungo!' the Director whispered. He staggered backwards as Mungo came towards him.

'You *know* this moleman?' Mr Jacobs asked, amazed. 'How is that possible?'

The Director's eyes grew hideously round, as if they were about to pop out of his head. His lips and nose became pinched and tight as the horror of the situation grew on him. 'Where are the guards? Guards!' he called hoarsely. 'There's a grubbin in the Academy! Guards?'

Stormy jumped down from Seraphina's back.

'This is Mungo Muddiman, the Director's *brother*,' he said very loudly, to make sure the students peering from the open windows and door heard too. 'That's right, this *grubbin* is his *brother*, and the Director had him locked up in the dungeon. You don't need guards, Director. This is your *brother*,' Stormy said. 'Now everyone knows your secret, don't they?'

'No, no, of course not, no guards.' The Director tried to smile. 'Stormy hasn't been here long,' he said, in a false cheery voice. 'He doesn't know what he's talking about. I suggest we go into my office and discuss this.' He spun round and headed quickly towards the house. 'Follow me, Mr Jacobs.'

'Just a minute . . .' Mr Jacobs said.

The gatehouse door opened and was flung back against the wall with a loud crash. Mr and Mrs Small ran out. 'Hang on! Hang on there!' shouted Mr Small. He cartwheeled across the yard and spun into a backflip, landing right in front of the Director, blocking his path.

'That grubbin *is* his brother!' Mr Small said, pointing a finger at the Director. 'The Director is a liar.'

'Yes he is,' Mrs Small, said. 'We know. We knew Mungo from long ago. It's all true.'

'How can you believe these two, these littles, I mean . . .' The Director began to edge backwards towards the house.

But everyone did believe them. The truth was written in the littles' round, honest faces. And the Director's guilt was obvious.

'Thank you, my dear vertically challenged friend,' Mungo said. 'Sylvester is my brother. Always has been, always will be; that's the sad truth. He locked me up because he didn't want anyone to see what *he* really was: half-grubbin. He's a thief, liar, cheat . . .'

'And he was training his Star Squad to rid the world of grubbins!' Stormy shouted, just in case they hadn't understood.

'These are serious accusations,' Mr Jacobs said nervously, looking from one person to another. 'I don't know what to say.'

Seraphina had been puffing out orange sparky smoke,

342

her eyes fixed on the Director. Now she began to shift towards him, inching closer and closer. Suddenly she charged the last three paces between them and jumped up, pushing him over with her front legs, toppling him as if he were a toy and treading him flat on the ground.

The Director opened his mouth but had no breath to speak.

'See!' Mr Small shouted. '*She* knows what's what!'

Stormy thought the Director's eyes were going to pop right out of his head.

'Stormy, remove your spitfyre,' Mr Jacobs said, but without much conviction.

'No, keep him there,' Mungo said. 'Hold him tight. He's not going to squirm out of this!'

Stormy went on talking quickly, fearing that if he didn't speak up now he might not get another chance.

'The Director has filled the dungeons with innocent grubbins,' he said. 'He's stolen their money. He's been deceiving you all!'

'I knew there was a lot of money,' Mr Jacobs said. 'I heard the spitfyres went out at night. Oh, dear, why did I never enquire . . . ?'

'They have been feeding them some nasty concoction made by Brittel, down in Otto's kitchen,' Stormy said. 'It makes them mean and horrid and determined to go after grubbins.'

'I did wonder, did worry, but not enough,' Mr Jacobs admitted, stopping as he saw Mr and Mrs Small running towards the door to the dungeons.

343

'Let them out!' roared Mr Small.

The guards had slunk away at the first sign of trouble; no one was protecting the cellars now.

Stormy and Mungo ran to help the littles unlock the door. Minutes later the noise of clanking chains and stunned voices filled the air.

The grubbins were free!

A crowd of convicts came up. They emerged blinking in the light and rubbing at their sore arms and legs, tugging their ragged clothes over their dirty bodies.

'I should have known,' Mr Jacobs said. 'And there are so many! Poor things. What a fool I've been.'

Mungo bobbed around amongst the prisoners and patted one or two on their backs, greeting old friends. 'Grand to see you! It's a good day, a fine day. It's all over, done with,' he said. 'You're free. Sylvester is finished.'

The grubbins cheered when they saw the Director trapped beneath the spitfyre's hooves. 'Down in the dirt where he belongs,' one said.

'What shall we do with them?' Mr Jacobs said.

'What shall you do?' Mungo cried. 'Why nothing, Mr Teacher. They do as they want to do themselves. They are living things like you and me and shall go free and live their lives as they wish to. Digging gold and silver and living where they wish and how they wish. That's what they'll do.'

'And what about him?' Mr Jacobs pointed at the Director, whose face was turning blue.

'Will you take him, Mr Jacobs?' Stormy said. 'Make

sure that he leaves the Academy and never comes back? He should never be able to work with spitfyres again.'

Mr Jacobs nodded. He beckoned to the other teachers, who had gathered on the Academy steps but had not yet had the courage to come down and find out what was going on.

'Come and help,' he called. 'Tell your spitfyre to release the Director, Stormy. What a day! I suppose this will be the end of the Academy,' he added sadly. 'I'll have the Director escorted off the premises later. Everyone leave the courtyard, please. Back to your rooms; no more excitement for today. I'll take over now.'

38

End

As Mr Bones came over to help Mr Jacobs with the Director, Mungo ran over to him.

'Brother, brother,' he said, catching hold of the Director's free hand. 'One moment, please.'

The Director snatched his hand free. 'Don't touch me!'

'All right. All right, but listen, all these years I've thought about my wife and daughter,' Mungo said. 'I must know what happened to them. Please.'

Mungo had begged Stormy to try and find out about his family and Stormy had done nothing. Except, he thought, smiling, quite by chance he had found something out. Something wonderful that would please Mungo no end.

The Director stared ahead coldly, refusing to look into Mungo's face. 'Your wife died,' he said. 'And daughter? What daughter?'

'You know there was a daughter!' Mungo cried. 'Don't deny it. Don't take away the only reason I've gone on living. Hoping to see her again. Hoping and praying she were alive . . .'

Mrs Small stopped him with a gentle touch on this arm. 'Of course you have a daughter. *That's* your daughter, right there!' she said.

She was pointing at Maud.

Maud was like a ghost. She didn't move. She had been watching and listening from the shadows, as she always did, and now she came forward hesitantly, staring at Mungo.

'She is your daughter, Mungo,' Stormy shouted, unable to stop himself butting in. 'Listen to me! I *know* she is. Look at the dimples! Same dimples! She's your daughter, all right!'

Mungo stared at Maud. A smile cracked his face and lit it up as if a torch had been shone on it. He knew his own daughter when he saw her. He tottered over to Maud and reached out a trembling hand to her.

'Little Maudie,' he whispered.

For a second Stormy feared Maud might be appalled at having a grubbin father, and at this moment Mungo was a very dirty grubbin, his clothes torn and his hair wild, but it was just the shock that held her back for a few seconds. Suddenly she smiled, dimples and all, and, taking a white ribbon from her hair, she handed it to Mungo as if it were a fine trophy.

'I knew you'd find me in the end,' she said.

Mungo put his arms round her and hugged her.

'I don't care about *him*!' Mungo said, nodding at the

Director. 'He is nothing to me. Now I've got me own dearest daughter, I don't care about anything. And it's all thanks to this lad here,' he added, patting Stormy on the back. 'Our hero.'

Stormy stared at the floor.

'I wish I'd never set eyes on your face, boy,' the Director said as Mr Jacob took one arm and Mr Bones took the other and they tried to move him on. The Director refused to budge. He went on addressing Stormy, staring at him intently, as if he was really seeing Stormy for the first time. 'Or I wish that I'd set eyes on you earlier, when you were younger . . . I could have moulded you into the perfect grubbin chaser. The most daring sky-rider ever! You would have been putty in my hands.'

'I never would! I never would have been!' Stormy said.

'That's what you think,' the Director said. 'But I *know*. You are a born sky-rider. You are a whisperer. Now you'll be *nothing*, because I'll make sure of that! I'm not finished. You'll see!'

'Never mind him,' Mungo said, putting his arm round Stormy. 'Never mind anything.'

The Director allowed the teachers to guide him into the house. 'You'll see!' he shouted back over his shoulder. 'You have no authority over me! I'm the Director!'

Stormy shivered. He hoped the Director was very wrong and would be banished from Dragon Mountain and sent somewhere far away.

Mungo was gazing lovingly at Maud. 'Dear little Maudie,' he said. 'My daughter.'

348

Stormy thought he'd better get out of their way. They'd have a lot to talk about.

'I suppose I should get Seraphina into her stable and get her rubbed down,' Stormy said, patting her shivering neck. 'Look at her, poor thing. She's exhausted. Oh, wasn't she marvellous?'

'What about Sparkit?' Mr Small said, nodding over towards the giant heap of sleeping spitfyre.

'He can wait,' said Stormy.

Araminta was standing in the doorway watching her father being brought in like a prisoner. She came slowly down the steps towards Stormy.

'This is all your fault,' she said bitterly, twisting her yellow skirt in her fist. 'You spoiled everything. I'll never speak to you again. Will you stay? Will you stay and help me? What shall I do?'

She was the same contrary girl, saying one thing and meaning another. Stormy shook his head. 'I can't help you.'

'Horrid stupid servery boy,' she said, stamping her foot. 'You don't understand, do you? I just want to be a sky-rider, that's all. You got to be one and you're just a pathetic little skivvy. Why won't he let me fly?' She nodded towards her father. 'Now he's nothing and now I'll never have another chance.'

'Araminta, I'm sorry, but –'

'No, you're not. No one is ever sorry for me. Not when I can't fly. Not when I had no brothers and sisters and was so alone. Not when my dear, dear, uncle died –'

349

'Araminta, you never even *met* your uncle, you told me that before . . . Oh!' Something had occurred to him. 'Actually, of course, you have!'

'What are you talking about?'

'The grubbin's your uncle. The Director said he was dead and took his money, but he wasn't.'

Araminta's expression was stony and cold. 'I do not have a grubbin relative of any sort!' she snapped. 'What a horrid thing to say.'

'And Maud is your cousin!'

Araminta swayed slightly then recovered herself. 'Maud is the maid. I couldn't possibly . . . she sweeps floors for her keep.'

'Poor Maud, she –'

'Poor me!' Araminta shrieked. 'It's *me* you should feel sorry for. I haven't got anything now. Nothing at all.'

Stormy took a big breath. 'What will you do?'

Araminta looked down her nose at him. 'How dare you ask me anything so personal? What impertinence from an orphan!' She looked up at the Academy. 'I shall stay with him. What else can I do?'

She followed the others into the house and slammed the door.

Stormy led Seraphina to her cave. She was tired now and limping slightly, exhausted by her final wonderful flight.

All the way Stormy talked to her and praised her and told her just how much he loved her.

Ralf and Purbeck greeted them.

'Well done, mate,' Purbeck said. 'Proud of you.'

'What about you, Ralf?' Stormy asked him. 'Happy to see me back?'

Ralf hung his head. 'I am, actually. Listen, I had to do it,' he said. 'I had no choice. Brittel said that if I gave them the powder just for the next six months I'd get to move on, get out. He said the Director would let me go. You know I hate it here.'

'Do you, do you really?' Stormy couldn't imagine anyone hating the Academy.

Ralf looked embarrassed. 'Well, I used to. Not so much now. Not since you two came.' He grinned at Purbeck. 'And if Hector's going to leave then Sparkit will have to go and . . .'

'And I'm afraid Bluey won't be back,' Stormy told them. 'Don't know about Polaris.'

'Daygo's in his stable but he's been hurt,' Ralf said. 'May never be the same again . . .'

'So it will all change up here,' Purbeck said.

'For the better,' Ralf said. 'I've thrown away the last of the yellow powder, Stormy, I promise. We just need Al to come back and then it would be perfect.'

'Let me help you with your spitfyre,' Purbeck said, falling in step beside Stormy as he led Seraphina to her cave. 'Shame she has to go back to that gloomy – hold on! Why not put her here, in Sparkit's cave? He won't be using it again, will he?'

'Perfect,' Stormy said, brightening up again. 'Thanks, Purbeck. Let's get it all clean for her straight away.' They set about changing the straw and putting in fresh water. Seraphina waited patiently, watching them with interest.

Soon she was settled inside. Stormy did not chain her up. 'No more of that,' he said. 'Though I suppose she might go for Al if he were ever to come back . . .'

'Al? Why?' Purbeck asked.

'Because she hates him.'

And Seraphina neighed shortly and pawed the ground as if she understood.

'Will she ever stop hating me?' a voice said behind them.

They spun round. It was Al. He gazed in at the spitfyre sadly. 'Not that I blame her, but will she ever stop?'

'Al! Where did you spring from?' Purbeck cried.

Ralf ran up to them. 'Al! Great to see you, Al! You look much better!'

Al did look plumper, and his eyes had a sparkle in them that hadn't been there before. He gave Seraphina a wary, sidelong look. She was watching Al carefully, but she wasn't showing any signs of distress like she had before.

'I was watching the flight from the valley,' Al said. 'I saw what happened, how she did the Spin, and I knew I had to come back. Well done for making her better, Stormy, and for being the best sky-rider I've seen for a long, long time.'

'Oh, thanks, Al.' Stormy's cheeks burned. 'Thanks a lot. But it was just because Seraphina –'

'Ahh, yes, yes, *Ser-a-phina*!' Al sank down to his knees. 'Ser-a-phina! How could I forget such a name.' His eyes were full of tears. 'She's a star, she's a beauty, my dear Seraphina. Dear, beautiful Seraphina.'

'You really had forgotten her name?'

Al nodded. He stood up and went closer to the spitfyre. 'Please accept my humble apologies for everything. Everything.'

Seraphina showered him with turquoise sparks and purple smoke.

'Is that her saying she forgives?' Ralf asked.

Al nodded. 'It's a start. It will take time, but I have that.'

Stormy said goodnight to Seraphina and they walked up to the servery together.

'I've stopped drinking,' Al said, sitting down in his favourite old place at the table. 'Otto stopped me. After Seraphina attacked me I made my way down the mountain and just as I feared, Otto was waiting for me. That ancient dog, Sponge, must be as old as the hills,' Al said, 'but he recognised me and barked like crazy so I couldn't sneak past.'

'What did Otto do?' Ralf asked.

'He forgave me,' Al said meekly. 'He's not the sort of man to seek vengeance in anything other than his imagination. He got me working in the kitchen. Got me washing and scrubbing and chopping. I felt like you, Stormy! Then I started eating. No alcohol, just fine food.'

'Good old Otto!' Stormy said.

'I'd seen Ralf with that little bottle of powder. Knew it wasn't right but didn't care enough to investigate, but after my brain cleared, after I'd been there a while, I asked Otto why he was sending up vitamins. Course he wasn't. Otto didn't know a thing about it. We went to Brittel's kitchen and had a look around. You should have seen what we found in his cupboards! Terrible stuff. Chucked it all away. We found a note from you too, Stormy.'

'From me?'

'Yes. Asking Otto if he knew the spitfyre's name, only Otto had never got it,' Al said. 'Brittel had hidden it from him.'

'I'd forgotten I'd even written it,' Stormy admitted.

'Otto threw Brittel out,' Al said. 'I didn't know such a bony bloke could bounce so high!' He laughed, then stopped abruptly. 'Sorry. You got thrown out too, Stormy, didn't you? It wasn't – I shouldn't have done that.'

'It's all right, Al.'

'No, it was bad. It was mean. I felt so mean then, Stormy. I wanted to stop you from interfering . . . Know who you reminded me of?' He went on before Stormy could interupt. 'Mayra. She was like you. Only saw the best in everyone, full of good thoughts. Sparky. Bright. Couldn't bear it. And there was pressure from Araminta too.'

'I know,' said Stormy. 'Forget it, Al. It's all worked out for the best.'

There was a knock on the door and Mungo put his cheerful face round, 'Hello! Anyone home?' he called. Maud came in behind him shyly.

Stormy introduced the boys and Al to Mungo and was pleased to see them greet him warmly.

'They've carted the Director off,' Mungo told them. 'There'll be some sort of trial and then hopefully he'll be gone for good. Araminta went with him. Hector too, and his spitfyre. All gone. The place is wiped clean.'

354

So Araminta had gone too. Stormy sighed. He would have liked to have helped her if he could have. She wasn't really bad, he didn't think, just sad. How could he ever have trusted her, that's what he couldn't understand. He had a lot to learn about girls . . . about everything!

Al seemed to understand what he was thinking. 'Girls are tricky, Stormy,' he said.

'Some of them!' Maud said, smiling.

'I'm glad they've gone,' Ralf said.

'We can start again,' Stormy said. 'If you'll be the new Director, Mungo?'

Mungo chuckled and shook his head. 'What do I know about spitfyres? I'm a grubbin!'

'You don't need to know very much,' Al said. 'You just need to be a good person who can run things smoothly. You're next of kin; I think the Academy probably belongs to you now. And Maud.'

'I'd need help,' Mungo said, looking around hopefully at their smiling faces.

'You've got us!' Purbeck and Ralf both said.

'I'd need a good spitfyre keeper,' Mungo said, staring at Al.

'I can't come back,' Al said gloomily. He began to rip a crust of bread into bits. 'I can't. No. I'm no good. I've let everyone down.'

Maud gently took the bread from his hands and set it aside. 'Don't,' she whispered. 'You *are* good.'

'Please,' Stormy said. 'It's where you belong, and the Academy can't exist without you, Al.'

Al stood up and took the crumbs to the doorway and tossed them up into the air.

'Why do you do that?' Maud asked. 'I've seen you do it hundreds of times.'

'Mayra,' Al said, and blew his nose loudly on a hankie. 'It's for Mayra. She never wanted anyone to go hungry. Give it to the birds, she used to say. She loved birds. Always had a little something for them.'

'Otto does it too,' Stormy said.

'We both loved her,' Al said. He limped back to the table. 'I'll think about coming back,' he said. 'I will.'

'I'll take that as a yes, then,' Mungo said, nodding enthusiastically. 'Good. I want you, Al. I want the Great Renaldo at my new Academy.'

'I never said –'

'Nonsense, you know you belong with those flying horses, and between the five of you – you, Ralf, Purbeck, Stormy and of course Maud – you'll make it the best Academy in the whole world!'

'Good, that's agreed.' Stormy thumped Al on his back. 'We'll get new rules and keep the dungeons empty,' he said. 'Mr Jacobs and Mr Bones and Mrs Lister say they'll stay on. We'll find more good teachers. This place will be wonderful. I know it will.'

Mungo and Al shook hands.

'It's a deal.'

Afterwards, when everyone had gone about their business, Stormy and Maud went down to say a last goodnight to Seraphina.

'Why did you give me those white ribbons?' Stormy asked Maud.

Maud looked away across the valley. 'I didn't have anything else to give,' she said simply. 'I wanted you to know that someone was thinking about you, wherever you went and whatever you did. I wanted you not to feel alone. I know what it's like to feel alone. I didn't know how to say it in any other way.'

'I wondered a bit . . .' Stormy began, then stopped, not wanting to admit he'd thought they were from Araminta.

Maud wrapped her arms around Seraphina's neck and laid her head against the spitfyre's warm coat.

'Oh.' She looked round at Stormy, an idea striking her. 'You never thought that *she'd* given them to you, did you?'

Stormy grinned. 'Of course not,' he said. He took the three lengths of white ribbon from his pocket and together they weaved them into Seraphina's glorious mane.

'Perfect,' Stormy said.

Maud smiled. 'Perfect.'

Rebecca Lisle

Rebecca Lisle was born in Leeds to two artists. Having studied Botany at Newcastle University she then completed a PGCE at Oxford. Rebecca lived in France, Manhattan, and England before becoming a 'proper' writer. She was awarded a distinction for her MA in Creative Writing at Bath Spa in 2006.

The Spin is her twenty-fourth book. Inspired by Dickens' *Great Expectations*, she's hoping it's her best book to date. Rebecca is a keen rider and had her own horse, Sylvia, when she lived in Australia. When she imagined the hero of *The Spin*, Stormy, flying on his winged horse, she was remembering the fantastic experience of riding over the wide expanses of New South Wales, which wasn't that far from flying and was certainly a highlight in her life.

Rebecca is married with three almost grown-up sons, who are the inspiration for many stories, along with her black and white dog Nike. When she is not writing Rebecca paints peculiar pictures of dogs. Find out more about Rebecca at www.rebeccalisle.co.uk